SILVER

OVER 100
GREAT NOVELS
OF
EROTIC DOMINATION

If you like one you will probably like the rest

NEW TITLES EVERY MONTH

All titles in print are now available from:

www.adultbookshops.com

If you want to be on our confidential mailing list for our Readers' Club Magazine (with extracts from past and forthcoming titles) write to:

SILVER MOON READER SERVICES

Shadowline Publishing Ltd
Box 101
City Business Centre
Station Rise
York
YO1 6HT
United Kingdom

telephone: 01904 525729
Fax: 01904 522338

NEW AUTHORS WELCOME

Please send submissions to
Silver Moon Books
Box 101
City Business Centre
Station Rise
York
YO1 6HT

Silver Moon is an imprint of Shadowline Publishing Ltd
the print publishing division of the Convecto Media Group
First published 2008 Silver Moon Books
ISBN 9781-904706-66-3
© 2008 Richard Garwood

JOANNE'S JOURNEY

BY

RICHARD GARWOOD

ALSO BY RICHARD GARWOOD
PAINFUL PERFORMANCES
PAIN ORDAINED
THE VICAR'S DAUGHTER

All characters in this book are fictitious, and any resemblance to real persons, living or dead, is purely coincidental.

THIS IS FICTION - IN REAL LIFE ALWAYS PRACTISE SAFE SEX!

Tuesday 23 April

I couldn't believe that I was to be punished just for standing in the forbidden triangle. So what if I could be seen by passers by? First of all they'd have had to have been craning their necks over the stone wall, and even then, what possible interest could they find in me? I've had a good look in the mirror. I am very ordinary. I know it's not helped by my rather lank hair and, of course, not wearing any make up. Despite liking athletics I've got a very ordinary figure. I'm about 5 feet 5 inches, I'm not overweight, nor am I super-model skinny. It's true, I could go anywhere and pass unnoticed, which is just how I like it.

I'd have liked to scandalise the whole lot of them. All sorts of pranks have crossed my mind. Cutting the elastic at the waist band of my panties and letting them fall to the ground when the visiting priest is in the hall, or perhaps losing a button or two from my blouse when the other priest is listening to confession. Now, there's an idea. I could make up a list of detailed sins so that he would whisk me away from here. I never wanted to train to be a teacher and most particularly not in this isolated dump where we are all girls together.

I know I shouldn't have smuggled in those copies of Cosmo after the Easter break. It's just that I haven't got over the contents yet. Clothes, make-up and sex seem to be the overwhelming interests of the readers. I haven't the money for fashion, make-up is virtually forbidden, so that leaves sex... I must have another look at the problem pages. I remembered that one woman was complaining that her partner wanted to strip her, tie her up and whip her. For some reason this made me feel all trembly. I've no idea why, though I'd like a masterful boy friend. What on earth I'd do with a boy friend of any sort in a place like this, I can't imagine. Creep out in the dead of night for an assignation on the forbidden triangle!

I'd better stop fantasising and do some work.

Wednesday 24 April

I didn't expect to have quite such vivid or unlikely dreams. It's as well that I have kept this diary very private. I dreamed that I was in a court because of a crime I had committed. The proceedings appeared to go on for ages without anyone referring to me. In the end the judge turned to me and asked if I had anything to say, but I was unable to offer any defence. He told me that normally my offence would carry the death penalty, but in view of my age and hitherto blameless reputation I would, instead, be publicly scourged. I had no idea what this meant but I bowed my head and was taken away by the court officers and locked in a cell.

My time in the cell seemed endless, but eventually two burly men dressed in black uniforms unlocked the door and dragged me along the corridor and up some stairs. I was taken across the road to the town square. A scaffold had been erected and I was hauled up the steps. The crowd seemed to press closer. A man in a leather hood and leather trousers, but wearing nothing else to hide the tremendous muscles of his chest, shouted something at the crowd about an auction. For a moment I thought I was going to be sold into slavery, but he was merely trying to drum up some enthusiasm so that he could make a bit of money. My guards undid the buttons on my blouse and stripped it off me. The man sold it to a woman close to the scaffold steps. My bodice was sold to the same woman and I found myself standing stripped to the waist in front of the leering crowd. Several remarks were made about me, but I could hardly make them out.

The man threw a rope over the top bar of the scaffold and my wrists were promptly secured to its end. In a moment I was hauled up so that my bare feet were just clear of the planks. I felt fingers at my waist and the slide of my skirt and petticoat down my thighs. Now I was naked before my persecutors. The executioner turned me round half a dozen times until I felt quite dizzy. When he let me go I began to turn as the rope unwound itself. I could hear the crowd shouting and cat calling. I closed my eyes against them, but opened them very quickly when there was a slash across my back. It made me draw in my breath and then cry out, but I had no means of defending myself as I turned and jerked at the end of the rope. A second slash hit me across my belly and a third burnt its way across my buttocks. A fourth and fifth sliced their way across the top of my thighs and then the small of my back. I could feel the pain from each of them burning on my skin so that I was breathless with the agony and tears were dripping down my cheeks. The huge man settled into a steady rhythm. The sixth slash caught me just under my breasts, while the seventh striped me across my back. These blows now alternated with the occasional strike across my breasts which bounced and compressed with the pangs inflicted by the plaited whip. I lost count after twenty slashes and the world began to fade and my sight grew dim. I felt the torment, but I could no longer cry out or do anything but hang listlessly from the rope, my body responding on its own to the biting of the whip by twisting and shaking. In the background I heard noises, but none of them made any sense, only the whistle of the whip and its crack against my soft flesh were real. I began to lose all sense of reality except that my thoughts were changed so that I was looking at myself hanging, nude, from the end of a rope and being ogled by the townsfolk. I saw every line of my body and every weal which the whip was putting on it. I saw my breasts, pulled high on my chest by the leverage on my arms and was amazed to see my nipples, twice as big as I thought they were, sticking out from the areolas and the tail of the whip biting them. My ribs were covered by only the slightest thickness of flesh and stood out white against my skin. My belly was elongated with my navel a direct echo of the lower slot which was concealed by my luxuriant bush of brown hair. My legs were slender and strongly muscled, but quite unable to support me as my feet were well off the floor. As I turned slowly I saw the curve of my back and my tight round buttocks dominating the length of the back of my thighs. I hadn't realised how small my waist was, nor how my hips flared out below it. All the time I was conscious that the whip was cutting into me and that the pain had gone past being unbearable into a purple miasma in my eyes and my mind. With the image of myself quickly fading from my eyes I felt my head fall back from between my arms and I heard a voice telling me to open my legs. As my feet swung apart a hand grasped my soaking cunt. I realised that I had been dripping for some time and now fingers were thrust into me from the front as the whip was plied on my back. I could feel the new pain and turmoil in my scored belly and the pangs of the whip receded as practised fingers worked on me, and the dripping turned to a spurt of juice. The crowd cheered and I once again hung immobile from the rope as the relentless thrashing continued.

I woke to find my hands between my thighs and the tail end of a scorching orgasm filling my senses. How on earth could I have got anything out of such an event: stripped naked, hung up for public inspection, whipped until I was almost senseless and then my incipient pleasure brought to full strength. I had a lot to think about.

Thursday 25 April

I hardly managed to pay attention in the lectures today, I found myself shivering at the recollection of what had happened to me the night before. I don't know whether it was a warning or an unfulfilled desire. In broad daylight the thought of being stripped naked and whipped in front of a crowd of ogling townsfolk filled me with horror, and yet... and yet there was something about it which made my breathing a little constricted and made my mouth dry and my heart thump inside my chest. Perhaps it was just being stripped naked and held up for everyone's inspection. Perhaps it was because, despite the pain, I seemed capable of deriving sexual satisfaction from being displayed and whipped. How perverse!

I really didn't know what to make of this. However, something made me think that my dream just might be a warning or perhaps an indication of my own secret desires. But that's silly. No one could possibly want to be displayed, naked, before the crowd in the town square and then whipped mercilessly. No, of course they couldn't. Anyway, what happened to me after the whipping? How silly, none of it happened.

Today I had to march up to see the Principal, Miss Readie, and account for my flagrantly immodest behaviour by which I had broken a college rule. I listened at length whilst she told me off, but my mind was full of my dream. Suddenly I became aware of what she was saying: "...and not so long ago you would have been stripped to your drawers and thrashed before the entire student body for your disobedience..."

I couldn't believe that my thoughts should have been echoed by the Principal. I felt a sort of vertical buzz from between my legs up into my belly. I just hoped there wasn't going to be any answering trickle in a downwards direction.

I seem to have got off lightly with a reprimand. I suppose this was because I didn't wear make-up or go out at the weekends, much as I would have liked to, but I haven't the money to spend. It looks as if I should have to go on living my dreams without telling anyone.

Friday 26 April

I was tired last night and soon fell into a dreamless sleep. Judging by a quick glance at my luminous clock I awoke at just after 1 a.m. I felt very uneasy, but I had no recollection of anything that could have woken me, or why I should feel so uneasy. I lay awake for a while and then began to drift off to sleep, my mind still full of disquieting thoughts. I'd never had a serial dream before but this most certainly was one. I could see my crumpled body, covered in the scarlet stripes inflicted by the whipping, lying on the scaffold in an untidy heap. It looked to me as if I had been thrashed until I passed out. The crowd, now that it was all over, was dispersing. A young man, dressed in a collarless shirt and thick trousers, stepped forward with a large sack in his hands. From my dream vantage point above the scaffold I looked down at myself as he approached me and lifted my legs into the sack. None too gently he drew the sack over my unresisting body and tied it off at my neck. It seemed to be no effort to him to bundle me up and throw me across his shoulder. I could see my head lolling against his back. My view point changed and as I hung over his shoulder I could see the backs of his legs and his feet moving purposefully away from the scaffold. I knew that I was entirely at his disposal. I had no one to turn to for help.

I had no idea where we were going and could do nothing except whimper as the coarse sacking chafed the weals on my skin. Eventually we arrived at a large building, of which I saw nothing except a wall made of closely fitting stones. I was carried round the building until we arrived at some smaller buildings. We entered the doorway to what looked like a stable and I found myself sliding from the man's shoulder onto a pile of hay. He undid the cord at the neck of the sack, turned on his heel and walked away. I was left, covered by the rough sack, waiting to find out what would happen to me next.

I hadn't long to wait. An old man unlocked the door. The light flooded in from outside casting him into shadow. I lay on the straw and nursed the fiery weals on my body. He told me to stand up. I got to my feet holding the sack at neck level. He told me to put both my arms in the air. I was panic stricken that he would take advantage of my nakedness. Very quietly he said, 'Do it now.' He didn't shout or threaten, but there was authority and command in his tone. I raised my arms as the sack slipped away to my feet. He stared intently at me.

'Turn round,' he commanded. I did as I was told. 'Made a mess of you. Never mind, we'll sort you out.'

I stood there with my hands over my head displaying myself to his gaze. He turned to the door and summoned two young men who came in to look at me. He gave instructions and the larger of the men picked me up as if I was a doll and carried me out of the cell. I felt the bumping of his feet against the cobbles relayed up his body and into mine. We went into another building, down a corridor and through a door where he tipped me off his shoulder so that I found myself sitting on a padded table. An elderly man in a white coat appeared as I sat huddled with my knees pressed tight together and my arms across my breasts.

He started to speak to me, but a loud noise disturbed my vision and I lost what he had to say and awoke. By some means I had divested myself of my pyjamas and I was lying on my side with my knees drawn up almost to my chest. I tried to regain my dream, but instead I eventually fell into an uneasy sleep.

Saturday 27 April

There was an opportunity for a visit to the college gym, or to go shopping in the nearby town. What I really wanted to do was to stay in bed and make up for my restless nights. I decided to go to the gym. I felt I needed some exercise and it was raining outside so that going for a walk wouldn't have been any sort of delight in my rather threadbare old Mac and leaky shoes. I put on my running shorts which fit me like a glove, and my sleeveless cropped top If I was going to get warm, that was OK, but I didn't want to get over-heated. My trainers are showing signs of age and the left sole has a crack in it. I'll have to try to save up for some new ones.

I had the gym to myself. I folded my towel and put it on a bench in the corner with my Mac. I thought that I might do some work on the wall bars. I climbed them and held on with my arms above my head, facing outwards. I lifted my legs to horizontal half a dozen times and then took a brief rest, another half dozen meant that I could begin to feel my abs working. A third set was half way through when I realised that my crop top was riding up with the pull on my legs and belly and the stretch of my arms. I was on my own. Why should I worry? By the end of the fourth set I looked down and saw that my breasts were almost completely uncovered and that my nipples were standing very much to attention. I was quite pleased. I recalled my dream adventure and at once felt a warm fluttering in my belly. I knew I wanted to be stripped in front of an appreciative audience. Perhaps my figure wasn't so bad after all.

I came down off the bars and did some stretching exercises. I've never been very clever using the rings, despite having quite strong arms and shoulders. As there was no one watching, here was my opportunity. There was a pile of practice mats under the rings. I stood on them and jumped up to grasp the rings. I had watched the proficient people and decided to do as many of their exercises as I could. This was another set of exercises where the benefit is gained from working against one's own weight. After a series of swings and lifts I managed to get upside down and hung with my knees above my hands. I wondered if I could twist the ropes round my legs and swing upside down without holding on to the rings. I found myself swinging free, but it was extremely difficult to get any proper momentum going. Eventually I settled for hanging upside down with just a slight swing. I wondered what I must look like and began to think of my dreams. I recalled last night's and as I thought about it my hands strayed to my breasts and my fingers began manipulating my nipples.

I had seen again the room with the table on which I sat and the man in the white coat examining me closely. He called for something which he explained he was going to use as a quick cure for my weals. A surly looking lad arrived with a ribbed bottle containing a dark slimy substance. He told me to lie face down on the couch and as soon as I had complied I felt his fingers sliding the unguent over my skin. He started with my shoulders. At first the effect was soothing and cooling but by the time he had got to my waist I felt increasing heat being generated. I told him what I could feel and he said that it was a good sign and that the ointment was doing its job. By the time he had reached my knees I was burning all the way to my bottom. He told me to turn over. For a moment I had hesitated, but I realised that this was helpful treatment so I turned and lay on my back with one hand and forearm across my breasts and the other hand concealing my bush.

Again he started at my shoulders and gently lifted my concealing arm away from my breasts so that he could spread the liquid over them. Once that was done he replaced my arm as gently as he had removed it, but now I knew I was safe in his hands and I let the arm fall to my side. His attentions were accompanied by a series of tutting noises and little comments about me being a poor thing. He removed my arm from across my belly. There was a pause. His fingers were in my bush. He told me it would have to go because he couldn't see what he was doing. He called out again and the surly youth reappeared. He was given instructions and very shortly he returned bearing a tray with a steaming bowl and various implements on it. The man in the coat stood back. I felt the fire spread over my shoulders to my breasts. I felt something odd about them, but I was more concerned about what the surly youth was doing. I could feel him tugging the fur between my thighs and I could hear and feel the snipping of scissors. In a few minutes he had completed that part of his task. I felt a hot wet cloth placed over my belly and between my now open thighs. The pain in my cunt was awful, but the warm wet cloth eased it a bit. The surly youth was apparently whisking up foam in a shaving mug. He transferred it to my skin with a small brush and then produced a razor and began to shave me. If it had not been for the pain left by my whipping and my fear that he might cut me I am sure that I would have found this process very stimulating. His hands were firm, but gentle. The razor made a tiny catching sound as it travelled over my mons and then attended to my labia. Despite his surly appearance he was obviously a very careful artist in his own way and he managed to avoid giving me any extra pain.

At last he rinsed my skin and dried it gently and stepped back. The other man peered at me between my legs. He muttered little curses as he very carefully parted my petals and examined my most intimate parts. He nodded his head and the surly youth moved behind me and caught my wrists in his hands. White coat had attached a strap to my dangling left ankle and swiftly caught my right ankle under the table, with the other end. I didn't struggle, but I very soon became aware of what he was doing. If the ointment had burnt my skin after it was applied it was as nothing compared with the fire which he ignited in my open cunt. He seemed to be sloshing the black liquid all round my belly and between my thighs, but then he opened me and thrust two coated, gloved fingers into me three or four times. As before, the immediate effect was quite soothing, but I knew what was coming. Even so I could not believe that he could have been so cruel as to soak my delicate membranes in this devastating way. I began to twist as I felt the heat build up. I twisted in the youth's hands and I jerked my pelvis up and down in an attempt to cool myself. I howled in agony. My mouth opened uncontrollably as I gulped in air. Tears ran from my eyes. I could feel the furnace in my vagina and then the scorching of my clit. No thrashing could compare with the acrid agony of this attack on me. I heard the man in the white coat trying to soothe me by telling me that it would be over in a few minutes, but with this sort of pain a minute feels like an hour. I squeezed the muscles of my vagina in an attempt to expel the boiling liquid that was scalding me, but this merely made it worse. I felt the muscles of my shoulders and then my thighs go into spasm, followed by the muscles of my belly. I began to cry out short gasps of explosive sound and then I realised that the pain was beginning to subside and that I was starting to generate lubricant which would cool my inflamed flesh. A finger touched my clit and suddenly I was pouring out juice and my head was filled with the roaring of my tortured orgasm.

As I gently swung I felt the brushing of my insides by the beginnings of my arousal as I recalled the events of my dream. I noticed the gathering tension within my cunt and felt it spread into my belly. My hanging head already had a confusion of noises within it, but suddenly I knew that I had to straighten my legs and press my thighs together. At once my juices started to flow, soaking my shorts and trickling down my belly and into the cleft of my buttocks. I was clawing my nipples and howling with delight. All too soon the passion was over. I waited a moment and then reached up for the rings, lifting my head and freeing my legs from the ropes. It was all a bit too much for me and I let go of the rings and landed in a heap on the mats.

Unfortunately, these were less comfortable than I had hoped and I rolled over with a view to getting up, only to find myself being looked down on by Miss Cotton, the physical education lecturer. She told me to come to see her after church tomorrow.

Sunday 28 April.

This has been a day full of surprises. For a change I was absorbed by the service and almost forgot the embarrassment of yesterday's encounter with Miss Cotton. But inevitably the time came when I had to stand up and face the music. I thought I would make a good impression by wearing the dowdiest clothes I possessed. Miss Cotton was waiting for me in her room. She had not been to church and was wearing a pale blue track suit with a pair of trainers I would have given anything for, except I reminded myself that I'd nothing to give. She seemed quite friendly but when I sat down I pressed my hands between my knees and hunched my shoulders. She asked me if I had any problems. Like what, I thought. She told me she was surprised to find me in the gym when I could have been in town enjoying myself. I looked her in the eye and told her that as I had no money I didn't go to town and this affected my relationship with many of the other girls who thought I was a stand-offish swot.

I was amazed at Miss Cotton's reply which invited me to call her by her first name, Mel, and she then told me that she had suffered from the same difficulty when she was a student. She told me that it would not make it better for me, but she could assure me that it got easier and then there was the enormous change of being employed. She told me how lucky she had been that a member of the staff had taken her under her wing and looked after her. If it wasn't an intrusion she would do the same for me as a sort of thank you to her own benefactor. I could hardly say I would struggle through on my own, and in any case I didn't want to. I was so relieved that she had not told me off that I felt tears coming to my eyes and I gave a most audible sniff. However, she was not done with me. She told me never to go to the gym on my own. She quoted Health and Safety regulations at me and then added, 'Besides which the two of us could have so much more fun.' I must have sat there goggling at her until she added, 'You know perfectly well that I saw what you were up to yesterday. I can assure you that it can be even better when you have someone to share it with.' I continued to be speechless and she looked at me quizzically.

'There's more, isn't there?'

I felt I had to tell someone and she was the only person on the staff who had shown the slightest interest in me. I told her about my dreams, though I played down my reaction to them. I hesitated when it came to the previous night. She encouraged me to go on.

I told her of the lead up to the previous night's dream and then described what had happened next. The man in the white coat had come to the head of the table and had secured my wrists to the tops of the legs at either side. The surly youth was just within my vision. I realised that he was taking off his clothes. Very quickly he was naked. This certainly took my mind off the agony I was enduring, but it hardly made it less. I tried to elevate my buttocks to get air to my burning cunt, but as I did so a rubber cushion was pushed under me. The man in white fiddled with something at the side of the cushion and then began to pump air into it, raising my buttocks and forcing open my naked cunt. There was some relief in this, though my position was now both wholly revealing and also very stressful. From my position on the table I was looking upwards, over my breasts, to the swell of my belly and I could just see the upper edge of my mons, now shorn of its previous covering. Before I knew what was happening, the surly youth was kneeling between my thighs. I saw him kneel up so that my view was dominated by his torso, which in turn was the backdrop for his rigidly erect cock.

I was fascinated to see that it nodded with every pulse of his heartbeat and that from time to time it twitched. He grasped the phallus in his hand and coated it with something. I feared that it might be more of the ointment which had burnt me, but then I hardly thought that he would apply such a thing to himself. He bent his knees and with no preliminaries he started to thrust his cock into my cunt. I don't know what I was expecting, but it certainly wasn't to be impaled on a piece of flesh that was as cold as if it had been in a freezer for a week. Whatever he had anointed himself with it had a wonderfully cooling effect on my boiling interior. He pushed slowly but hard into me until I thought that he would do me some damage. Inevitably the tip of his cock came into contact with the neck of my womb. He pulled back until I could feel the icy thing touching my outer lips. I wanted him to take me with all his strength, I wanted to feel that he wanted me more than anything in the world, but in this I was to be disappointed and he just repeated his thrusts time after time. He showed no sign of excitement; probably as a result of whatever it was that he had spread over himself. I, too, began to feel vaguely anaesthetised. I began to count his thrusts, but lost count at twenty two. Eventually it was the mechanical reaction to the thrusting and the friction on his cock that made him stiffen his body and grunt. At once he pulled out of me and I saw his cock throbbing wildly. Before he could reach down to it, it gave a violent twitch and a fountain of jism spewed out of it and spread across my belly. The fountain seemed to work in pulses, each one producing its quantity of sticky fluid shooting as far as my ribs and across my hips. I was fascinated by the power and quantity of his ejaculation. Despite his rather sour appearance I knew that I could want this man in me at some more propitious time. As it was he had lessened my pain and coated me with his richly smelling viscous jism.

As is so often the case with dreams, the next scene seemed unrelated to the previous one. I found myself in a four poster bed with a great depth of feather mattress above and below me. I was reclining on a pile of pillows and had obviously just awoken, for I started to stretch. I turned on to my back, and as is my habit I held my breast in my hand for a moment and then pressed my hands up between my thighs, amazed to find that the luxuriant bush had gone and that my cunt was just smooth skin. I didn't know whether I liked this or not, but I touched it gently and was pleased with the effect my questing fingers were having. I looked round the room, I was alone. In the far corner there was a long mirror beside an armchair. On that there was a black and red dressing gown. I slipped out of the bed and stood in front of the mirror. I looked at myself, truly naked, and was surprised at the sight of my body. My breasts were fuller than I thought and the nipples quite surprisingly erect. I carried not an ounce of surplus flesh so that my collar bones and my ribs were as clearly defined through my skin as the terminal points of my pelvis. I had no idea that there was such a substantial difference between the narrowness of my waist and the broad swell of my hips. My navel was a cleft in my slightly convex belly and between my thighs, visible for the first time for many years was the cleft of my cunt with its pale folds and vertical division. My thighs appeared rounded and strong with some muscle visible and my knees were far less grotesque than I had expected. My calves were slender but showed an almost vertical crease at the side where the muscles divided, and then, wonder of wonders, I realised that I had small and very pretty feet. I began to think that I had been looking at a mirror which was magicked to show only what I hoped to see. But I realised that I had not looked at my face. I lifted my eyes to see my nondescript features and mousy slightly lank hair, but I was amazed to see that I had been transformed. My hair had been cut short and curled and dyed a rich auburn. Taking my hair away from my face revealed a good jaw line, a firm chin, lips that were full and spread with carmine, a small nose and, with the aid of more make-up, eyes that shone out of my face below well drawn almost straight eyebrows. Whilst I had been asleep someone had worked hard on me, but how could this lovely, sharp looking girl have been hiding behind the facade of my plainness? I turned to put on the dressing gown, still fascinated with myself, when there was a knock at the door and a man in uniform came in.

It all seemed to stop there and my dream dissolved very disappointingly. Still, I had found a new appearance and with it a new confidence, at least in my dream. Unfortunately, in my day to day reality I was still the dull uninteresting girl I had always been. Remarkably, Mel sought to disagree. She told me that she would send for me and that we might have another chat and perhaps something agreeable for both of us might come out of it.

Monday 30 April

I've spent far too much time getting into bothers and writing up my diary. Yet how could I not want to record these amazing dreams, and then there was the promise of some reality with Mel. She made me tremble just to look at her in her track suit. I should have been getting on with my revision because there will be an exam on Friday morning. I should, but I can't resist putting down a few details of my dream last night.

I couldn't wait to get into bed and draw the duvet up to my ears. Instead of drifting off to sleep I thought about Mel. Perhaps I could be rich in terms of relationships rather than cash, though a bit of cash would be helpful. I realised that I had never noticed Mel in anything but her track suit. They're handy things, are track suits, but they hardly flatter or reveal the wearer's figure. Mel is a nice looking woman; she's been kind to me and hasn't embarrassed me as she could have done. I must have sunk into sleep with Mel on my mind.

The next thing I knew I was being supervised by the uniformed man walking down the corridor. He told me to stand still outside a big wooden door. He knocked and I was admitted. Sitting in a large armchair was the elderly man who I had first met when I was brought here. He smiled at me and asked me if I was all right. I managed to whisper a reply that I was, but I felt afraid. He told me that I now belonged to his community and that I would, in future, do only what I was commanded to do. The alternative, he pointed out, was to have been allowed to stagger away, naked, from the gallows and be the prey to any passing rapist or cut throat. I shivered at the reality of this description of my fate, but I wondered what the alternative might now be.

He smiled at me. He told me that I was a very beautiful girl and therefore a valuable asset, though the drawback, if that's what it was, was that my will was in his hands. He asked me if I had looked in the mirror. He asked me if I was pleased with what I saw. He knew that I was. He pointed out that he had transformed me physically in the course of a single night and without my agreement or co-operation. He would ensure that I continued to be happy, but that happiness would depend on my submission. He promised me beautiful clothes, an attentive companion and experiences which would change me forever.

The uniformed man took me back to my room. There, to my amazed surprise, was Mel, but nothing like the Mel who I had spoken to so recently. Gone were the track suit and the trainers. Instead she was dressed in the tightest of amazingly low on the hips red leather trousers which relied wholly on the swell of her buttocks to be kept from descending to her knees, and a matching sleeveless top which came just to the lower curve of her breasts. She looked stunning. I stood in the doorway entranced by the sight of this friend and her gorgeous outfit. She smiled and asked if I was pleased to see her. My response was to run to her and fling my arms round her. I thought she was being stand offish when she detached my arms from her, but I very soon realised that this was no more than to ensure that we could embrace with greater effect. I had never before pressed my body against another woman, but I was delighted with the embrace.

I asked her what she was doing in this strange place and she smiled sweetly and told me that she was fulfilling her promise to look after me. Thinking about it afterwards it is strange how reality and fantasy can coalesce in dreams and also how unrelated elements slip into what seems like a narrative. How did Mel turn up in this exotic dream location?

Her first job was to teach me to dance. I can get by on the dance floor, but this was quite different. In a typical dream anachronism she put a CD on the player and from it came music with a slow, seductive rhythm. It was the sort of thing to which my response might have been to put my arms round my partner's neck and hold him as close as possible and hardly move my feet. There was more to it than that. It seemed very intense and somehow, as it played, I began to twist my hips as I stood quite still. Mel suggested that I should put my hands behind my head. I felt the unaccustomed thick curly hair, and at the same time I found that I should move my legs apart and twist the upper part of my body against the movement of my hips. Suddenly I realised that I was the embodiment of writhing. Mel seemed to be very pleased with my performance. She told me to turn round slowly. I presented her first with my side view and then my back. She told me to swing my bottom more and I was happy to oblige. The music penetrated every part of my consciousness. I moved with my eyes open and then closed them as I turned. I felt as if I had been taken over and had become sinuous where once I would have been awkward.

Mel suggested that I should dress the part. We went to the wardrobe and she selected a costume for me. There was a wreath of glittering emeralds to put in my hair, my breasts were covered by a strapless confection made of scintillating garnets on golden threads, and precious little of them at that. The skirt was made of thousands of threads of silk with jewels sewn in to many of them and each one with a scintillating jewel at its end. I turned away from Mel to put the costume on but I realised there was nothing to put beneath the skirt. Mel assured me that it was intended to be like that. She found me some high heeled slippers encrusted with jewels and I stood before her, trying to work out how to secure the skirt. She told me that it was not intended to go round my waist. I looked at her trousers and understood. I undid the Velcro fastening at the top hem and lowered the skirt to my hips. Mel laughed and reached towards me. This skirt was intended to give a complete view of my belly with the upper part of its band revealing the crease between my belly and my thighs almost to showing off the plumpness of my mons. Mel re-opened the wardrobe door and I saw myself reflected in the mirror on the inside of it.

She told me I was gorgeous. I put my hands behind my neck and started to dance again. She suggested that there might be a bit more foot movement and that where the music quickened I might try a twirl. I practised for three quarters of an hour, adding more and more alluring elements at Mel's direction. The brushing of the silk strands between my thighs became stimulating and I felt a tiny flush build on my chest, echoed by a buzz between my legs. Mel laughed again and told me that if I enjoyed the dance, so would my audience. She suggested another costume. This time there was a band of gold set with diamonds to be clipped to my hair. My breasts were to be left bare apart from an ornament clipped to each nipple which was a series of tiny rose petals. Mel pressed a jewel into my navel and I was allowed to keep the skirt. This time the music was much faster. I listened to it and then asked Mel what I should do. She asked me what I felt like doing and I blushed. She told me to do it.

It didn't take me long to fall into pace with the music. I stamped my feet, I twisted round rapidly, the skirt flew up, and I felt the breath of air on my naked cunt. I shook my breasts. I became one with the music in a way that I had never experienced before. Mel told me that if I was called on to perform I should take the ornaments from my breasts during the dance and put them behind my ears. She seemed to think that I should twirl my skirt and perhaps even use it as a prop whilst I danced naked. The music came to an end and the scene faded from view.

Tuesday 1 May

Mel invited me to her room this morning. I sat, demurely, on the low armchair whilst she remained behind her desk. My mind was full of the sight of her in her revealing red leather. I raised my eyes to take in the usual track suited figure and was delighted to see that the top had been discarded and she was wearing a skimpy sleeveless T-shirt through which I could discern the outline of her breasts and the points of her nipples. She had obviously been involved in some very vigorous exercise as sweat on her skin made the garment cling to her. Her face was a little flushed from the efforts she had been making.

Mel raised the matter of my feelings of isolation. I told her that the only reason for them was that I had little cash and what there was had to be spent wisely and carefully. I didn't want to go down the road of major debt. It might not matter to some students, but I had always been hard-up and also very careful. Mel seemed to be moving uncomfortably in her seat as I spoke and she interrupted me and told me she hadn't had time to have a shower after her training run and would I mind if she had one now as she was getting chilly. I hadn't realised that the door in the middle of the wall opposite where I was sitting led to her personal shower and changing room. As she opened the door she asked me to lock the corridor entry door and told me we could keep talking.

I had seen Mel only partially clothed in my dream. I had not expected to see her naked soon after. She stripped off her T-shirt and dropped her track suit bottoms after pulling off her trainers. She had turned away from me and I had looked away, rather embarrassed, but I turned my head back to find her standing under the shower, water streaming off her perfect figure. Everything about her was quite understated, but bronzed and well toned. I took in the small, strong breasts with the nipples pointing slightly upwards, the muscles of her belly and the perfectly shaved cunt. I found her as exciting in the flesh as I had in my dream. This was a case of reality matching fantasy. After a few minutes in which I tried to give her an edited version of the dream I had last night, she stepped out of the shower and started to towel herself vigorously. She asked me if I could dance and I replied that I could get by but didn't think I could equal my dream performance. I was amazed when she said that I ought to try. She smiled at me and pointed out that if I had looked to her to teach me in my dream then I should accept that she could do it in real life. I smiled at her rather tremulously. Still naked, she stuffed her soiled clothes into a basket and put on another track suit and clean trainers. 'Come on,' she said, 'a dance will do us both a lot of good.

She took me to one of the small practice rooms at the side of the gym. I was wearing the regulation blouse and skirt with flat shoes. Mel sorted through a pile of CDs. I stood feeling rather awkward.

'The first thing you have to do is to be certain that you enjoy what you are doing,' she told me, echoing her dream advice. 'Let's see what you can do with this.' She started the CD of Ravel's Bolero. Without thinking I raised my hands to the back of my head and started the hip and upper body movements I had seen myself do the night before. Mel stood opposite me and imitated my stance and actions. I was delighted with her movements and moved more freely as I watched her.

After less than a minute she stopped and switched off the CD. I was disappointed and thought that I hadn't been doing well enough. I was surprised by her next words. 'You're doing really well, but somehow you seem to be constrained. I bet you gave yourself to the music in your dream. You can do that here, but I think we should strip off.'

Before I could respond she had stepped out of her tracksuit bottoms and I began to unclasp the waist band of my skirt. I had already seen her naked, and she had seen me pretty much so and enjoying my secret pleasure. Even so, I was hesitant and I stood in front of her in my bra and pants whilst she laughed and told me to come on. She was so open and friendly that I had no alternative but to shrug my way out of the two concealing garments. Mel looked at me and told me that I had a beautiful figure which would benefit from a bit of toning. I was embarrassed by the luxuriance of my bush compared to her neat nakedness. She told me not to worry and added, intriguingly, that she would see to that.

We stood opposite each other, quite naked. I recalled my dream. She had seen all this before, I remembered, and suddenly felt better. The music began and we twisted and then began to turn. We stamped our feet, rotated our buttocks, jiggled our breasts together, thrust out our hips, displayed our cunts and spun, seemingly quite consumed by the music. We were so close that I could feel the warmth from Mel's body and the rush of air as she twirled. I had eyes only for her erotic movements and ears only for the building tension of the music. As it ended we were facing each other and as one we stepped forward and pressed our bodies together in a gleeful hug. She asked me if I had enjoyed the dance, but she knew that I had. I knew that I had thrown off a number of useless inhibitions. Mel suggested that I might like to do a few toning exercises. I looked for my clothes, but she laughed again and said, 'No, as we are.' And why not, I thought.

We started hanging from the wall bars and lifting our legs. She could do fifty without effort. I stopped at twenty. We did press ups with the same score. We bent and twisted,

Mel did a back somersault, she developed a rosy glow, and I panted. 'Have you ever had a leather massage?' she asked me. I had no idea what she meant. She punched a security code into a door lock and in a moment was back with a length of leather about five centimetres wide and a metre long. 'I'll try you with this,' she said, and then you must give me one. Just jump up on the rings. We'll see if you like it.' My mind filled with the fantasies which had delighted me the last time I used the rings, but this time I was naked and Mel was there. I hung from the rings and felt my body lengthen and everything about me stretched out. Mel told me that she would stimulate my blood flow until I decided I had endured enough. I only had to drop from the rings and she would stop. All I wanted was for her to begin.

Her first strike was no more than a gentle slap across my back, the second was no harder but made my buttocks bounce. The third crossed the first one, the fourth caught me in the small of my back and made me shake, the fifth slammed up from my thighs and caught the underside of my buttocks. I rocked my body and in exchange received three more on my back and thighs. I could feel my breathing become faster and shallower. The blows were now paced more slowly, but were increasingly hard. I couldn't see Mel and I wanted her to whip my front. I pulled on the rings until I managed to draw the ropes together and twisted myself round to face her. She looked hard at me and swung the leather until it cracked against my right thigh. I shook and uttered a small cry, but I knew that this was the way that I could gain access to what I most desired. I shut my eyes when Mel caught me across my left thigh and opened them as the leather creased my belly. This was a biting blow and I let the air out of my lungs in a hoarse huff. Her next strike caught me just below my breasts and spread across my ribs. I wanted her to hurt me almost past bearing.

As far as I could I thrust my breasts out towards her. She looked at me and raised an eyebrow, I whispered 'yes' and received a cutting slash across my breasts which made me howl and shake. The next hit caught my belly from hip to hip. I swung my legs to ease the pain and felt a flutter in my belly. I opened my legs and thrust my pelvis forward. Mel raised her eyebrow again, but this time she didn't wait for an answer and struck me twice between my thighs, squashing my cunt and making me gulp for air which I wanted to use to scream, but found my throat constricted and my cunt reacting of its own volition. Juices spurted out of me and as I closed my eyes I saw that Mel had discarded the leather and had one hand between my thighs and the other on my breast, tweaking my nipple with her finger nails and squeezing my breast unmercifully. She prolonged my climax as I hung there and I gushed and dripped into her hand. She seemed to know just how to manipulate my clit and find my G spot with her savage fingers. I began to swing, shake and buck my hips. The last thing I recalled before I let go of the rings was the triumphant smile on Mel's face.

I landed sprawling on the mat. Mel stood over me, her eyes fixed on my awkwardly disposed limbs. She reached out a hand and I grasped it as she pulled me up. I started to apologise for having given myself over to my pleasure, but she stopped my words by laying her fingers on my mouth. She told me not to be silly and asked if I thought there was anything better than giving someone else such delight. I knew the answer to that one, it was enjoying it completely myself. Mel lay on her back lifting her feet and arms together. I didn't wonder she was so toned.

Without touching the floor with her hands she bounced herself into a standing position and sprang onto the mats. 'Your turn now,' she said. I picked up the leather and felt sick at the prospect of hitting her with it. I swished it in the air as she jumped up to the rings. For a moment I hesitated and then I wondered if the effect might be the same for her or whether it was just something which she enjoyed so that she might show off her beautiful body.

I struck her across the buttocks, quite gently, but enough to start her swinging. I tried to remember the sequence which she had used on me but decided that I might just as well go at it free style. When I struck her across the back there wasn't a quiver from her body. She seemed to be all muscle and in perfect control of herself. I drew back the strap and caught her across the small of her back and her waist. I slammed it into her tight little buttocks, but with apparently no effect. Two more to her back and a very sharp cut at the join of her thighs and her buttocks and I wanted to see her face and how she was faring. She continued to hang there waiting my next attentions. I walked round to her front and saw that she was breathing quite deeply with her ribs expanding so that every one was visible under her skin. I marvelled at the spareness of her body and wondered if being so slim meant that it hurt less than if she had had a little more covering.

My first strike caught her across the top of her thighs. It was harder than I intended, and she swung and twisted. The next strike was across her belly. I saw the muscles contract and then return to their relaxed position. I realised that she was looking straight at me. I caught her a sharp cut below her breasts and she shook and uttered a little mew. She had struck my breasts, so I gave hers a double slash first from left to right immediately followed by right to left. For the first time she cried out. Before she could fully recover I caught her across the tops of her thighs, she let out a low howl and bucked her hips. I pulled back my arm to repeat the blow, but Mel had lifted both legs so that her body was bent forward and her knees were on a level with her ears. I was presented with just one target, her naked and unfurling cunt. I struck it and she jerked and twisted. In a moment she had twisted her legs round the ropes and had let go of the rings and was hanging upside down with her legs apart and her cunt an easy target. I brought the leather down across her cunt and the cleft between her buttocks. At the moment of impact I heard her howl and received a spray across my waist. The target was seeping juice. I decided that I'd see if I could make the whole thing a bit more adventurous. I struck her once, twice, three times on her cunt, eliciting sprays of juice and cries from Mel. I stepped back and watched her body undulating from her shoulders to her thighs. I struck her again and this time the juices overflowed and began to run down her body towards her breasts. I discarded the leather as she began to howl and writhe and sank my fingers into her, pressing the thumb of my other hand against the little crater between her buttocks. She attempted to pull her body up, but my fingers were doing their work too well. Juices oozed and then gushed again. I held her close to me and the slightly sticky issue spread over my hips. I continued to apply my fingers to their task as she subsided and then renewed her orgasm. After four of these climaxes whilst hanging upside down she began to unwind her legs and I held her with my lips on her open petals and my tongue licking her erect clit. She couldn't take any more and I lowered her to the mats where she lay in a much more tidy pose than I had managed, but with much the same response as mine had been.

We hugged, showered, hugged again and dressed. I went back to my room in the hostel and clambered into bed. I almost immediately fell asleep.

Wednesday 2 May

I could hardly be disappointed that no dreams came to me last night, given the experiences I had shared with Mel. On the other hand I will have nothing to report when I see her next. I shiver whenever I think of what it felt like to inflict pain on her. At the start I had been apprehensive almost to the point of refusal, but towards the end I wanted to hurt her so that she could have the same response as I had. I realised that it was about power. I had enjoyed power over her when I pushed her into slashing at my cunt and making me come. I had power over her when I thrashed her between the legs until she had climax after climax. She was completely at her mercy, even to the point of penetrating her with my fingers. In the clarity of the working day this seems incredible, yesterday it was an instinctive reaction to prove that I could do as well as she could, at least in this one thing.

I had learned at last what it meant to give my body over to music and to enjoy the display of my naked body alongside another. I want to hold Mel in my arms and fondle her and kiss her, and sometime I'd like to thrash her into orgasm again, but this time I will dictate when it finishes. I suspect she will be unable to walk when I finish with her. I realise that this is sadistic, but I want her to do the same to me.

Thursday 3 May

I worked hard yesterday and am almost up to date with my revision. Mel didn't call me to see her, which I was not surprised about, though my mind was full of her every time I paused from my concentration on work. Quite late I went to bed and lay naked under the bed clothes. I put my hands between my thighs and I could feel the tickle of the hair of my bush on my wrists. I got up and went to my bathroom. I got out my nail scissors and began to prune away the fur between my thighs. It took a long time to reduce it to being short enough to shave, and I had a fair pile of cuttings on a paper towel. I turned on the sink tap and ran hot water into the sink. I soaped my flannel and applied it hot and soapy between my thighs. The pressure was distinctly pleasing as was the wet heat. I rinsed off the soap and applied shaving gel, but I realised that I really couldn't make this into a foam or it would be difficult for me to see what I was doing. I got out the razor I use for under my arms and opened my legs about as far as they would go. I was very nervous about cutting myself and so I started in the crease between my thigh and my belly. I thought it would be painful but it wasn't. Despite this I remained nervous and the presence of the razor at the gates of my sex made my heart beat fast and my breathing became a bit difficult. I drew the razor carefully across my outer lip towards the cleft. I had difficulty in keeping my hand steady and getting to the edge of the stubble. I got a mirror and inserted it under my thighs so that I could see exactly what I was doing from as many angles as possible. I had never looked at myself from this angle before and I was quite startled by what I saw. I drew the razor across three or four times. The skin appeared white and smooth underneath. I had managed to shave and do myself no damage, so far. I shifted my position and tried shaving with my left hand, but I was far too awkward to manage it. I opened my legs further, stood up over the mirror, pulled at my self with my left hand and ran the razor across the remaining bristle until I was completely free of any signs of my bush. I washed off the remaining gel and looked at myself in the mirror. This would take some maintenance, but it was really worthwhile. I was delighted with my naked, vulnerable cunt. Now I wanted something to happen to it.

Friday 4 May

This has been such a strange time for me that I forgot that next week is a reading week. We are supposed to go home. I don't have anywhere to go and I'd left it a bit late to organise my usual cleaning job at the hotel where I could always find somewhere to sleep and I could scavenge the kitchen's surplus. Things didn't turn out to be quite the disaster which I feared. Mel summoned me to her room at the morning break. She looked at me rather oddly and then after a moment's hesitation she asked me where I was going for the reading week. I was embarrassed and tried to think of a quick explanation. She saw through that straight away. She told me that she was going to stay at her uncle's house and that she would welcome my company. It turned out that her uncle was abroad. I went through the usual ritual of making sure that she was quite certain and thanked her. She told me she was going tomorrow and would be coming back on Sunday the 13th. I told her that I was pretty much penniless and didn't want to be a drain on her resources. She said I could help out with looking after the house and she'd welcome my company because she needed to do more work on her thesis and I could work on my studies. She told me to be ready at six thirty tomorrow morning so that she could make an early start.

I collected up all the books I needed and my few clothes and packed them in my ancient rucksack. The rest of the day I spent in the library until it was time to go to bed. I had a shower, checked my packing and slipped beneath the duvet. I was agitated by the prospect of a week with Mel in a strange place. I knew it was risky, she might come to dislike me and there was the risk that I might like her too much. After a good deal of tossing and turning and running over in my mind all the events in my dreams and the even more amazing experiences with Mel I must have slipped into that essential stage just before sleep when pictures form before my eyes. These are not dreams, they are usually very fleeting, but they are heavily influenced by recent events. I saw ropes and swings and garishly coloured drapes and then I was back with my master.

I was lying in bed when there was an abrupt sound and I awoke to find a servant with a silver tray in his hand standing beside the bed. He said nothing and I took a piece of paper from the tray. It commanded me to be ready for the women who would prepare me for that night's dancing.

I found two women by the bath, pouring scented lotions into it. The bath had very high sides and they helped me into it. I almost totally submerged in the warm, scented water. They whisked up bubbles to amuse me and then their hands were everywhere, soaping and rinsing me. I stepped out of the bath onto the warm floor and they patted me dry in every part of my body. The taller of the women led me by the hand to another room and there my hair was tinted to ensure that it was the same colour all over, my feet were massaged and the nails painted. One of them produced a razor and attended to my underarms and my shins and then I had to lie back and open my legs so that I could be shaved with infinite thoroughness and care. I knew I wouldn't be cut this time so I was able to relax as the girl's fingers pulled and squeezed the flesh of my cunt and drew the razor over every crease and fold. Make up was applied to most of my body. I had to stand up so that I didn't smear any of the work that they had done. Yet another woman came in pushing a trolley with a clothes rail on it. From the rail hung numerous garments. What I was to wear had already been decided. She showed me a green costume which consisted of a single layer short skirt and what I took to be a blouse which crossed over at the front and was secured by a hook and eye so small they were virtually invisible. The double layer of the cross over made a good attempt at concealing my breasts, but the cross over itself was low enough to show a good deal of cleavage. I wondered what sort of dance I was to perform in this outfit, but Mel appeared, this time in a dark blue leather outfit which emphasised her slenderness and left a great gap from the lower curve of her breasts to ten centimetres below her navel. She was wonderfully stylish and I envied her ability to be poised at all times. She started to instruct me in the dance that I must do, but it was more athletic than I thought I could cope with. She unhooked the coiled whip which hung at her side and showed it to me. She warned me that any short comings would be immediately rectified by the application of biting leather to my skin, and perhaps something worse. We had some more practice and then she led me to stand behind a pillar in a large room liberally furnished with huge sofas on which sprawled men and women wearing frightening animal masks. To one side was a small group of musicians who were quietly performing what I thought of as wallpaper music. This background didn't interfere with their conversation, nor with the various embraces and groping that were in progress. Several of the women were no longer fully dressed. I thought this was hardly fair to the dancers as they were an obvious distraction to the men.

The pace of the music changed and a man clad in a top hat and formal evening wear called for a dancer. From the side of the room opposite me a petite blonde girl, stepped into a space formed by the arrangement of the sofas. She was dressed in a number of lengths of coloured cloths, some apparently attached to a collar at her throat and some secured by a thin golden rope at her waist. I guessed that she was to lose some or all of these, but I hadn't realised that she was about to perform the dance of the seven veils. She made her way round the sofas swinging her body in time to the music, pattering her bare feet on the tiled floor and closely approaching and then dancing away from the audience.

Her dance was pleasingly erotic with quick glimpses of her legs and then her breasts as she turned and twisted, but they were only glimpses. I began to wonder what she would do next when she came close to a sofa where there was a couple, both with owl masks. The man was lying back, clearly happily intoxicated, but the woman was sitting upright and obviously very much in command of herself. As the girl turned before them the woman reached out and grasped one of the pieces of material. Her grip was firm and it came away in her hand. The loss of one veil made little difference, but the means of its removal woke up several of the audience. The dancer drifted across the square and turned before what appeared to be a very relaxed couple, but this time, as she moved away, there were two of her veils in the man's hands. I had a fine view of a naked leg and buttock and just the briefest vision of the side of a breast. She danced on without hesitation, twirling and twisting and sometimes just standing in the middle of the square moving her body in sensuous turns. She was remarkably adept at teasing her audience, all of whom concentrated their attention on her whilst she danced.

She set off once more to circle the lounging spectators. She passed a couple whose clothes revealed more of them than her veils did of her. As she turned away from her they both reached out and tore off two more of her veils. Now one hung from her collar and another, below it, from her waist. They were both at the front of her body and she managed to spread the upper one so that it covered her breasts. I was entranced by the way in which she twirled and the seductive movements of her hips, shaking her neat high buttocks as the music called for action. She was one of those rare women whose back view is as delightful as their front. She had slender arms, quite wide shoulders sloping down to a tiny waist and buttocks which were like two small footballs and as firm and strong. Her legs were shapely and slender and her tiny feet had toes each of which carried a jewelled ring.

She danced so that the audience had a brief and incomplete view of her breasts and belly. She trailed the veil at her collar in her hand so that as she turned it continued to cover her. I wondered what she was going to do next, but apparently she was not going to let the spectators remove any more veils. Instead she pulled at the veil at her waist, undid it and began to use it to cover herself as she danced. She was very clever and she managed to detach her collar veil without any of us realising until it floated to the floor, whereupon she received a round of applause. Now she was naked apart from two fine gold cords and the veil she held in her hands. The music was reaching a crescendo and she twirled faster and faster. Suddenly she raised her hands above her head and there she was, quite naked, revealing her beautiful body to the delighted spectators. She danced on until the music stopped and then curtsied to everyone present. A large man in a lion mask beckoned to her and in less time than it takes to tell she was curled in his lap with her arm round his neck and her head on his shoulder. He began to fondle her and she pressed herself even closer to him.

The music had stopped and then the master of ceremonies talked to the group for a short while. I had forgotten, just for a moment, that it was my turn next. I watched as the blonde girl moved in the man's lap as she opened his trousers. I could not see what she had found, but she moved her position so that she was sitting with her back to him, her hands on his knees and her legs widespread. She began to move her arse up and down, so I assumed that she had found a peg to steady herself on. He seemed to be enjoying the contact and I had a sudden impression of that small back and tiny waist blossoming out into superb buttocks bouncing on his rigid shaft. It made me wonder if I would have the same treatment. The master of ceremonies called my name and the music started again. I stepped out from behind the pillar and into the middle of the floor.

I was aware that all eyes, except perhaps those of the man the blonde was pleasuring, were on me. I started in on the routine which required me to do a good deal of writhing interspersed with gymnastic tricks. The first of these was a cartwheel which gave them all a very brief glimpse of my body up to my waist. I felt I wasn't as fit as I ought to be, but the cartwheel was complete and quick. I danced on as I had started and then bent backwards into a crab. I knew that at the end of drawing my feet closer to my hands I ought to be able to flip my legs over my head and bounce into an upright position. I also knew I couldn't do this so I opted for an easier way out and twisted over onto my knees and then stood up. Brief as my skirt was I knew that so far they had seen very little of what they wanted. I raised my hands above my head and turned the backs together, interlacing my fingers in the classic belly dancer's stance. I rotated my hips and shook my breasts, but I remained covered. It was almost as if I didn't want them to see what I was supposed to show.

At this point a bar, supported by a rope at each end was lowered from the ceiling. I jumped up to it and began to swing on it by my arms. Having got a good rhythm going I hauled myself up to get the bar under my arms. I raised my legs and moved them apart. The motion of the swinging moved my skirt up my thighs, but still I was preserved against their sight. I pulled myself up until I was sitting on the bar and swinging in time to the music. Then I dropped my body down backwards with my legs entwined in the ropes. As I fell back I managed to unhook the fastening of my blouse. This should immediately have given them a good view of my breasts, but I had to move awkwardly to pull the blouse behind me. As I hung upside down I tried to take the blouse off, but this proved very difficult and I failed to take advantage of my situation to make it seem as if I was being deliberately teasing. At last it fluttered to the floor and I hung upside down with my arms trailing out from my shoulders. I knew I had to try something else. There had been no applause.

I unwound my legs and pulled myself up onto the bar again. I went from sitting to standing and began to swing much more violently. I twisted so that the Velcro fastening of my skirt caught the rope and began to separate. A bit more and the skirt separated into a length of material and descended to the floor. Even then there seemed to be more interest in the blonde's antics than in my display. I dropped down so that I had a leg either side of the bar and lifted my arms to catch the rope behind me. I could feel the bar pressing against the cleft of my buttocks and separating the petals of my cunt. This would give them something to look at. I squirmed on the bar trying to get my clit in contact with the wood. I crossed my ankles and began to move so that my clit was getting the benefit of the pressure and the rubbing of the wood. I hoped that I would begin to feel the fluttering which announced I was on the way to a climax, but I caught sight of the blonde and lost the edge which would have driven me forward. I went through the motions, but there was no passion. At last I reached both ropes, pulled myself up, bent down to the bar and jumped backwards, swinging by my arms. There was a faint murmur of interest, but at that moment the blonde jerked her head back, clawed at her breasts with her hands and uttered the howl of the satisfied she-wolf. I dropped to the ground and was about to curtsey and depart when a powerful hand caught the upper part of my left arm. I stood still.

A woman in a tiger mask pointed at me and spoke, 'No passion, not even enough of interest for a pub stripper. She should be warmed up.' At once other hands seized me and I found my wrists attached to the ends of the bar on which I had just performed. I was hauled up until my feet were just clear of the floor. I didn't mind if they were going to take out their displeasure by whipping me, I knew I could go through the pain barrier and come out the other side to an all embracing climax.

I looked round to see the blonde curled up again on the big man's lap, but this time holding the rather flaccid remains of a quite huge cock. No wonder she had cried out. I knew that they would hear plenty more from me as the leather struck my skin.

Hands grasped my ankles and pulled them apart. I felt something cold penetrating my arse and then my cunt. Someone was counting, five, four, three, two, and one and then there was a sudden pressure at both my holes and I felt as if I was being inflated by a pump. The counting was shorter this time and at 'one' both the instruments with which I was being invaded were withdrawn. I hung quite inert for many seconds until I began to feel a heat developing in my arse and my cunt. It started as a not unpleasant warmth, but this grew rapidly to an increasing heat until I felt as if I had been transfixed by red hot pokers. Some substance had been pumped into me which was igniting me. Suddenly the pain took me over. I began to scream and twist and writhe. I moved my legs up and down together and alternately, but this had no effect on the fire burning within me. I howled at the pain. I had a sudden vision of a flaming torch being thrust between my legs. I tried squirming and lifting myself to try to cool myself down. I opened my legs as far as they would go, but all I achieved was the display of my cunt to the spectators who now seemed to be concentrating all their attention on me.

I tried to spin the bar so that cool air might waft between my legs, but nothing reduced the agonising fury of the fire. I felt my breathing become stertorous, I was sure that my heart rate had doubled. I felt that I would be the slave forever to anyone who would put out the fire. I could hear my howls and screams as if they were from a huge loud speaker. I began to dribble from my mouth and then, involuntarily, I felt the flutter which I had hoped would come earlier. I swung the upper part of my body against the lower part so that I was bouncing on the fastenings of my wrists. I was completely out of control of myself. Tears ran down my face and then the tortured membranes took their own way out and I began at first to seep juice and then to drip. I pulled my knees up to my head so that the juices would run down my perineum and penetrate into my open arse. At once gushes of juice started pouring from my cunt. I knew that I could manage three or four substantial pulses, but this time there was pulse after pulse. I could hear myself groan and howl. I could feel the liquid splashing from my cunt. I could no longer hold my knees up and I let them drop and hung inert and flaming between my legs.

Saturday 5 May

I waited for Mel for a couple of minutes and she turned up exactly on time. We put our bags in the trunk of her car and I sat beside her as she drove away from the college. She asked me if I had finished having dreams and I told her an abbreviated version of the night before. This took some time and when I mentioned that she had again appeared she put her hand on my thigh and squeezed gently. She asked me what she looked like in my dream and I described the leather suit which I had seen. She told me that my vision of her was most remarkable and was about to add something else when we got stuck behind an ancient heap driven by an even more ancient pensioner. At last she found enough room to overtake safely and we were soon back to something rather more than the legal maximum. I had no idea where we were going and asked her. She told me the name of a village near Cape Cod, but I was really none the wiser given that there were numerous villages on the Cape. We found our way beyond the conurbation and I saw high hills in front of us. Mel swore under her breath and headed off the Interstate onto a narrow, winding road down the side of a valley. There seemed to be trees everywhere. We crossed a bridge over a stream and then, in the middle of a wood, turned sharp right through a gateway. We carefully made our way up a narrow track with a big drop on the driver's side, turned at a sharp bend and were presented with an almost impossibly steep section of tarmac with trees which overhung like a tunnel. Very shortly the gable end of a large stone barn came into view and then on our left, a large and oddly arranged house. Beyond it was a stone garage with a large shuttered door. Mel told me to pick up the remote control in the open ash tray and press the button. At once the door began to rise and without stopping Mel drove in on the right hand side. To the left was a beautiful racing green Aston Martin. It was as well that Mel's Chrysler was relatively small.

We got our bags out of the trunk. Mel pressed the remote again and the door started to close. We walked under a large chestnut tree to what seemed to be the back entrance of the house. Mel's key opened the door but there was then the sound of an alarm. We went hastily through another door into a rather untidy room and Mel dropped her bags and punched numbers into the security pad. Everything went quiet.

She asked me if I would like to sleep in the old part of the house or the new. I had no idea what either would be like, so I opted for the old. She took me up one of the staircases and opened a door off a gloomy corridor. The room was large - well, large by my standards. The floor was of highly polished oak planks, but not very flat. Dominating the room was a four poster bed complete with a valance at ceiling height and curtains caught back at each of the posts. It was a high bed, almost as high as the table in the corner. A door close to one corner led to an elegant bathroom with walls and floor covered in very large grey marble slabs and a long bath with spa and Jacuzzi jets. I hardly had time to take it all in when Mel said that she would have the room across the corridor. I dutifully followed her leaving my rucksack by the bed. This room was similar to mine, but as well as a row of small windows high up on the long wall, the end wall was glass from floor to ceiling and virtually the full width of the room. A big climbing rose spread its blooms along the windowsill. Her bathroom was similar to mine except that the marble was pink.

Mel said she'd like a wash and then she'd show me the kitchens. There were two. One was a galley kitchen for breakfasts and small meals whilst the other was down yet another flight of stairs at a different level from the old part of the house. This was an ultra modern and sophisticated kitchen/diner with a magnificent oak table and chairs and an oak dresser. Patio doors led into a steeply sloping garden. Mel sorted through the contents of the fridge and the freezer and thawed a loaf of bread. In a very few minutes we had toast and marmalade, egg and bacon and Jamaican Blue Mountain coffee with hot milk and Demerara sugar. I hadn't realised how hungry I was. Everything was put into a dishwasher and we sat on a huge leather sofa enjoying the view.

We went upstairs and Mel opened the door of the room over the one downstairs. Apart from its size the most obvious feature was the roof which had huge exposed oak beams connected by an intricate framework of stainless steel bars. I said it looked like a gym and Mel added, 'Yes, and something else.' There was an en suite bathroom and another room which turned out to be a vast walk in wardrobe. There were racks of clothes and carefully labelled drawers for various items of underwear. There were three drawers for gloves and on the back wall was a floor to ceiling rack containing shoes of every imaginable variety. Mel's aunt had been on the stage, her career cut short by an aeroplane accident in Colorado. No wonder the clothes looked exotic.

We went outside. There was a high, old fashioned barn that Mel took me into. The inside of it was like a medieval cathedral with huge beams and innumerable rafters. Mel suggested that we should explore the grounds after lunch. And in the meantime we returned to the house and Mel led me into a cosy sitting room. She clapped her hands and the fireplace was at once alive with a flame and crackling wood. She smiled at her party trick. Mel produced a lap top computer and a note book and settled to work. I collected some books and followed her example.

Lunch was followed by a stroll. Some of the grounds were ancient woodland, some more modern plantations. There were pleasant open gardens, well tended, and shrubberies with disappearing passageways in them. We returned to the house for tea and a slice of cake. Mel attended to her studies again and I followed suit.

About half past six Mel got up and refused my offer of help. In fifteen minutes she was back, wearing high heels and a long velvet coat. I hadn't realised that she was going to dress for dinner and wondered how I was going to cope. She walked about for a short while and asked me if I liked the coat. It was beautiful, and I said so. 'Then what about this?' she asked, and threw off the coat. Mel stood there dressed as I had seen her before, but only in my dreams. She was wearing a dark blue backless leather halter top which failed to cover the whole of her breasts and was secured with a thin leather thong at the back. The whole of the lower part of her chest and almost all her belly were bare. Her leather tights were cut so low in front that another centimetre would have shown the cleft below her mons. They were slightly higher at the back, but there was still cleavage on view there. They were so tight that I had no idea how she got them on until I noticed a flap concealing a zip which ran up each leg.

'Is this what I wore in your dream?' she asked. She beckoned me to follow her and I walked behind her admiring the tilting of her hips and the dimple on each side of her spine above her buttocks. She opened the vast wardrobe door. 'I thought you might like to choose a costume. Take your time. You might want to find something to dance in.' I felt a little shiver as I realised that she wanted to replicate the dream I had told her about. She went into the big empty room next door whilst I moved from one rack of clothes to the next. Eventually I found what I guessed must be there and took a hanger which held a pale blue chiffon top and skirt. I stripped off my dull day clothes and put on the skirt which was caught at the waist with a lengthy strip of Velcro. This could be made to fit almost anyone. I wrapped it round me and with the top it looked like a diaphanous chiton, all too suitable for gymnastic exercises. I went into the big room to find Mel sitting on a window seat. Her attention was at once entirely on me. She told me that she thought I needed toning and that we might as well have a session before we ate. She started with press ups, followed by exercises for abs and then simple bending and stretching. I was sure that it was all very good for me, but that was about it. I puffed a bit but although I wasn't toned I was quite fit so I managed without too much difficulty. She told me to jump up and hang on to one of the steel bars which supported the roof. This was easily done, but my top pulled out of the waist band of my skirt and opened at the front. Mel laughed. I was about to try to hang on with one hand and adjust my gaping garment when she gave a sharp pull on my skirt which obeyed the laws of gravity, leaving my front elevation quite naked. Mel looked at me appreciatively. She told me that she noticed that I had made a small improvement to my appearance since we were last together and I shivered slightly as the air touched my unaccustomedly naked cunt.

She instructed me in lifts of my feet, raising my legs so that I could double my body up, twisting my legs in the rope and hanging head down, whereupon I lost the top I had been wearing. She taught me how to spin whilst holding on to the rings, and then, sensing that I was becoming tired she allowed me to lower myself to the ground. I stood before her awaiting her next instruction, but she reached out her right hand, grasped my left nipple and drew me close to her.

'You're lovely now, but just you wait. I've all sorts of things in mind for you.' I was tempted to ask what these might be, but I didn't. I had a shower, put on a pair of jeans and a T-shirt and went in search of Mel. I found her in the kitchen dressed in a patterned silk kimono and with an apron tied round her waist. She was preparing a fruit salad. The first course was in the oven.

She told me that we were to have a visitor after dinner and she smiled secretively when I asked her who it was. At exactly eight o'clock there was a ring at the front door bell. Mel went to answer it and ushered in a middle aged woman in a white coat who was pushing a large trolley. We all adjourned to the kitchen. The woman took the cover off her trolley and then spread a big plastic sheet on the floor. Mel put a chair in the middle of it and I was invited to sit down. I was at once enveloped in a large blue cloth which was secured at my neck. Mel told me that Mrs Jones was the best hairdresser in the area and that she would cut, style and colour my hair. She thought auburn would be nice and she smiled again at me. I knew that this was another stage in the change of the dowdy me to the interesting and exciting person I always hoped was lurking behind my normally dismal appearance.

It was well after eleven by the time Mrs Jones finished. My hair was now short, curly and a beautiful shade of auburn. She had made up my face and she left me with instructions on the maintenance of my hair and with lots of cosmetics. Mel saw her out and I indistinctly heard a conversation about payment. When she came back I told Mel that I wanted to pay for the transformation, but she refused, since it was her idea, and led me into the bedroom so that I could get a full size look at myself. I shouldn't say so but I had become amazingly attractive, at least compared with my normal dowdy self. I turned to Mel and caught her in my arms.

Sunday 6 May

I don't know what I had expected last night, but I slid into the beautiful feather bed, switched off the light, hoped that Mel might join me and was cast into a dreamless sleep within a couple of minutes. When I awoke this morning I went into the bathroom and yawning, looked in the mirror where I was greeted by a total stranger. I just stood there, unmoving, for several seconds before the surprise wore off and I was able to take in this new image.

The day was quiet. We got on with our studies quite companionably. We ate, walked in the grounds and enjoyed the spring weather. In all sorts of ways it was close to being paradise for me. Every so often I sneaked off to the bathroom to take another look at myself. This would take some getting used to. Besides which, for the very first time I was pleased with what I looked like.

In the late afternoon Mel suggested that we might have a toning session. We went to the empty bedroom. Mel handed me a tiny green thong and a matching bra with two small triangles of silk and bootlace straps. As I was putting these on Mel echoed my dress but in yellow which stood out on her tanned skin. We went through yesterday's exercises together with a good deal of aerobic stepping up and down on a low stool. After a session of press ups and running on the spot we had both managed something of a sweat. Mel looked at me approvingly and told me I was fitter than she thought. I suspected that this was down to having to walk everywhere.

Her next remark left me breathless. She stood in front of me and looked me in my eyes, 'I want you to do to me exactly what it is you would like me to do to you, so that I may have the experience and know how to treat you.'

She handed me a leather whip about a metre and a half

long. I must have stammered. I told her that I couldn't, despite the fact that I already had. She told me not to be silly. Her manner was direct and matter of fact. I stood there dry mouthed and trembling. Once more I felt slightly sick at the prospect of whipping Mel's beautiful body. I tried to refuse. She told me she would take me back to the college that very moment if I found her repulsive. There was no question of that. I swallowed hard and asked her to grasp the rings. She removed her bra and lightly sprang up to the rings and hung there. I realised that although I had seen her unclothed before I had not really looked at her closely. A certain shyness had prevented me from examining her as I would have liked to have done.

This was soon rectified. I found myself standing at one side of her looking at her face and body in profile. Her hair was caught up at the nape of her neck in a French plait. She had small ears and high cheekbones. Her eyes were a penetrating blue and were separated by a slender, short nose over full lips slightly parted. Her arms were well muscled and shapely whilst her breasts, emphasised by the pose she had adopted, were of medium size and very pointed with nipples which protruded from them as if they were erect. Mel has not the slightest evidence of surplus flesh and her ribs showed through the covering of skin. The pull on her arms had elongated her body and her buttocks stood out in sharp relief. To my surprise I gathered the courage to rip off the thong she was wearing so that I might see every part of her. Whilst her belly was quite flat, her mons dominated the naked, closely furled gap between her legs. Her thighs were strongly provided with muscle and her calves matched them, leading to small elegant feet. I thought she was lovely. I took a couple of steps to bring me to her back and I gazed in wonder at the clearly defined muscles and the way her waist appeared to be dovetailed into the spread of her hips. In a moment I was at her front looking at my victim hanging there naked. I had not realised how striking her features were with her hair drawn back, or how her breasts were pulled together with her arms above her head. I wanted to run my hand over her breasts and down that beautiful, taut belly and press my fingers into her. Then it dawned on me that if this was what I wanted her to do for me, I should now take up the opportunity to do it to her.

She shivered as I brushed my palm over her breast and took hold of her nipple between my finger and thumb. I shifted my hand so that I could hold her buttocks and put my lips to her breasts, nibbling at her nipples and sucking them out to their fullest erection. I ran my finger tips down the crease between her buttocks and found her secret place. She uttered a little whimper as I pressed my second finger into her. I bent my head to her belly and licked round her navel. I could feel her legs moving as she thrust her pelvis out towards me as I traced a line down the crease between her legs and her belly. There was only one place I was going and she knew it. I kissed the fleshy top of her mons and nuzzled the cleft below it. She opened her legs as far as she could and my lips contacted the slightly open petals of her cunt. I sank my tongue between the first and second layers of her protective lips and by luck my protruding tongue caught her clit. Mel gave another cry and I lapped at her bud feeling the sheath open and the little roseate button moved out to meet my intruding tongue. I pressed harder between her buttocks and I felt her push herself into my mouth. The muscles in her belly tightened and I knew it was time to move on. Mel howled as I removed my mouth and my finger from her. She shook her body and crossed and uncrossed her legs. I had left her nearly at the point of her climax and I knew she would be deeply frustrated.

I stood back and enjoyed the image of her body writhing

to make herself come, but without success. She presented a deeply and darkly sexual image, hanging helpless and frustrated and still writhing with her eyes closed and her mouth open. I watched her movements wondering how she would respond to the whip this time. I was determined to find out and so I stood behind her and to her left. I held the handle almost at its end so that I could get the maximum purchase on it. I swung it about several times in order to get the feel of its weight and be sure that I had total control over it. The end, with its hard leather keeper whistled as I struck the air. This was a formidable weapon. I would have to be careful that I inflicted no damage. After a couple of minutes whilst Mel continued to hang from the rings I turned the whip so that it sliced upwards against her buttocks. I had intended it as a warming up shot, but it was obviously harder than I had expected. Mel uttered a muffled snort and swung her body. I counted to five and placed the next strike across her back to reach the tip of the whip just over her shoulder. After another pause I caught her across her waist and she drew up her knees as if to relieve herself of the pain. The fourth strike was across her buttocks and I saw the white weal develop across the globes of her arse and begin to turn pink to match the others. I began to speed up my attack on her, striking her back repeatedly as the end of the whip curled round her body, into her arm pit and then biting the side of her breast, or swinging from her back across her belly. Mel was suffering now and her mouth was permanently open with her head well back between her arms and tears running from her eyes whilst she uttered long drawn out howls but still she hung on to the rings. If she had let go it would have been all over. I walked to her front and saw the patches of bright pink where the end of the whip had caught her. I moved to her left side and as she hung in her agony. I swung the whip against her, catching her across the belly. She made a strangled gurgling sound and lifted both her knees. I swept the whip up from the ground and caught her across her buttocks from underneath her legs. She immediately dropped her knees and I slashed her across the top of her thighs and followed this up with a strike just below her breasts. I could see and hear the vigorous rise and fall of her chest which took her breasts with it. I couldn't resist the sight of her breasts buckling and creased by the blow from the whip and then springing back to their original shape. I felt a sudden desire to haul her down from the rings and kiss and console her, but the trial of her courage was not yet over.

I wanted to attend to that beautiful, neat crease at the base of her belly. I wanted to bury the tail of the whip in there so that she would scream and weep and shake so that I could comfort her. I caught her again across her belly and again she raised her knees as if to protect her body. I saw that her knees were open and shortening my grip on the whip I struck up between her legs and surprised myself with the force and accuracy of my strike. I saw the end of the whip disappear between her buttocks, and the next length cut its way between the guarding lips of her sex. For a moment everything was quiet, but then she dropped her legs and drew in her belly as she filled her lungs with air to create the most dreadful howl of agony I had ever heard. She was swinging on the rings and twisting her body in an attempt to reduce the pain. Her head was as far back between her arms as it would go and her body was contorted into a rigid arc. She drew up one leg and as her foot came level with her belly I struck her again and then again as she appeared to be paralysed by the pain. Then I saw the juices gathering at the lips of her cunt. I dropped the whip and adopted the position I had taken just before I started to whip her. Her cunt was sticky with her sweet juices and once more I began to use my tongue, this time to lap up the juice she was producing and then to stimulate her further with my teeth at her clitoris. I pressed into her underneath with my fingers and she began to buck her hips so that I had difficulty keeping engaged with my tongue and lips. I transfixed her with my long finger in her arse and held on to her left buttock with my free hand, digging my nails into the bright red weals unmercifully. I felt her belly begin to throb and I knew that I must complete my work on her as quickly as possible. I poked, sucked and nibbled as hard as I could. Suddenly the trickle became a flood and Mel seemed to go into a paroxysm of release. Juices gushed into my mouth and over my face. I could hear her crying out with that unmatchable howl of the female who is at the very peak of her sexual delight. I continued with my efforts until she became quiet and ceased to move. I knew that I had come close to a release myself and that I was distinctly sticky between my thighs.

I tried to pull her off the rings, but her grip was so strong that I had no effect at all. I stood holding her round the waist and with my face pressed against her breasts. I spoke soothingly to her and after a while she started to relax and then her grip left the rings and I held her close as she slumped forward. I lowered her to the carpet and cuddled her and kissed her, telling her how beautiful she was and how brave, and reassuring her and then saying how much I admired her while cradling her in my arms. The touch of her trembling naked body was utterly wonderful. Mel lay in my arms quite unresisting. She was mine to do whatever I wanted with. One part of me wanted to kiss her and be gentle with her, another part wanted to stand back and make her crawl whilst I thrashed her.

Mel's eyes fluttered open and she looked at me with a strange mixture of love and awe. She lifted her face and I kissed her eyes and then her mouth. She opened her lips to me and I thrust my tongue into her. She lifted a hand and touched my breast. I feared that she might want her revenge there and then, but her fingers were gentle. She enclosed my breast with her fingers and I kissed her again. I shifted my position so that I could hold her more comfortably, only to find that the movement had enabled Mel to put her free hand on my knee. She slid her fingers along the soft inside of my thigh and in a twinkling she had opened me with her thumb and forefinger. As our breasts and mouths pressed together in a passionate embrace, she inserted two fingers deep into me and used her thumb to agitate my clitoris. I was absolutely ready for her penetration, but I had not expected her to find my G spot again. In all too short a time I was pulsing into her hand and she was kissing my breast, my eyes and my mouth as I had hers a little while before.

We managed to recover, put on some clothes, eat a very light meal and retire to my bed complete with books and notepads. Being in bed with Mel in companionable affection was a wonderful end to the day. I wasn't at all surprised that when it happened my sleep was quite dreamless.

Monday May 7

I rolled over in bed as the light came through the shutters and found Mel looking at me. I asked if she was all right and she pulled down the bedclothes, kneeled up and showed me the front of her body. There remained numerous weals and small darker patches where they crossed each other. I started up in the bed and clasped her in my arms. I was utterly overcome by her beauty and the damage I had done to her skin and burst into tears. I should have been consoling her, but she comforted me. After a shower she handed me a bottle with a hand-written label telling me that the contents were glycerine and ichthyamol. She gave me a small pad of cotton wool and instructed me to go over her body with the lotion. She assured me that so good was this mixture that by tonight just about all the marks would be gone. I loved touching her, but hated the signs of the damage I had inflicted. After breakfast the post van was admitted through the gates and Mel extracted a letter from among the plastic covered catalogues and read it. Her face lit up. She told me that the letter was from her cousin who was coming back from Australia and wanted to stay at the house. I held my breath. I wondered when this was likely to be. My query was answered much sooner than I had expected. Mel's cellphone made a peculiar singing noise and she delved for it in her bag. It turned out to be a text announcing that her cousin was on his way from Boston, hoped to catch the 10.35 and could she pick him up at New Bedford where Amtrak said they would deliver him at 12.45.

My face must have given away the disappointment which I felt. Mel put her arm round my shoulders and told me not to worry. 'We shall do whatever we want, just as if he wasn't here. But I can promise you that he's a really nice man with a great sense of humour, very broad minded and likely to love being with you.' I hardly thought so and felt that my paradisaical existence was about to be ruined by the advent of a serpent.

We had some elevenses and then Mel drove us to New Bedford. Finding a space in the station car park we awaited the arrival of her cousin. I realised I didn't know his name. He was apparently called Kerr, which also didn't endear him to me, but then, what could?

Mel let out a little shriek, pointed, and made a bee line for a man who was coming through the barrier. That was the first time I saw Kerr. He was about six feet tall, wide in the shoulder, narrow in the waist and hip, sun tanned, dark haired and so good looking that I felt my knees go weak. I pulled myself together because if he was anybody's he was Mel's. She flung herself at him. He dropped his case, picked her up, held her close and laughed, swinging her round as if she was a child. He put her down as she said something to him and he looked across at me and gave me the benefit of as beautiful a set of even white teeth as I'd ever seen. I walked towards them and he held out his hand. His hand was big, slightly rough, dry and completely enfolded mine. Without any warning he drew me towards him and I found that his free hand was at the nape of my neck and he was kissing me as if we had known each other for years. I was totally overwhelmed. I must have looked it because Mel said that she had warned me that I would like Kerr. I felt a profound buzz at his touch and revelled in the slightly musky, clean smell of the man.

We made it home with Kerr sitting in the back of the car with his head between us, talking happily. He was amazing for someone who had travelled for eighteen hours. Mel had got ready a meal of soup and salad with an apple crumble and ice cream to follow. Kerr produced a bottle of Australian wine and we sat having a pleasant lunch followed by coffee and chocolate mints. After it was over we all cleared away. Once the dishwasher was going I tactfully suggested that they might like to be alone, but that was immediately denied and we went out on to the terrace and lolled in the loungers with soft drinks.

Kerr sat between us. He looked first at Mel and then at me. He flattered us by telling us that we were the two most beautiful women he had seen in the last six months. He was definitely the handsomest man I had ever spoken to. I didn't tell him. He gave the impression of great physical strength, but there was more to him than just that. The sun had become quite hot. Kerr was obviously uncomfortable. Mel suggested that he might like to do a bit of sun bathing. He lay back on the recliner having removed his shirt to reveal a strongly muscled torso. He gazed up at the tree above him watching the gently moving leaves. Mel winked at me and put her finger to her lips. Kerr slept.

She suggested that we might follow his example. She collected the thongs and bras we had worn so briefly the day before. I demurred, thinking that it was showing off. Mel told me that Kerr would be his friendly, laid back self if we were both naked. I hoped not. We put on the scraps of material and started work on our books.

An hour passed and then another. Kerr lay back, quite unmoving, until suddenly he was wide awake with his legs straddling the recliner. He apologised for sleeping and said he'd follow our example. In a couple of minutes he reappeared dressed only in a pouch at his groin which bulged interestingly. I caught myself staring at him and looked away in confusion.

He produced a paperback and laid back, 'soaking up a few rays,' as he put it. I wanted to touch him and investigate the contents of his pouch, but I tried my hardest to suppress these thoughts. I was trying to give my full attention to a book on classroom discipline. It described the sanctions of the past in great detail. I found myself becoming more interested than I should have been. It was an academic text, after all. I glanced across at Kerr as he turned the page of his book, revealing the lurid cover. It was a photograph of a naked young woman on tip toe facing the reader with her wrists chained above her head. I didn't quite catch the title or the author's name, but it was clear to me that Kerr was reading a very sexy novel. When I glanced up at him again I saw that his pouch was much fuller than it had been and he was moving his bottom to get more comfortable.

I saw that Mel had not missed either the book or the effect it was having on the reader. She laughed and told him that if he would read erotic novels he might just get a frustrated buzz out of them. Kerr laughed in return and replied that he felt he was strangled by the laws of decency. I saw that Mel was undoing her bra and was showing him her pretty breasts. She nodded to me and I started to remove mine. Kerr stared straight at me and told me that my breasts were beautiful, just like the rest of me. Mel told him that he could relieve himself of his strangulation if he wished, but he said he didn't want to shock us. Mel undid the cord of her thong and with my heart beating fast and a dry throat I undid mine. In a moment we were both quite naked. Kerr made no attempt to follow our example. Mel looked at him and then at me. 'Do you suppose he's got anything in there?' she asked me, pointing at Kerr's pouch. 'Go on, fish it out,' she commanded.

I was immobile and speechless. Kerr turned his head to me and told me to help myself, if I wanted to. If only he knew how much I wanted to. Mel told me to come on and I swung off the lounger and knelt on one knee by Kerr. I looked into his face and he smiled at me. Taking courage I looked at the bulging pouch and unhooked the bootlace strap which was pulled up to his waist. Without looking at him I took hold of the top of the pouch which was much thicker and more rigid than I had imagined, and drew it down his groin. At once a superb penis unbent itself and stood out from his groin and belly. I couldn't resist touching it and I tried to get my thumb and second finger round it without success. Kerr laughed and told me that he had got me measured as a very prim and proper lady, but if I liked his equipment it was mine to do with as I liked. I gave a few trial rubs up and down and caught Mel's eye. I was about to let go and apologise when I saw the radiant smile on her face. I tried a few more and his cock became noticeably harder. As I looked up again I saw Mel stand up with her fingers in her cunt. She looked at me, reached over Kerr and squeezed my breast, and then she told me it was her turn. All sorts of thoughts had been racing through my mind, mostly connected with getting Kerr to penetrate me. I was amazed to see Mel put my desires into her own practice. She kneeled on the recliner with a knee either side of Kerr's waist. Reaching between her legs she got hold of Kerr's cock and levered it up to vertical and then rubbed it on her sex as she lowered her thighs. She lowered herself steadily on to him whilst her fingers were busy with her clit and her breast. She slowly raised herself and as slowly re-engaged with Kerr. He had brushed her hand away from her breasts and had a hand on each of them, cupping them in his palms with his thumbs pressing and rotating her nipples. I saw that there was virtually no evidence of the thrashing I had given her the night before. She repeated the slow descent and lifting perhaps twenty times before I saw that she was beginning to gasp and utter little cries whilst Kerr's dick glistened from the gathering juices of her orgasm. I counted three more, rather quicker descents and Mel howled her characteristic cry of release. I watched as she shook her breasts, worked her buttocks on to Kerr's thighs and spurted onto his groin and belly.

All too soon I found that the show was over. I was rather disappointed that Mel had enjoyed this beautiful experience, but I was again left with so little.

Mel bent forward and kissed Kerr on the lips. He held her against him and said something to her. She nodded and slowly sat up and then levered herself across Kerr's body. As she stood up I was surprised to see that Kerr's cock was not only still rigid, but nodding gently. He smiled at me, moved a bit on the recliner, patted the space he had made and invited me to sit next to him. I did as I was asked but had great difficulty in preventing myself from following Mel's example. He searched under the recliner and came up with the book he had been reading. He held it towards me, with the cover fully visible. The naked redhead was chained to a post. Her body showed the weals of a recent whipping. There was a sheen on the inside of her thighs and her nipples stood out from her breasts as if they had been sucked into erection. She was very pretty and very vulnerable.

'Mel says she owes you one. This picture reminds me of you. Could you bear it if I was to whip you?' My heart seemed to turn over in my chest. My mouth became dry. I was filled with a mix of fear and desire. Whatever this man wanted he could have from me. I whispered 'yes' as I lowered my head. Kerr made a gesture towards Mel and then, sitting up, he held me in his arms.

'There is nothing, absolutely nothing like being whipped into orgasm and then kissed and comforted and at last fucked into mindlessness. Do you like the menu?' I nodded my head, wondering if I would be able to cope. I wanted him so much and I knew the pain would eventually bring me some relief, but what was that compared with the comfort of his arms and the pressure of his cock inside me?

Mel reappeared with a basket in her hand. Kerr swung

off the recliner which tipped and deposited me on the tiles. He reached down a hand and helped me up. As he did so I found that I had pressed myself against him and that he had a hand on my arse. I could feel his cock pulsing against my belly and I longed to seize it in my mouth and, having got him to the point of no return, get him to plunge himself into me. I was awakened again from a fantasy by Mel inviting me once more to 'come on.'

We walked into the garden and Mel pointed to an old oak with many calluses on its venerable bark. I was instructed to stand facing it. I could feel the faintest of tremors in my cunt as I moved towards it. Without any warning I found that they had each grasped one of my wrists and had pulled me so that I was embracing the trunk with the rough bark pressing against my breasts and belly. They secured my wrists and they then took an ankle each and repeated the process so that I hung with my legs apart as if I was making love to the old tree. I could feel a hard lump of bark between my thighs and I pressed my cunt on it. I turned my head to the right and saw Mel hand the still rampant Kerr a black leather tawse. I knew that this would hurt me and I clung to the tree for consolation and support.

There was no pause in the action. I heard Kerr swing the tawse through the air. It was a trial run. The next swing caught me across my back and I squeezed my body as hard as I could against the tree, chafing my breasts, belly, cunt and inner thighs on the bark and involuntarily uttering a squeal. I recalled that only a few days ago I had wanted to be involved with a strong, dominant boy friend, but what I would have done with him there I didn't know. I knew I couldn't count on Kerr as a boyfriend, however much he fitted into the other criteria. What I hadn't expected was that he would turn out to be so immediately what I thought I had wanted, and fierce as well. These thoughts flashed through my mind during the pause after his first strike. I turned my head to the right and I could see Mel, looking simply beautiful standing naked a metre or so away and looking at me intently. The second slash was across my buttocks and forced my belly and cunt hard against the tree. I cried out as much against the pressure between my legs as the slash to my buttocks. They stung and quivered. I opened my eyes to look at Mel, who stood just where she had been, still watching me. The third and fourth strikes came in rapid succession, one across my back and the other at waist level. I wanted to shake my body to relieve the pain, but the rough bark caught at my breasts.

I was unprepared for the next two strikes which swept up from the ground scraped the bark of the tree and bit me between my thighs. The pain was excruciating, but I could do nothing to relieve it except howl. Even that was limited by my inability to get enough breath into my lungs. I shook my head in protest, but I knew that I would have to put up with far more than this, just as Mel had done, except that her immolation had been voluntary. There was a pause in the proceedings and I felt a hand on my right buttock. In a moment a thumb dug into my arse and fingers opened further my bruised petals. I put my head back and looked up into the branches of the tree and the dense dark foliage above them. I had no way of avoiding the penetration of my body by these fingers, even if I had wanted to. My body stung with the whipping I had received, but the pain diminished as the exploring, penetrating fingers worked on me. I began to feel a flutter in my belly and my cunt began to feel turgid. I knew it would not be long before I started to drip and then to gush. I was breathing heavily, drawing lungfuls of air into myself against the pull of the bonds that secured me. Almost all of my attention was riveted on the space between my legs and my belly. A knot seemed to form just below my navel. I felt the beginnings of a trickle from within me and suddenly the intrusive hand was withdrawn and it slapped me across my buttocks. I pressed myself as hard as I could against the big callus on the side of the tree and twisted in the hope that pressure here and contact with my clit would complete the work started by the penetrating fingers. I became desperate to reach a climax, but the knot had loosened and I was too slow to achieve what I wanted.

My legs were being undone and my feet dropped onto the visible roots of the tree. I was relieved when my arms were released, though I had underestimated how much I had depended on the tree to keep upright. I was about to fall backwards when Kerr turned me round and in a trice secured my wrists to a rope whose end he expertly tossed over a low branch. He moved it so that it was in the fork where the branch met the trunk of the tree and then hauled me up until my feet were clear of the ground. For Mel and Kerr it was the work of only a moment to bend my legs behind me and secure them so that my ankles were either side of the trunk. My buttocks were compressed by this manoeuvre and thrust my cunt out at them. I looked out from my bonds at them. Mel was standing close to Kerr looking at me. He had his left arm across Mel's shoulder with his hand draped over her breast and the tawse hanging down her body. His other hand was wrapped round his cock which had become as solid as it was before Mel had made use of it. Although only vestiges of my previous excitement remained I could feel a new stirring as I looked at Kerr.

Still looking at me, Kerr said that it would be a pity to spoil the beautiful skin that I was showing him. I had no desire for my skin to be spoiled, but I didn't see that I had any choice. Mel moved back several steps and Kerr raised the tawse, shaking it in front of me. I was justifiably frightened of what he was going to do to me, and felt a pressure in my bladder as well as my belly. He looked at me as if he was hungry and then swung the tawse in an arc whose end was its impact with my belly. I was grievously hurt and screamed out to announce my pain. He ignored me and I saw the tawse hanging in the air before it struck the lower part of my ribs. The pain seemed to double at each cut of the tawse. He slashed me across my thighs, the lower part of my belly, below my breasts and then across my breasts which buckled under the force of the blow, only to return to their original shape with tramlines of weals across them. I was beyond crying out, so ferocious and continuous was the attack. I knew that he would soon slash me between my pinioned legs and that I might quite possibly avoid the agony by fainting.

Instead he came close to me and he took my right breast in his hand, pulling at my nipple as if he wanted to draw it out into a shape and length it had never had. He kissed my mouth whilst his right hand slid down my body towards my thighs. My mouth was open to his probing tongue and his fingers carefully opened my cunt, sliding two long fingers deep inside me whilst his thumb cruelly engaged with my bruised clitoris. I could feel his fingers exploring inside me as I tried to contract my muscles on to them. I couldn't believe that this beautiful, civilised man could be so barbarous. I had no defence at all against his probing, and slowly but surely he changed my situation to one where again I was just a willing partner in the brutal game, displaying my naked cunt and hoping that I would get the satisfaction of an explosive climax.

It was certainly coming closer. He transferred his fingers to my left breast and held it cupped in his palm. He squeezed in rhythm with the frotting he was giving my cunt. I knew the time was close and a dribble came from the walls of my vagina. At once his hands were withdrawn and he sliced into my engorged cunt three times with the tawse. I could distantly hear the awful howl I was making, part of agony, part of frustration. I was deprived of my ability to gush my vaginal juices in a splendid orgasm, but my bladder gave up its control and I streamed from between my legs, at least relieving that pressure. At once he was back, standing in front of me as the last shaming trickle poured on to the dust in front of me. He pressed his body against me and in a moment I felt his hand and then, I guessed, his cock at the tender gates of my sex. He gave a sudden jerk of his back and legs and he had impaled me. I was completely open to him and he was all too keen to take me. Despite my pain I thought that if he was to thrust himself into me several times I would most certainly come.

Whilst he held himself against me I felt Mel untying my ankles. My legs slid forward, but most of my weight was still carried by my aching wrists. Mel unwound the rope so that it was free to run over the branch from which they had hung me. As my arms came down she untied my wrists, but my arms wouldn't answer my command to put them round Kerr's neck. His arms were round my body, and still locked on to his cock he carried me from under the tree to a rug laid out in the sun. He used all his muscular strength to lower the two of us to the ground, never for a moment risking a disengagement from between my legs. I was lying slightly on my side facing up towards him as he loomed over me. He brushed my hair back with his fingers and started to say sweet things to me. Tears of frustration, pain and joy rolled down my cheeks. He swept them away with his fingers, and bending further over me kissed me on my mouth as he thrust himself into me as far as he could. I was still lying, virtually unmoving, trying to return my limbs to their former strength. Kerr was telling me that I was his darling and was slowly, but inexorably thrusting himself into me and then withdrawing. I felt the tip of his cock against the outer petals of my cunt and the pressure began to build up until they parted and he was able to enter me like a conqueror. I could do nothing but lie back with my legs and arms splayed whilst he took me without hurry or hesitation. I hoped beyond hope that he could delay his orgasm until I had achieved mine. I had been so close but had been deprived of satisfaction more cruelly than if I had received several whippings.

Kerr changed his position and began to draw his knees under him whilst grasping my buttocks in his hands. He drew me unresistingly up towards his groin, over his thighs, whilst he raised his torso and head to vertical. I had not noticed Mel beside me, but I became aware of her as her fingers made their way across my belly to my open cunt and they pulled back the lips and began to gently finger my clitoris. Mel was clever and gentle. She managed to synchronise her massage with Kerr's thrusts. These were no longer from the gates to the neck of my womb, but were limited to two or three inches, every movement of which I felt within my steeply tilted vagina. I was still unable to take an active part in the congress, but I needed only to lie back, abandoned to the thrusts and fingers of the two of them. Mel bent her head and took as much as she could get of my left breast in her mouth, flicking her tongue across my nipple and sucking on it.

I knew that they were doing everything they could to give me the orgasm I so much desired. The sun beat down on our bodies and in the distance I could hear the cry of wheeling sea birds. I looked at Kerr's rugged body, with his abdominal muscles clearly defined and the pressure of my buttocks on his wrists reflected in the tension of his arm muscles. He was smiling at me. I tried to see where he was penetrating me, but the angle of my body made this impossible. I turned my head to Mel and saw the determination on her face as she gripped my nipple between her teeth. It was this which thrust me over the edge and I felt the knot in my belly grow wings and fly through my body to my head. Mel pressed more urgently on my clit, Kerr thrust more deeply, I closed my eyes and saw the gold and red cloud of passion which was enveloping my mind and body. The luminescence grew to a painful brightness, there was thunder in my ears, my throat contracted so that I stopped breathing, and then there was that sudden, explosive release, which soaked Kerr's belly and our thighs. I was pumping out my juices in a great, joyous pulsing stream. I could see and hear nothing, but I could feel the great gift of ultimate pleasure and for a moment the true nature of happiness. I opened my eyes to find Kerr pulling out of me and spurting a great arc of jism over my belly and thighs. I watched the pulsing nod of his cock until it began to do no more than dribble and he leaned towards me and kissed me, telling me that I was wonderful. At last my arms began to work and I enclosed his neck with one fore arm, and Mel's with the other. They cuddled against me, stroking and kissing me. It was my first experience of unconditional approval, love and acceptance. I knew what I had been missing all my life.

Tuesday May 8

Yesterday was the greatest experience of my life and it took me many hours to come down from it. Eventually I apologised to Mel and Kerr for following them round like a besotted puppy, but they did no more than embrace me in a communal hug and told me that there was a lot more where that came from. I lay in bed at the end of the day and became very sad as I realised that there were only a few days left before we should pack up and go back to the college, leaving Kerr to his own devices. I don't know if I was sorry for myself or for the loss of Nirvana. I reached for a tissue and wiped away a tear. Slowly the room became lighter and I realised that the door was being opened very quietly. Mel whispered to me and asked if I was asleep. I sat up in bed, foolishly clutching my wisp of a pyjama jacket to me. She suggested that if I liked we could all three sleep in the super king size bed that Kerr was occupying. Nothing could have appealed to me more.

Mel led me along the corridor to a huge bedroom illuminated by a single bedside candle. The bed must have been eight feet wide and lost in the middle of it was Kerr with his head on a long soft bolster. I got in on one side and Mel the other. Kerr reached out his arms and scooped us towards him. I lay on my right side with my head on his shoulder. My left arm drooped down my body until it rested on his belly. I realised that he was quite naked, but I felt that I should keep my hands to myself. Very shortly afterwards I felt Mel's hand touch mine. She told me that she had found a little toy and put my hand on Kerr's soft cock. Both of us played with it for a while with what seemed an inevitable result. Kerr kissed Mel and asked her to excuse him for a while. He turned towards me and asked me to lie on my side facing away from him. He bent me forward from the waist and held my hips whilst his erection nuzzled its way between my legs. I lifted my right leg and reached between my thighs for him. In a moment he had brought his hips up so that he penetrated my cunt from behind. I could feel the hard pressure of the tops of his muscular thighs against the globes of my arse and the increased penetration of my foreshortened cunt by his cock. I didn't need another climax, but he gently stoked my fires, holding on to my breasts to pull me towards him as he pushed in. I was truly content. I didn't need passion, but I loved the idea that this gorgeous man wanted me and that he was inside me, pressing and probing with his splendid tool. Eventually I had a tiny, happy climax and turned over towards him. I realised that Mel was lying pressed against his back throughout the time he had been fucking me. He kissed me and again begged to be excused and turned to Mel who he arranged as he had me. I cuddled his back and in a daze of happiness, in the middle of his congress with Mel I slipped into a sweet and untroubled sleep.

Today we have taken things easily. Kerr has found another paperback. I had a quick look at the first one, only to find that the story was reflected by my own experiences. It was almost as if someone had been present at what I had dreamed and experienced and had written down a fictionalised account of it all. I only read a few chapters so that I wasn't disappointed when I found that reality wasn't at all like the delights of fiction. Well, we shall see.

Mel and Kerr had attended to my weals last night. After lunch Mel received a phone call from a friend who lived about ten miles away. Mel asked me if I would like to go out to a party with Kerr and herself. I became diplomatic and said yes, but only if she didn't think I would get in the way. Then there was the matter of what I was to wear, but the big wardrobe settled that. By 7 p.m. we were all ready. Kerr was dressed in a close approximation to the tight, smart three piece with high heeled boots, so beloved of Mississippi gamblers of the early 20th century. Mel had on a pale blue silk dress which came up to her neck in front but was almost completely backless. This was the sort of dress that could only be worn by someone with a flawless back and very firm breasts. Mel had both, and a bottom to match. My dress was of dark green velvet, cut very low at the front in a sort of sweet heart shape, so that the shape showed off the upper curve of my breasts and the décolleté revealed the whole of the inner curve of both of them. I asked if this wasn't a bit too revealing, but I was assured that there would be others present revealing much more (how was that possible?) To be careful I took a silk pashmina the same colour as the dress. I was none too skilled at applying make- up but I sat next to Mel and she guided me. I brushed my hair and shook the curls into a mass on my head. Some high heeled sandals and I was ready. Kerr looked at us and told us we were sensational and that he had no reason to change his opinion from when we met at the airport.

We climbed into the Aston Martin and began the journey to Calumet. The house was typical of the oldest New England buildings with a gambrel roof and projecting bays, many small windows and a great deal of ancient oak in the structure, filled in with bricks, mainly at a diagonal. The front garden was hidden by a high wall, pierced by a small, solid gate for those on foot and a big double oak gate peppered with heavy wrought iron studs for those with transport. There must have been a TV camera somewhere because there was only the slightest hesitation before these gates opened and we were admitted. I caught a flash of radiant colour from the flowers in what I took to be the front garden as we swept along the drive to the South facing side of the house, with its views over sloping gardens, woodland and then the sea. Mel parked next to a huge pale blue Cadillac and we turned towards the back of the house. This had a long terrace in front of it which was accessed by stairs at either end. There were several people on the terrace, all of them with glasses in their hands. I didn't expect to recognise any of them, but both Mel and Kerr waved in response to greetings.

Once on the terrace we were greeted by a tall woman of about thirty. Mel introduced me, and I discovered that her name was Alys. She was an imposing figure seen at a distance, but close to she was quite remarkable. Her hair was perfectly white and matched her skin and eyebrows. Dominating her face were her lips which were a slash of purple lipstick and her eyes which matched the lipstick. I had never seen an albino before and there was something both wonderfully beautiful and quite frightening about her. She was warm in her greeting and kissed both Mel and Kerr. She turned to me and I found myself suddenly enfolded in her arms. I realised that she was a woman of remarkable strength. In contrast to her own colouring she was wearing a black dress of some material which clung to every voluptuous curve of her body. Quite out of character I suddenly wondered what she looked like without her clothes. As she stepped back I realised that her dress was designed to reveal rather than conceal and my errant desire was almost immediately satisfied.

I suppose that all my years of being dismal had made me uninterested in other people's beauty. It came as a great surprise to me that I had this new interest, but I was determined to pursue it.

We were taken to meet the other guests. There was an elderly man with a neat white beard who had an air of having had command of a ship, with his wife who was considerably younger and sported shoulder length blonde hair and a dress which made me blink. There was as much on view as there was covered, which would have been entirely in keeping with a sultry evening, except that she was covered in all the areas that didn't matter. What was on view was delightful and as we fell into conversation together I told her so. She seemed pleased with the compliment and politely asked me if she might make a slight alteration to the dress I was wearing. I could hardly refuse, but I was astounded when she folded back the upper part of my dress until it hardly hid my nipples. 'I'm a bit blatant,' she told me, 'but really I usually like to keep them guessing, but not too much. I think that is just about right. From her bag she produced a brooch which matched the colour of my dress and secured one of the folds with it. A small gold safety pin secured the other side. 'Don't turn sideways rapidly,' she advised me. She took me by the hand and led me to a small group who were earnestly discussing something. Once again the women were wearing revealing dresses whilst the men were dressed like gangsters or members of the Mafia, which perhaps they were.

'We were just discussing,' said the man who I had been told was Pietro, 'what it is that most turns us on.' I sipped from my glass and looked over the rim at the speaker. 'It seems that Charles here is at his best when he is fucking a girl in one room whilst his wife and her friends are doing the same in the next one. Jerry likes a bit of violence, and he is at his best stripped naked and whipped by his partner,' I shivered at this revelation. 'Jane likes it best out of doors, and preferably up against a tree.' I shivered again but he went on. 'Miranda likes masks and best of all enjoys not knowing who it is that is taking her.'

He smiled rather wolfishly at the rest of us. 'Paula likes just about anything that is going with a man or a woman, and perhaps both at the same time. But best of all she likes a new experience' Paula looked as if she didn't mind who knew provided she got what she wanted from the encounter.

I wondered how they could be so open about their preferences. Pietro turned to the lady who had adjusted my dress. 'And what about you?' he enquired, raising an elegant eyebrow. There was a moment of hesitation.

'I share Jane's preference for out doors. In our bit of woodland we have a shallow pit full of clay and water. I like to feel the cling of the mud against me, the covering of my body with sticky clay and the wrestling interaction with my partner's body and before you ask I can get as much out of a woman as I can from a man.' She smiled in my direction and I took a long draught of whatever sort of powerful alcohol was in my glass. I wanted to leave the group, but I knew that I would be labelled a spoilsport if I did.

Pietro raised his eyebrow and looked straight at me. I had already thought how to get round this one. 'I'd like to know what is best for you, Pietro,' I told him. There was a good deal of laughter from the others. The woman called Jane told me that past experience made them think that Pietro managed to keep quiet about himself. 'So this is the opportunity for him to reveal all,' I replied. Pietro didn't look delighted, but he knew that he would have to say something, and probably the truth, since he had so little time to think up a lie.

'I like women with beautiful breasts, like yours,' he announced. 'And I like them to have a curvaceous arse, also like yours.' I began to think he was getting a bit personal and turned abruptly to the lady who had just spoken. 'I warned you,' she said, and I realised that my breasts were on view. I was about to adjust my dress when she told me to leave them alone. Pietro seemed delighted. He smiled at me showing big strong white teeth. 'I like a bit of violence. Tearing off the lady's dress always appeals, and then I like to work on her with my fingers and tongue until she comes. It's even more fun if her hands are tied behind her back.' I became interested and returned his steady gaze. 'Then I like to dip myself in her cunt, withdraw, turn her round, bend her over at the hips and press my dick into her arse. I like to feel the grip and hear the squeals.'

By the time he had finished I was getting quite breathless and my pulse was thumping hard between my thighs. It was my turn. I thought I'd embroider my story a bit. I looked back at Pietro. 'I like being stripped naked and tied up dangling from a tree branch so that everyone can see every part of me. I like an appreciative audience, but I need at least one person to seek out my pleasure zones and bring me to a climax, with fingers or tongue. I need to hear admiring comments on my figure and then I like a little gentle flagellation before being taken down, cuddled and amorously fucked.' I smiled at Pietro and the group who managed a round of applause. Oh dear, that drink must have been very strong and I had opened my mouth far more than I intended.

'Well done,' said Pietro. 'I thought you might have decided on a censored version. I'm so glad you didn't. I should have told you that one of the aims of the party is to give each of us a chance to experience someone else's turn on. Before any of us had any chance to get out of it he had written our names on scraps of paper which he folded, shuffled and distributed. I looked at mine. It had the name of the lady beside me. I had no idea how they could provide a mud bath, but if I was lucky I was going to be fucked in one.

Pietro took back the scraps of paper and handed each of us a different one. I drew Pietro himself. Wrestling him in the mud would be quite an event. Two people had swapped over because they had their own names. Pietro asked Jerry where his wife was and he pointed to the other end of the terrace.

'Right,' said Pietro. 'Here's a mask each,' and he gave

one to Jane. 'We'll adjourn to the other end of the terrace and see if you can live out Charles and Miranda's fantasy. We all moved off to the slightly shadowed end of the terrace. Jerry looked a bit uncertain and asked Pietro a question. 'Of course, naked,' he replied. Jerry began to fumble with Jane's dress, but she brushed his hands away and as we formed a loose semicircle round them she took off her dress and laid it over the balustrade. Fortunately Jerry was a lot more adept at getting his own clothes off. Jane was a lovely young woman and as soon as his body touched hers Jerry's erection stood up strong and sharp. He kissed her mouth, caressed her breasts, bent to lick her breasts and nipples and dipped his fingers between her thighs. Jane was becoming distinctly interested and had backed against the rough corner of the balustrade which pressed into her buttocks. Jerry continued his work between her thighs and then dropped on one knee and stuck out a surprisingly long pointed tongue and licked between Jane's petals. She hung on to the balustrade with both hands whilst he probed and sucked until her eyes and mouth opened and she told him to fuck her. In a moment Jerry was on his feet and was holding her against himself whilst pressing her buttocks back against the rough stone f the balustrade. She reached down between them seized his cock and rubbed it between her thighs and then aligned it so that a thrust would take it into her. Jerry put all his strength into the penetration and began pumping for all he was worth. Jane howled and juices ran down their thighs as Jerry announced his climax with a roar. As he subsided, he kissed the masked Jane and stroked her flanks. The two of them got a round of applause for their efforts. Jerry told Charles that he'd better get some advice from him because it seemed too frightening to cope with and in any case he liked it to last rather longer. On being told that his wife was looking for him he clambered into his clothes and acted the part of an innocent bystander. It would have been better if he had zipped up his bulging fly.

It was Charles and Miranda's turn next. I realised that I hadn't worked out who they had drawn. Pietro gestured to us all to follow him and we trooped off down the terrace steps into the garden and from there to the orchard. Pietro was carrying a bag. We stopped at a large pear tree. From the bag Pietro produced two long leather straps and a rope. 'You have both drawn some flagellation. I suggest that we decide who is going to be whipped first and then see what follows.' They removed their clothes and looked at each other ruefully. Miranda looked as if she was going to try to back out, but one glance from Pietro dissuaded her. They couldn't choose so Pietro told Charles he was to be the first. He hung the rope over the nearest branch, attached it to Charles's wrists and hauled him up until his toes were just in contact with the ground. I was collecting some excellent views of men's cocks, but this one nestled in its surrounding bush and was totally withdrawn.

Miranda took the strap and appeared not to know what to do with it. Pietro told her to wrap the end a couple of times round her hand and then waft it about until she got used to it. She seemed far from able to do anything successful and burst out that she was quite unable to whip anyone. Pietro asked her if she would rather he did it, because if he did, Charles would not be able to stand up when he had finished. At that Miranda decided that she would try, however unhappy it made her. All this time Charles had been hanging quiescent with his head forward between his arms. He was a good looking guy, about thirty, with a nicely toned body.

Miranda waved the strap in a circle and caught Charles across the back. It was a dilatory sort of strike, and though Charles felt it he gave very little evidence of its impact. Pietro looked disapprovingly at Miranda, who swung the strap again, a great deal harder. There was an audible crack as the leather contacted Charles's skin. He jumped forward as far as he was able and uttered a gasp. I was standing to one side of the tableau and I at once noticed that his cock was unfurling itself. Two more hard strikes followed and Charles appeared to be fully erect. His face was scarlet and he puffed and grunted as Miranda's blows caught him. After ten strikes Pietro told Charles to turn round. Those who hadn't shared my viewpoint admired his erect cock, glistening at the end. Miranda slashed him across the chest twice and then across the waist. Her next strike took the strap across his thighs, the following one caught him across his navel and he uttered a cry. Miranda looked at Pietro, who nodded. She had five strikes to go and it was apparent to me where she would aim them. She stood beside him and shortened her grip on the strap, bringing it up to her shoulder and then accelerating it down so that it struck the upper part of Charles's rigid shaft. Before he had a chance to recover she hit him again in the same place and then reversed the strike so that the strap came up from somewhere below his knees and bounced his cock against his belly. Pleased with this she repeated the strike and Charles let out another cry of pain. Her final strike was a bit off target and caught Charles's balls before striking his cock. I had heard of the tenderness of men's testicles, but I was unprepared for the despairing howl which Charles emitted as his head jerked back and the muscles of his belly went into spasm. Miranda started to apologise, but Pietro cut her short. He lowered Charles's arms and untied his wrists. Charles gasped and doubled up, gently massaging himself. After a minute he seemed to recover and his erection returned to its earlier tumescence.

Miranda put her arm round his shoulder and touched his arm and side with her breasts. This seemed to take his mind off his pains and he was about to seize her when Pietro stepped between them. Miranda's face was filled with apprehension as her wrists were pinioned and she was drawn up as Charles had been. She had a beautiful figure which was truly feminine. Sizeable rounded breasts, a narrow waist, wide hips, superb buttocks and elegant legs. It was a body designed for fucking, we were going to see if it was made for whipping.

Charles stood off to her side and without more ado caught her a slicing blow across her buttocks which bounced delightfully. He followed it up with another in the same place and Miranda let out a whimper and twisted slightly. His third strike was across the small of her back followed up almost immediately by two to her back. Charles ignored us all and moved to Miranda's side. He kissed the angle where her neck joined her shoulder and ran his hand over her breasts, cupping the right one in his palm. I saw him squeeze her breast, gently at first and then more firmly until his pressure distorted the shape of the orb. He slid his hand from her breast down her chest to her belly and then to her cunt which he opened with two fingers which he pushed inside. He seemed to me to catch her clitoris with his thumb as he moved his fingers in and out and stirred her insides. Miranda began to lift her feet alternately and he pressed himself against her so that his long cock was across her belly. She began to breathe heavily with her head back between her arms. Charles deemed this the time to continue whipping her and laid on another five strikes, the last of which curled up under her buttocks and made her jump and cry out.

She turned unwillingly to face us and we admired the slight swell of her belly and the neatly trimmed covering of her cunt. I liked the crease down each side of her belly where it met the muscle at the top of her thighs and her hips, framing her elongated navel. I thought she was quite beautiful.

Charles resumed his attack on her with a strike across her waist, followed by one across her belly and a third at the top of her thighs where the strap was likely to contact her mons or the cleft below it. Miranda had given herself up to a series of groans and cries. Her head was well back between her arms and her mouth and her eyes were wide open, though it was unlikely that she was getting anything into focus or able to utter articulate phrases. Three more caught her across her ribs and then her breasts, which provoked a despairing howl. There were four to go and Miranda hung with her head back and her body bent at the hips with her pelvis tilted outwards. Charles didn't need any encouragement and sliced his way across her mons with his first cut, a couple of inches further down with the next one, and then as Miranda sagged and her knees opened, two more brought up between her legs to strike her cunt. She emitted a dreadful groan at this excruciating pain, but seemed to be able to withstand the agony better than Charles had done.

I noticed that there was a sheen down her thighs which I put down to Charles working on her after the first five stripes. As Pietro released her, Charles threw down the strap and encircled her with his arms. He lowered her very slowly to the grass and held her in his arms, kissing her and touching her eyes with his lips. Miranda began to relax and he licked her breasts again and touched her belly with his fingers. Her eyes were closed but I noticed that she opened her legs to his gently questing fingers. In a surprisingly short time she had recovered enough to reach her arms up to his neck and pull him towards her. He went on kissing her as he knelt between her thighs, still gently touching her most exciting places. I saw her belly contract and he leaned down over her as she grasped his cock and at once guided it into her.

Neither of them lasted long before they were consumed

by their climaxes. Charles lay beside her on the grass pillowing her head on his arm whilst he kissed her and stroked her as his almost flaccid cock dribbled its last traces of jism onto his thigh. It was a classic performance and deserved the round of applause it received.

We were half way through and I thought it would be my turn next, but I had reckoned without Pietro's role as master of ceremonies so it was Paula and the lady who had been beside me, who I found was Sophie. They seemed to have collected each other's wishes, which was good for them as they had both indicated their ability to cope equally well with both sexes.

I wondered what they might do, and I hadn't long to wait to find out. Sophie was shorter than Paula and her hair was mid brown. The dress she was wearing was a halter neck in dark blue with the neck line descending almost to her waist. There was no back as far as her waist and the material was cut to enclose and reveal the whole of each breast, with her nipples trying to poke through the apertures in the lace. Her skirt was a double layer of chiffon which ended just below her knees. Her feet were encased in matching ballet slippers which reinforced the impression of being tiny. Paula was much taller and had a mop of black hair to go with her polished dark brown skin. She had chosen to wear a white dress to contrast with her own colouring. A thin strap went round her neck and held up two very small panels of satin which were not wide enough to cover her breasts. The panels narrowed below her breasts and descended well below her hips where a micro skirt whose upper seam was several inches below her jewelled navel, ended about an inch below the join of her thighs. A thin white cord was tied tightly round her waist with a bell at each end which tinkled as she moved. Her figure could only be described as magnificent: wide shoulders, very large breasts, a narrow waist, a rounded belly, wonderfully rounded buttocks and thighs of sculptural proportions. Paula was a heroic figure and had a directness of speech to go with her physical power.

Paula and Sophie faced each other. Sophie looked up and Paula bent her head to kiss her. The touch was delicate and relatively brief. They continued to stand close to one another but hardly moving. It was then I noticed that Sophie had drawn aside the left hand panel of Paula's dress and had revealed a magnificent dark brown breast capped by a darker nipple which pointed up from her areola. She at once applied her lips to it. Paula meanwhile had drawn Sophie's halter over her head so that as she took her lips away from Paula's breast she was revealed naked to the waist. Her body was pretty almost beyond words, with small firm breasts pointing outwards from near the top of her chest, ribs that were visible within her skin without an iota of surplus flesh. Her waist was so tiny that Paula could encircle it with her hands. She bent her knees and putting her hands round Sophie's waist she dug her big thumbs into Sophie's navel, which made Sophie gasp and she then lifted her off the ground. She kissed her lips and then licked each of Sophie's breasts. Sophie hung in her grasp like a doll.

Paula slowly lowered Sophie to the ground and as she did so Sophie reached out and pulled at the tape round Paula's neck which parted almost at once. The panels fell as far as the white cord showing off Paula's powerful chest and solid breasts. As Sophie's feet touched the ground she tugged at the bell on the end of the cord and the granny knot which joined the two ends unravelled and Paula found herself naked to the upper seam of her skirt. Sophie stepped forward and buried her face between Paula's breasts. She reached up close to her ears and took a sizeable portion of breast in each of her hands. Her nails were busy pressing into the flesh of Paula's breasts and tweaking her nipples.

Paula reached over Sophie's back and caught hold of the waist band of Sophie's skirt tugging it down over her buttocks. She stepped back drawing Sophie with her. Sophie stepped out of her skirt, but was quick to strip Paula.

We were now presented with a remarkable tableau. The statuesque Paula facing the diminutive Sophie. The black skin made a perfect foil for the white. The difference in size and strength emphasised the beauty of each of them. Paula kissed Sophie and sat down on the grass. Sophie kneeled between Paula's outstretched legs. She pushed Paula's shoulder. Paula lay back whilst Sophie knelt between her legs and lowered her body so that she could suckle Paula's breasts. Paula ran her fingers through Sophie's hair and then reached her long fingered hands on to Sophie's breasts, her long sharp nails engaged with her nipples. Sophie pushed her bottom up in the air so that we could see the cleft at the top of her thighs and slowly moved her tongue down over the curving swell of Paula's breast and on to the rib cage below it and thence across her belly until she reached the fold between Paula's belly and the beginning of the muscles which held her thighs. She licked all the way down the crease whilst inserting her left thumb in Paula's navel. Paula gave a gasp as Sophie's thumb was pressed into her and another as Sophie reached the promontory of her mons and took a small fold of her flesh in her teeth and bit it. Before there was any time for Paula to relax, Sophie opened Paula's cunt and darted her tongue between the fleshy leaves and beyond into the pink softness of Paula's hidden parts, catching her clitoris with her flickering tongue. Paula lay back fingering her own breasts as Sophie continued working between her legs. I could see Paula's face become shiny and she turned her head from side to side and groaned. Sophie pulled her tongue out of Paula and substituted her fingers. She was working her way into Paula when she encountered a small dribble of lubricant. At once her fingers clenched and she started to press her fist up into Paula's vagina. Despite her size Paula was obviously quite tight and Sophie exerted a good deal of strength and determination until her fist and half her forearm were buried inside Paula who was making small choking noises. Sophie began to twist her arm and wrist as if she was trying to screw something in place. The effect on Paula was obvious. Both her hands were cupping her own breasts and her finger and thumb were ravishing her nipples. Her mouth was wide open and she was breathing heavily through it, letting out great gasps of breath and licking her lips. Sophie's attack on Paula's cunt was vigorous and relentless, her arm moving like a piston shoving itself into Paula, withdrawing, entering and twisting. After a little while, Sophie pulled her thumb out of Paula's belly and used her fingers to locate Paula's pleasure bud. She had been there earlier, but this time she was using her thumb and forefinger to scrabble against its all too sensitive membrane. Paula had begun to kick her feet and was lifting the heavy cushion of her buttocks to meet Sophie's invasion of her. Sophie continued working on Paula, occasionally putting her head between her arms and biting Paula's mons, until Paula began to go rigid and scream out a long series of jerking, howling shrieks as she reached her climax. I had a particularly good view and I could see the spurting juices wetting Sophie's thighs and knees.

I thought that now there would be a little time for Paula to recover and then she would engage with Sophie. I had reckoned without the determination which Sophie showed as she continued her pumping and tweaking throughout the time that Paula was coming. For such a delicate looking creature she had great reserves of strength and even greater ones of determination. Paula lay as if struck down by a lightning bolt after her climax and then shook her head at

Sophie and moaned a long drawn out 'No'. But there was no question of Sophie giving up and we all watched in fascination as she changed hands and then thrust her long finger between Paula's buttocks as she continued to push and twist with her other hand. At first Paula appeared to clench her buttocks to try to deny Sophie entry to her hidden crater, but after a little while she shifted herself so that her buttocks must have opened slightly and Sophie drove home with her finger through Paula's well lubricated sphincter. I think I was the first to see that the finger had been followed by another and then two more until Paula was penetrated in both orifices by Sophie's fists.

Sophie was now dependent for her balance on working her arms alternately. Her breasts jerked with every jolt of her pumping of Paula's well filled orifices, her nipples erect and her breasts themselves as beautiful in their hanging position as they had been when she was standing up. She was smiling in a sort of grimace with the effort which she was making. I think everyone was amazed at the effort she was expending in subduing Paula. She was certainly winning and once again we were treated to the sight of Paula twisting and writhing under Sophie's merciless onslaught until the screams came again and she pumped her juices over Sophie's arms and thighs. This time we were certain that Sophie could find no more strength and Paula had come enough to satisfy even her. But we were wrong and for a further five minutes Sophie worked her ruthless magic on Paula until she cried out and lay totally supine. Sophie slowly withdrew her hands from Paula and walked them up her body, pausing for a moment at her breasts until she was stretched out along Paula and her head was just above Paula's. She started kissing the inert woman whose mouth was open, but whose eyes were fast shut.

Paula started to revive and moved her right hand so that

her arm was across Sophie's back, holding her tight against her. She moved her left arm to enclose Sophie completely and gripped her own wrist. She began to tighten her grip on Sophie's back until Sophie pulled up her head and began to gasp for breath. Paula lifted her head and pressed her mouth against Sophie's. She must have relaxed her grip and as their mouths parted Paula moved her hands to Sophie's buttocks and dug her fingers into her, pulling her cunt hard against her own body. Paula closed her legs on Sophie's and turned her body so that they were lying side by side. As soon as this seemed to be a settled position she moved again and now Sophie was under Paula and quite unable to move. Paula stretched out over Sophie, pressing her right breast against Sophie's face. Her fingers caught at the clothes which she had removed and from the pile she retrieved a wisp of silk.

Paula grasped Sophie's wrists and tied them together with the silk. She held on to Sophie with one hand and hauled herself into a kneeling position and then a bent over standing position. She stood at Sophie's head and grasped her arms. Hauling Sophie's elbows apart Paula pushed her head between them and having put her hands on her knees she started to stand up. I could only admire the sheer physical strength which Paula exhibited as Sophie's body, facing the same way as Paula's came up from her lying position until, when Paula was standing up fully, Sophie was hanging from Paula's neck. She grasped Sophie's left leg and bent it up slightly putting her foot on her own knee. For a moment Sophie scrabbled with her right foot until her delicate toes found a purchase in the muscles just above Paula's right knee.

Paula now stood erect with Sophie's body bent outwards from her own like a decorative bow. Sophie had managed to get her head on to Paula's right shoulder. Paula put her hands round Sophie's waist and started to move her feet so that she turned in a complete circle so that we could see Sophie's exquisite white body tensely bowed out from her magnificent black one. As she came to a halt, Paula ran her hands up from Sophie's waist to her breasts. I had noticed before how long her fingers were and how strong her nails appeared to be. She turned her head and kissed Sophie, whilst her fingers started to pull at Sophie's nipples. Sophie gave a little cry. The nails must have hurt her. Paula continued working on Sophie's nipples with her left hand whilst her right drifted down over Sophie's chest to her belly. To get a reasonable purchase on Paula's legs, Sophie had found it necessary to open her knees. This had given us all another view of her delicate cleft, now almost parted and open to Paula's long fingers.

It was evident that Paula was intent on equalising the score between them. She sank her fingers into Sophie's cunt. The angle was wrong for more than fingers, but in any case there was no way in which Sophie could have accommodated Paula's large fist. Paula continued her work on Sophie's breasts and cunt and then took her fingers out from the front of Sophie's body and transferred her hand to Sophie's rotund little buttocks. I thought that this was no more than offering support to Sophie, but I soon observed a long thumb pushed between Sophie's buttocks and even longer fingers gripping her cunt. At first Paula worked on Sophie's clit and Sophie began to wriggle as far as she could and then utter little sounds. It seemed that Paula wasn't prepared to put as much effort into rousing the completely exposed and vulnerable Sophie as Sophie had with her, or else she expected a more rapid response. Paula leaned her body back to counterbalance Sophie. This caused Sophie to have to lean back even further, pushing out her hips and inevitably thrusting her open cunt into Paula's hand. I stood in front of them to see exactly what tricks Paula could pull on Sophie. I watched Sophie's small frame twitching and I couldn't understand the reason other than Paula's fingers on her clit. But these weren't the twitches of a woman who was just being pleasured. Only Paula's forefinger was pressed against Sophie's clit. Three more were inside her vagina, with her thumb dug deep into Sophie's arse.

Paula's other hand was engaged in manipulating Sophie's breasts, the long finger nails leaving weals and tormenting her nipples. In the midst of my fascination and slight puzzlement with this scene, Sophie let out a shriek. This was not the cry of someone approaching or achieving orgasm but a shriek of pain. For a moment I wondered if the contorted muscles of her thighs had become cramped, but then it dawned on me that Paula was closing her fingers relentlessly within Sophie and that her sharp finger nails were giving Sophie agonising pain. Sophie's breasts rose and fell as she took shallower and more frequent breaths. She was breathing through her mouth, but remained in what could only be a muscle tiring and very vulnerable pose. She was crying out 'No! No! No!' repeatedly, but Paula showed no signs of relaxing her grip, let alone releasing it. She had Sophie, already unnaturally bowed backwards, in the dreaded scissors grip.

Paula removed her hand from Sophie's scratched breasts and replaced her forefinger at Sophie's clit. I could see by the way her fingers were bent that she was clawing Sophie with her nails. Sophie began to cry out an inarticulate howl, but in the midst of her agony I could see that she was dribbling from between her legs into Paula's palm. Paula must have given her just enough encouragement for her to start to spurt her juices and lay back her head on Paula's shoulder and howl again and again.

I thought that Paula might want to be as unrelenting as Sophie had been, but instead she put her arms round Sophie and lowered her so that her feet were on the grass and then she ducked out from between Sophie's arms and turned her to face her. She held Sophie in her arms for a while and then released Sophie's wrists. I could see Sophie's thighs quivering from the stress which had been put on them. Paula kissed Sophie very delicately and drew her down to a sitting position on her left thigh. Paula began to caress Sophie and told her she was beautiful and stroked her breasts and brushed her hand up the inside of Sophie's thighs. Sophie began to relax and held on to Paula, gently touching her breasts and running her hand over Paula's belly. This went on quietly for a while and was hardly exciting, but it must have led to a great deal of mutual satisfaction, because as I was losing interest I saw Sophie snuggle against Paula, and then she bucked her hips twice and uttered a little cry and achieved a loving and affectionate orgasm. They seemed to be content to hold each other in their arms so the rest of us gathered together. I had almost forgotten that it was my turn next.

Pietro extended a long forefinger and crooked it. I was happy to be summoned in this way because he also smiled at me with every evidence of pleasure. The six of us left the flower garden and through an archway of laburnum we entered the vegetable garden. As we walked along the grassy path Pietro pointed and I saw a scooped out part of the garden. In the bottom of the scoop was water, what lay beneath that I could only surmise.

'Will you leave your dress in the shed?' he asked. Having been a witness of the others I knew I had to do my bit, though I hardly knew just what was expected of me. I went into the shed, followed by Pietro. He turned away from me and started to strip off his jacket and shirt. I fumbled with the closer on my dress.

'What do you expect me to do?' I asked him.

'Enjoy it, fight me if you wish, get well fucked and exceedingly muddy. There's a hose by the pond so we can get ourselves clean afterwards.'

I nodded and stepped out of my dress and my sandals. I put my clothes on a box and turned to see Pietro. He was a fine looking man, but his most noticeable feature, for me at least, was the rigid shaft protruding from the black curly hair at his groin.

I turned to go out to the others but he caught my arm. 'I cheated, you know,' he told me. 'I fixed it so that I could share this little adventure with you. I think you are absolutely beautiful.'

I had forgotten my changed appearance and for several seconds I stood gaping at him until I got myself together and whispered, 'I'm so glad you did.'

The rest of the party were awaiting us, sitting on upturned boxes or on the grass which surrounded the pool. The water seemed clear, but it was impossible to guess how deep it was or how thick the mud underneath it might be. I slithered down the bank and found that there was little more than a two inch depth of water and beneath that enough mud to reach my shins. The water was quite warm and the mud glutinous in the extreme. I felt Pietro enter the water behind me and I took a couple of awkward steps forward and with some difficulty turned. Pietro seemed to tower over me. He held out his hand to shake mine, but I thought I ought to get an immediate advantage if I could so I seized his wrist and jerked it as hard as I could towards me. He was already leaning forward and was caught completely off balance. He waved his arms about and tried to step forward to keep himself upright, but I eluded him and he fell flat into the muddy water. As soon as he was down I pulled my feet out of the ooze and straddled him, sitting on his buttocks and holding his head out of the water by pulling on his hair. Poor Pietro, I thought, so much for fighting.

I hadn't expected him to be able to do much, given the grip I had on him, which I observed was causing the others a good deal of amusement. However, I felt him try to draw his legs up so that he could force me off his back and himself out of his prone position. I wasn't having any of that, so I increased my pull on his hair. His ability to withstand pain was greater than I had bargained for. He suddenly drew his arms and legs together and I found myself floundering as I fell off his back. I got one foot down into the mud, but it was so slippery that I was unable to keep my foothold and I fell, none too gracefully, in the mud and water. Meanwhile Pietro had regained his feet. He was facing me as I started to lever myself up from the clinging mud. He looked like a 'swamp creature', covered in mud from head to foot.

I was amused by his appearance and not properly prepared for his sudden lunge towards me. I had already learned that sudden movements on a very slippery surface were not a good idea. Why this lesson had escaped Pietro I had no idea, but his lunge took his feet from under him and he fell on me, his substantial weight thrusting me back into the mud and making me fight to keep my head above the liquid. Pietro had forced my legs open in his fall and I had every reason to be aware of his rigid shaft pressing against my belly. He showed no signs of wanting to remove himself from his position, but I felt him twist against me and he took some of his weight on his left forearm, for which I was grateful. His movements were slow and calculated. He used his right arm to hoist himself into a kneeling position whilst his left hand transferred itself to between my breasts where he pushed me down further into the ooze. I could feel the thick mud grasping at my back, buttocks and legs. I seemed to be sinking slowly further and further into it. There were sticky fingers of mud probing their way between my buttocks and against my cunt. I looked at Pietro wondering what his next move might be. The viscous sludge was slowly draining off his chest and his cock was dripping thick black mud. It remained difficult to make out details of his physique, but I was in no doubt, from the pressure on my chest, that I would have little chance of winning any sort of fight against quite so powerful opponent. I decided on a different tactic and raised both arms towards him in as inviting a way as I could manage. Pietro seemed to be delighted and lowered himself towards me. As he moved towards the horizontal I made a grab for his balls. Probably because of the mud I found myself holding his cock instead. Always anxious to make the best of a bad job I proceeded to tug at it which produced a few comments from the audience as the mud splashed over me. He lowered himself further towards me and I knew that he intended to penetrate me with this monstrous, long, filthy thing. I started to protest, and tried to push him away with both my hands, but it was impossible to stop him and I felt the tip of his cock at the portals of my sex and then he thrust himself into me. I had a sudden vision of this great muddy staff stabbing into me carrying the mud and water from the pond deep inside. I tried twisting like a fish on a hook, but he had no interest in releasing me from his thrusts. Mud crept over the tops of my thighs, it oozed over my belly, it spread up to my breasts and then almost covered them, and still he jerked himself into me and withdrew again and again. I realised that this action was pumping the sticky mire into me. I could feel every bit of his cock as it pushed and squelched within me. He reached forward and caught my arms forcing me still further into the mud. I could only just keep my head above the black slime. It crept to my chin and I tipped my head back as it slid over my tightly closed mouth. My hair and ears were full of it; I began to be afraid of what more he could do to me as he continued his unremitting thrusts into my body. I knew that I was no more than an orifice for him to force himself into and eventually derive some satisfaction.

I realised that I could do nothing and that I might as well accept him as he strove to sink me into the black mud.

The audience had begun to count his thrusts so he changed his rhythm, interspersing short pressures with deep insertions. I could see his white teeth shining between his drawn back lips. He paused in his penetration of me and removing his hands from my arms he caught my right thigh over his forearm, lifting it out of the liquid and putting my leg on his shoulder whilst still deep inside me. I used my arms to push up from the mud, but I achieved very little because he suddenly ducked his head under my knee and turned me over so that I was facing down into the black liquid. I could use my arms to keep my head and shoulders out of the mud, but it was at the expense of my cunt being thrust even more deeply down into it.

I felt Pietro withdraw and then an unnerving pressure between my buttocks. I drew up my legs to escape this intrusion, but I achieved no more than presenting my arse more accessibly to him and he thrust himself into me with a cry of triumph which I echoed with a howl of pain, fear and horror. Pietro inexorably drew me backwards on to his cock with my thighs either side of his bent knees. I felt the whole length of him penetrating my arse. He pulled me back as hard as he could with his fingers round each of my breasts clutching them in a grip which made me squeal. He pushed me forwards and I found I was on my hands and knees in the mud with his shaft thrust into my arse. At last he had found a pose which enabled him to complete his orgasm, though he had done nothing for me. He leaned back, detaching himself from me. I was full of mud, water and his jism. Slowly he began to stand up and I felt his hand under my armpit holding my breast and drawing me up to stand with my back to him, mud pouring off my body and a slimy mess trickling from my arse and my cunt. There was something strangely comforting about being held close to Pietro's body, despite the smothering of black mud over both of us.

I leaned back against Pietro and thrust my buttocks against his thigh as he gripped my breasts and pulled me back so that my head was against his shoulder. I wondered if I would ever get my hair clean again. I made the mistake of wiping my face with the back of my hand, spreading the black stuff further across my forehead and my right eye. I supposed that we both looked like mud wrestlers, which we had ineffectually tried to be.

Pietro gave me a gentle push out of the pond and we stood on a concrete ramp which led down to it. I turned towards him, wondering what would happen next. I couldn't see that we would be very welcome wandering back to the house and dripping slime all the way to the nearest bathroom. Almost at once I felt what I thought was a push to my shoulder, but this eased off and I realised that one of the party was holding a hose in his hand and had just adjusted the stream to a reasonably gentle shower. He started with my hair and as I turned to see who it was he washed both our faces with great care. He certainly knew what he was doing, starting high, the water ran over our bodies and took the mud with it. I turned my back and felt the spray across my shoulders with the water running down my back and between my buttocks. I was apparently clean down to my thighs. I felt the nozzle thrust up my arse and the water penetrated me. He kept it going for only a few seconds, but it was enough to wash out where Pietro had enjoyed me.

Although the water was quite warm, it was less than body temperature and I felt threatened and chilled. The washing continued and I turned towards the hose man. He started again at my shoulders and worked down over my breasts, which again was a pleasant sensation, making them jiggle and my nipples become erect. I held up my arms so that my armpits could be washed clean and I shook a lot of water out of my hair.

The spray washed over my chest, my waist and my belly. I saw him come closer and he held the nozzle between my thighs. A lot of the water splashed back down my legs, but a good deal penetrated my cunt, massaging it very effectively. I perversely wondered why I had never tried this in the shower. It certainly gave me a pleasing tickle and then a frisson which the hose wielder noticed. By some means he managed to increase the pressure of the jet and caught my clit with a powerful massage. I supposed that it was being frustrated by Pietro's penetration which did it for me, but I stood with my legs apart and my eyes closed, with my hands on my breasts and my fingers on my nipples, willing him to go on with his target practice on my cunt. I wasn't disappointed, and in very short order I felt a knot forming in my belly, a pressure mounting in my body, a roaring sound in my ears, sparks forming before my closed eyes and then the knot suddenly unravelling with a feeling like the beating of wings as I added my juices to his spray.

I assume that he saw me thrust my hips forward suddenly as I achieved relief, and then as I opened my eyes, with my legs trembling, he washed my thighs, shins and feet. Up to that point I hadn't realised that there were now two people wielding hoses, but as I turned towards Pietro I saw that he was completely clean and that the massaging effect of the water had apparently brought him back to an erection. I realised that though I would probably enjoy a good clean fuck, what I would like even more was to find Mel and Kerr and see what had happened to them. Someone had thoughtfully laid a large white towel by my clothes and I dried off my body and my hair. What I really needed was a little while before a mirror with the contents of my clutch bag. The group began to make its way back towards the house, en route picking up Sophie and Paula who hardly seemed to have moved from the position in which we left them, and trailed by a rather disconsolate Pietro. Never mind about Pietro, I could have a share of Mel and Kerr if I continued to be lucky.

At the house we were shown to ornate bathrooms attached to equally ornate bedrooms and were left to get on with the tidying process. Downstairs someone had laid out a substantial buffet and I suddenly realised that I was hungry. Joining the others I found Mel who looked just a little bit dishevelled. I raised an eyebrow to which she replied that she would tell me later. I wanted to hold her in my arms and kiss her, but at that point Kerr appeared with rather more buttons undone than I expected. He came straight up to me and kissed me and told me that I looked wonderful, which I knew was far from true. Mel began to look a bit pale. I asked her if she was alright and she said she had a headache. I asked Kerr if it might be a good idea if we went home. I took Mel outside whilst Kerr sought out our hosts and thanked them for their hospitality.

WEDNESDAY MAY 9

It was as well that we came home early last night. Mel was busy throwing up, Kerr was very concerned and as I was unable to be useful I wanted to get on with my diary. I knew we would not be together that night and that Kerr wouldn't join me. I was first up on an unexpectedly damp day. I took Kerr a cup of coffee and looked in to see how Mel was faring. She sat up in bed and told me that she had been unwell until 3 a.m. and then things had settled down. I asked her if she would like a peppermint tea and she told me yes, and an arrowroot biscuit. She asked me to bring my tea back with hers. In a few minutes I had tucked my legs under her duvet and was leaning back on the pillows. As she drank the tea, colour came back to her cheeks and she cheered up. She asked me what I had been up to at the party and I told her.

'Oh,' she said. 'If that isn't typical of Pietro. To get the best out of the mud he should have made sure that you came before you got mucky. I suppose his masculinity was offended by your flattening him at the beginning. Never mind, Kerr isn't at all like that.'

I asked her what she had done and she told me about the men dipping their cocks in hot curry and the women having to suck it off, which made me flinch. Mel had drawn a very unappealing fat man who on the third dip had wanted to shove his curry laden shaft between her breasts and then lick that off. It had not been a great experience and Mel thought that her sickness was probably entirely psychological. We had finished our tea and Mel put an arm round my shoulders and kissed me on the cheek.

We snuggled down into the bedclothes together and I turned towards her, slipping my arm under her head and stroking her flank with my other hand. Mel reciprocated and kissed me on the mouth. She turned slightly so that I caught her breast in my hand and I was not at all willing to let go. She stroked my breasts gently and I began to quiver as her fingers brushed over my nipples. I slid my fingers down her belly until I encountered her mons and then I very slowly and gently prised her open. I felt her fingers between my legs and I knew that this would make up for the frustrations of last night. Mel was so deft at handling me that I knew that it would only be a matter of a couple of minutes before I was ready to come. I went through all the warning signs as quickly as I could list them as I continued to work on Mel. She started to gasp as I began to feel the knot tighten in my guts. I thought of nothing but getting us to come together and I achieved my wish with our mouths joined in a sweet kiss. This wasn't the lovemaking of lust, but the lovemaking of affection.

We had sunk back into the bed with contentment and satisfaction with one another. My dressing gown seemed to have provided no cover at all and was now round my back apart from the ribbon across my waist. Mel was deliciously naked. We must have fallen into a happy slumber, because the next thing we knew was a gentle rapping at the door and Kerr, in jeans and T-shirt with a tray in his hands.

Eventually we all met downstairs. Kerr was using part of the table as a prop for a very impressive book from which he was making notes. I went to do the washing up and on my return I found Mel also involved with notebook and pen. I followed their example and for a couple of hours we all worked together in companionable silence. Mel broke off to make us all a cup of tea and we then continued working until lunchtime. I hadn't realised that Kerr had set up three plates of salad which we had with French bread, followed by stewed pears. I was glad to see that Mel had managed all this, and breakfast, without difficulty, so her diagnosis must have been right. Mel asked Kerr who he had drawn the evening before, but he blushed and faltered. Mel, probably deliberately misinterpreted his hesitation, but eventually he told us that it was the voluptuous blonde, but that his reputation was now completely shot because his thoughts had been on Mel and me and he couldn't rise to the occasion.

I was very flattered to be included with Mel and imprudently told him not to worry about his reputation as I would always vouch for him with delight. I'm glad Mel laughed. We did another hour after lunch and then Mel asked Kerr if he had ever been down in the basement. With a promise that there were all sorts of interesting things there she led the way to a room off the back porch. This was in the oldest part of the house and was quite empty. The door was locked but Mel found the key on the lintel over the low door. She opened the door and we were confronted by a set of steep steps which disappeared into the gloom. She told us to be careful and let our eyes adjust to the dark as she started down the stairs. Kerr followed her and I brought up the rear. The old door swung quietly closed behind us shutting out the principal source of light.

We arrived at the bottom of the stairs and I heard Kerr whistle. I could see very little, but as Kerr moved to one side I saw that we were in what looked like a workshop, except that I didn't recognise what the equipment was for. I asked Mel what was manufactured in the basement and she said one word: 'Agony.'

I was about to ask for an explanation when Kerr remarked that someone seemed to like to push themselves to the limit. 'Or other people,' Mel remarked. In the gloom I wandered round the huge room. Kerr had followed me and I pointed to a strange looking chair. There was something about it that was distinctly odd, but I had no idea what it might be for. It seemed that Kerr was as ignorant as I was. There was a wheel with what looked like leather tags mounted on the circumference. Kerr shook his head. I pointed at a sort of clamp mounted on the edge of a table.

Perhaps we were both ignorant and unimaginative. This was certainly not true of Mel, but then she had been here before.

I found a swing suspended from the roof but tied neatly against the wall. I wondered what possible harm could come to anyone who enjoyed a swing. Over to one side, in an area which was quite clear of other paraphernalia was an eight foot diameter ball made of wickerwork. Kerr shook his head and we wandered on down another crowded aisle. At the end of it we found Mel. She had her skirt hem round her waist and she was sitting in a carver chair holding a little box in her hand. She seemed rather abstracted, but something she was doing seemed to be pleasing her. I asked her what s happening and she gave me a rather dreamy smile and said, 'The chair is making love to me.' I had no idea what she meant and I asked her to explain. She pulled up her skirt and for the first time I noticed that her legs were wide open with her knees pressed hard against the supports for the wooden arms of the chair. She pressed a button on the box see was holding and I was suddenly aware that there had been a faint whirring noise coming from the chair. Mel laid the little box on a low table which was beside the chair and then heaved herself up from the seat. In the centre front of the seat was a circular hole, through which jutted the head of what looked very like a big black dildo. 'It's better when someone else controls the box and your wrists and ankles are tied to the chair,' she told us.

There was no lack of straps and rope so we attached the mildly protesting Mel to the chair.

I wanted to hand the box to Kerr, but he refused it. I was about to ask Mel what I should do when I noticed that the various buttons had labels on them. She seemed to have re-engaged with the black shaft so I selected 'pulse' and waited to see what might happen. From what little I could see the dildo was thrusting itself into Mel and then withdrawing. She seemed to be enjoying the sensation, but I was more interested in the other buttons. I pressed 'vibrate' and I could hear a new noise over the previous whirring. Mel began to look a little flustered. I came to a sliding button which was set a quarter of the way along a track which went from slow to fast. Before I gave that a push I found another which was labelled 'depth.' I thought Mel ought to be given a good seeing to so I pressed depth and then pushed the slider towards fast. The whirring and buzzing increased in intensity. Mel began to gasp and attempted to lift herself in the chair. I was sorry that Mel's folded skirt was hiding the penetration. Kerr was less reticent than me. He reached from behind her and pulled her skirt well away from her open legs and tucked it in the front of her T-shirt. We could now see the bulge in her belly each time the dildo rose to intrude itself into her. She was hanging on to the ends of the arms of the chair as tight as she could. The dildo was rising and falling like a piston. I increased the speed to almost as fast as it would go and then pressed the depth button for a moment. Mel began to cry out and attempt to pull herself up from the seat of the chair, but the position was not one which she could maintain for more than a very brief time and she sank back on the pumping, pulsating and vibrating shaft. Kerr looked at me and raised an eyebrow. I told him that I wished that Mel was naked. He smiled his agreement. We watched Mel as a flush rose up on her neck and her eyes dilated and her mouth opened. I pushed both depth and speed buttons to their maximum setting and the machinery emitted a low pitched throb. Mel began to call out and howl and we were able to see just enough of her belly and the beginnings of the open lips of her cunt to know that she was in the throes of an orgasm induced by the machine. I wondered when I should switch the apparatus off and then realised that I had no idea what to press to achieve my aim. Mel's juices spurted onto the seat of the chair, the pulses coming almost perfectly in time with the thrusts she was receiving. By now her head was thrown back and her howl had become a despairing moan. I pressed several buttons but without effect. I handed the control box to Kerr, but clumsily I dropped it and it fell among some equipment under the table. We both were on our hands and knees looking for the controller and eventually Kerr found it and started to press buttons starting at the ones at the bottom row. Nothing stopped the reaming of Mel's cunt. He pressed six buttons which seemed to achieve only what looked like a rotary action for the dildo. Mel was far gone into a second orgasm, when Kerr turned the control box over and found a labelled pad inscribed 'emergency stop'. He looked at me and then at Mel who was dripping and on her way down and then pressed the stop button. At once everything became still and silent. Mel maintained her pose for several seconds and then opened her eyes and closed her mouth. She looked from Kerr to me and licked her lips. We began to release her, but she was quite unable to get the strength back in her legs. She was certainly returning to normal, but had some way to go. I touched her face and asked if she was all right. She told me that one would have been enough and shuddered. I remembered the word she had used when I asked what was manufactured in the basement and asked her if she was in pain. She shook her head and whispered, 'Imagine what it would have been like to have been impaled there for an hour, or two hours, or to have to endure that thing thrusting, twisting, vibrating in my belly for as long as someone else determined.' She looked appalled, but Mel has great reserves of strength and in a few minutes she was back on her feet. I asked if she wanted to go back upstairs but she told me not unless I did. I was intrigued enough to want to see more.

It was hot and stuffy in the basement. Kerr removed his sweat shirt, looked at both of us and stripped naked. We followed his example and for a moment had a comforting hug. I loved the touch and pressure of the other two bodies, so different from my own, but now so familiar and comforting as well as exciting. We broke off to continue our exploration. Kerr had found again what we had taken to be the clamp and asked Mel what it was for. Mel gestured for him to stand in what looked like stirrups, but as soon as his feet pressed into them they clamped him to the floor. Mel took Kerr's right wrist and gestured to me that I should take his left. We held them behind his back and Mel strapped them together, leaving Kerr rather uncomfortably and precariously balanced. The clamp was on a trolley. She pushed it close to Kerr and retracted its wheels. Kerr's dick was flaccid, but Mel's clever fingers soon altered that. As soon as she had got his shaft rigid she adjusted the clamp so that it encircled it. She made a small adjustment and the clamp tightened itself. Mel and I stood back and admired Kerr's beautiful body. He looked puzzled and asked Mel if that was all. She asked him how much he would enjoy standing there for two or three hours, unable to move and with the clamp tightening itself if he became less than turgid. Kerr indicated that he hoped that wasn't going to happen and Mel laughed.

She went to the back of the clamp and moved a switch. At once the shaft on which the iron fingers of the clamp were mounted began to rise and fall slowly. Kerr said 'Wow!' and sweat ran down his forehead and trickled from his arm pits. Mel pressed another switch and Kerr jerked his entire body as much as he was able to. 'Electric shock on the up stroke,' she explained to me, 'not enough to burn, but enough to bite.' Kerr was going 'Oh! Oh! Oh!' in time with the movement of the clamp. 'He's getting off lightly,' Mel said. 'If I wanted to be really nasty I'd have clamped his scrotum and quadrupled the voltage. That really gives results. Eyes light up when that happens.' I had no doubt that she was right. She reached up and kissed Kerr, remarking that his lips tingled. I wanted to lick my lips and see what the effect might be, but she towed me away. 'Come on. It's your turn. Here's something nice.'

At this promise I didn't resist and placed my feet in a pair of quite widely spaced stirrups, facing Kerr. I submitted to Mel strapping my wrists behind me, but said 'No electric shocks,' to Mel, who repeated what I had said. She turned away and pulled another trolley towards me, settling it close in front of me. This one had three wheels on arms. The wheels themselves were like the bigger one that Kerr and I had seen earlier, with tags all round the circumference. Mel took a cable from the trolley and pulled the end between my legs and hung it from my wrists. She made an adjustment and I felt a quick pressure between my buttocks. Before I had time to ask she had moved one of the wheels to touch the nipple of my right breast. 'If you attempt to move away from the wheels you'll get a nasty sensation, keep still and there will be no electric shocks.' She placed the largest of the wheels between my thighs. She opened me and touched the rim against my clit. The third wheel was pressed against my left nipple.

'Just a little trial run,' she said. I watched Kerr suffering the pleasuring of the oscillating shaft, marred by the repeated electric shocks. With the one he might have come in a minute or two, but the other prevented the usual performance taking place. My concern for his pain and frustration was soon diverted by Mel starting the wheel she had first set up. A tiny whirr came from the axle and the wheel began to turn slowly, as it did so each of the leather tags touched my nipple. The wheel turned quite slowly and the sensation was not at all unpleasant. She started the second one with much the same result. The third one began to agitate my clit at once. I had never realised how sensitive my little pleasure bud was to being touched. Almost at once I began to feel a slight stirring within me. Mel must have noticed just what was happening and she reduced the speed of the wheel between my legs to almost nothing, until I waited in a froth of excitement for the next touch which seemed to take ages to come. At the same time she increased the speed of the nipple wheels until each was getting an almost continuous series of small slaps, pushing the nipple up and hitting it again before it had fully bounced back into its usual position.

Mel left me to it and went back to Kerr and turned off the machine. I could see that Kerr's dick was sticky with some pre-come, but that he had not been able to ejaculate because of the grip of the clamp and the firing of the electric shocks. He stood quietly as Mel released his feet and then his wrists. He tottered slightly, but at once recovered and stepped towards me. I realised that I could have a climax at any time if the wheels were adjusted just a little for speed and pressure.

Mel asked him if he had enjoyed the little game she had played with him. At the most ten minutes was all that he had endured. She told him that the story was that one unfortunate had been trapped there whilst his tormentor went upstairs and had a lengthy lunch. It was obviously a machine for those who can endure frustration and pain and those who like inflicting it. I stood quite still to avoid any sort of retribution caused by inadvertently moving away from the wheels. Kerr stood beside me and cupped my left buttock in his hand and squeezed. I was already breathing deeply and feeling the early stirrings of an incipient orgasm, but the pressure of his fingers made me close my eyes and concentrate all my energies on trying to bring myself to a much desired climax. Kerr released his hold on me and stood behind me. My wrists were tied so that my hands were about my waist level. My fingers were quite free to touch Kerr and I did, coming into contact with the rigid tip of his cock. He pressed himself between my buttocks and unthinkingly I moved backwards to gain more of the pressure he was exerting. At once we both got our reward and a powerful electric pulse was delivered to my arse where his cock was upstanding between my buttocks. I was glad we shared it, but it had the effect of getting him to stand back very abruptly.

Kerr recovered quickly as I thrust myself back into the ministrations of the wheel. He laughed and told us that this was the first time he had literally felt the ground move, and certainly no other arse had given him such a vigorous welcome. I blinked and licked my lips and took several deep breaths of air, but I didn't dare move away from the wheels and I just hoped that I could get some satisfaction out of them, though I'd have been happier sharing a bed with Kerr and Mel. Mel told Kerr that he could operate the machine if he wished. He took up position where Mel had been standing and she instructed him on the effects of the switches and dials. Seeing his naked body with his twitching cock made me keener than ever on having an orgasm, preferably one induced by his hands or his cock or both. He was a bit heavy handed with the controls and increased the speed of first one wheel which was flicking my nipple and then the other. He looked at me and smiled and slowly turned the switch which increased the speed of the wheel between my legs. I moved forward slightly so that I could get the whole buzz that it imparted. As I did so he increased the speed again and I stood still, trembling with desire. I could feel that it was making my vagina pulse and that a pressure within me was ascending upwards towards my chest. My throat constricted and I closed my eyes as the steady series of stimulating slaps caught my nipples and my clit. The last thing I saw before I closed my eyes and opened my mouth to howl out my orgasm was Mel's fingers on Kerr's cock. The last thing I heard was her invitation to Kerr to take her upstairs and fuck her.

I was beyond caring. I stood as the wheels revolved and the little flaps contacted my nipples and my clit, I slid into an all-consuming orgasm which poured my juices out of my cunt in a stream of amazing lubricant. My head was full of thunder, my knees wobbled, my belly felt as if someone had trodden on it, I had come again and again and now I was being ravished by the pitiless wheels. I swallowed several times and attempted to think how I might escape the machine which was torturing me. I feared that in the fullness of time I would be brought to another climax and then another until I was unable to stand and in my fall I fired off the electric shocks which I had shared with Kerr, but which, on my own and in my over excited state I wondered if I could endure. The very thought made me go weak at the knees and I began to shiver and tremble violently. How long would I be left to this implacable machine? Would I be ruined by it before the others returned from their pleasure with one another. I felt the need to hold my head in my hands and call for help, but I knew that nothing that went on in the basement could be heard in the house and the straps at my wrists prevented me from moving my arms.

I stood, slightly hunched towards the wheels, and prayed for release. I felt a deep groan mounting in my throat and the feeling that my treacherous cunt was about to do its magic again. I doubted if I could stand it. What if I collapsed and the others didn't come? Would the electric shocks be continuous? What if I lay there in the spreading pool of my juices and the shocks rendered me unconscious? I thought all these and other despairing thoughts whilst my body prepared itself to respond again to the continuous stimulation which it was receiving. I gave myself over to what was inevitable and felt the pulsing against my clit echoed in the pulsing of my vagina, the beating of heavy wings in my belly, the gasps of my breathing, the constriction of my throat, the drumming in my ears and the annihilation of everything about me in the inexorable pressure and release of another climax. It seemed to go on interminably. I could see flashes and glows before my eyes. My breathing and my heart beat became erratic. I knew I was going to pass out but I made every effort to hold myself upright and still to avoid the electric shock. I could hear myself making a low pitched howl of complaint. The last thing I remember was the lights which flashed before my eyes being extinguished.

I started to recover to find that the electric shocks had not happened. What's more, Kerr and Mel were releasing me from the bonds which held me. Mel told me that she had played a trick on me and that the electric shock apparatus had been turned off and that she and Kerr had stood in the shadows watching me and had caught me before I had fallen. I rubbed my arms and Mel cradled me, whilst Kerr massaged my ankles and feet. I was surprised that I didn't feel quite empty, but I thought that what I had wanted all along was the touch and presence of other bodies, and now that need was being satisfied. I snuggled against Mel and almost drifted off as Kerr continued his massaging. I felt Mel nod to Kerr and she leaned slightly back from me so that he could slip his arms under my knees and across my shoulders and pick me up. There was something wonderfully comforting and reassuring about being carried up the stairs and then being kissed and cuddled whilst Mel ran a bath for me. Kerr must have been far stronger than I thought as he stood with me in his arms and then gently lowered me into the warm scented water. He picked up a large jug and streamed water over my shoulders and back. The water lapped round my belly as I sat in the bath and I opened my legs to investigate my cunt. Despite the attentions of the wheel and several mind blowing orgasms I seemed to be exactly as I usually was. I relaxed and leaned back in the bath with just my knees and my breasts above the water. Judging by Kerr's erection, which was pointing at me over the edge of the bath, it was a sight which he enjoyed.

I realised that only Kerr had not achieved any sort of release. I wondered what Mel had in mind for him. Us, I hoped.

Thursday May 10

The time has gone so fast! I realised, when I woke up this morning lying in the comforting crook of Kerr's arm, that there were only two more full days left of this new life. I should have to go back to college and resume my penniless, dowdy life, except I was changed. My appearance was nothing like it was when I came here. I am as different inside myself as I am outside. I'll let my appearance speak for the other changes. The girls who despised me aren't going to be able to take away my lovely auburn hair and they won't see where there isn't any. I have made friends with and become the lover of the most interesting, beautiful and well regarded of the members of staff. I've even acquired some interesting clothes, some of which will be all right for day wear.

Last night Mel and I cuddled each other and Kerr and then Kerr had each of us, which just about rounded off a perfect day!

Today has been largely given over to work. Kerr tidied up and made the meals whilst we sat on the terrace with our skins bronzing in the early summer sun and stuck our noses in books and journals assiduously taking notes. It was a useful, pleasant, relaxing day, but Mel wasn't prepared to let it go at that. 'Time for some more entertainment,' she announced. Kerr and I looked up to see what she had in mind. 'The basement, I think.' I hoped that it would not be as frightening as yesterday. She cajoled us and we put down what we had been reading and followed her. The basement was gloomy and stuffy. 'Off clothes,' she said in a tone that brooked no disagreement. Kerr showed no signs of interest, but then he had enjoyed both of us the night before. We were well used to each other's skin and as at ease with each other's naked bodies as we were with clothed ones.

Mel took charge. She led us to the side of the basement and unhooked the swing. 'Ever tried one of these?' she asked. Neither of us had. 'This one is a bit special. Come on, we'll see if we can make it work. She gestured to me to sit on the seat. I held on to the supporting ropes and almost automatically started to move backwards and forwards. It was another life and another person when I had last tried a swing, but I hadn't forgotten the trick of getting it moving. Mel called 'Whoa' to me and I let the swing slow down until it hardly moved. 'You haven't got your feet in the stirrups,' she told me. I hadn't realised that there were stirrups, but Mel caught hold of my right ankle and moved it round to the side of the swing, inserting my foot in a stirrup. She did the same for my left ankle. I found that I had to sit forward on the seat with my legs splayed to either side of it. Kerr gave the swing a little push and I moved forward. The sensation was pleasant enough, though the only way I could relieve the pressure on my thighs was to move even further forwards on the seat. Mel asked me if I liked the swing, and I admitted that it was pleasant enough. Kerr stood in front of me and my swing pushed my knees either side of his thighs. He almost began to show an interest and I could imagine swinging towards him and happily impaling myself on his rampant cock. So far, at least, this didn't look likely and I could hardly blame him after last night.

Somehow this device seemed out of kilter with the apparatus we had used before. It provided neither pain nor stimulation. I didn't know whether to be pleased or sorry. However, I was wrong. Mel appeared with yet another trolley. She efficiently attached two cords to the swing's supporting ropes and then spent some time with her back to me fiddling with something I couldn't see. Much to my surprise the cords pulled the swing forward a little way and then released it, only to repeat the process at once. I began to swing in an increasing arc, but not before I had seen what Mel had been doing. Mounted on the trolley was a length of rod with a circle at the top of it. Through this circle protruded a blunt ended tube. As I swung towards it I felt an unexpected and not entirely pleasant jab in the lower part of my belly. Mel was doing some rapid adjustments as I swung back. On my return my open thighs received the tip of the tilted up tube, bang on the slightly parted folds of my sex. I felt the spray of something between my thighs and as I looked down I saw that I was shining all round my crotch. The swing was dragged forward even faster and I looked at the tube which had become slightly more extended from the ring as it sprayed me again and the end thrust its way into me. . I thought it might hurt me, but instead I felt that though rigid it had about it a degree of flexibility which allowed it to adapt itself to me. I swung away from it, quite happy with this game.

The next stroke drove the tube deep inside me and I felt it touch the neck of my womb. Suddenly it seemed to swell inside me and as I swung away from the ring it came with me, and was followed by a lengthy corrugated pipe. I swung forward, but the corrugated pipe travelled back through the ring so that no harm was done. The swinging continued for several minutes with the tube inside me as I gripped it with my pelvic floor muscles. This was quite pleasant once I had got used to it. I dared not take my hands off the ropes of the swing in case I fell off. This would have been disastrous before the pipe entered me and even more so now.

I was hoping that there might be something more to this apparatus when I felt the tube becoming warmer and beginning to vibrate. At the same time it seemed to be pumping something deep into my cunt. This was becoming more interesting. Mel and Kerr were sitting on a bench behind the trolley watching every move I made. Mel didn't touch anything on the trolley so I assumed that the tube was programmed to provide a pleasing set of activities. Apart from being careful not to alter my position, I couldn't quite see where the pain came in. I hadn't long to wait. The vibration increased and the girth of the tube seemed to grow greater. I felt something protrude from the side of the tube and press against the delicate membranes of my vagina. No sooner had one pressure point developed than I felt another, and then another. Unless there was a way of disabling the whole contraption, there was no way in which the tube could be withdrawn.

My next sensation was of both heat from the tube and the pressure, not only of the prongs which had extended, but of some liquid that was being pumped into me. I was now swinging in a ninety degree arc, being hauled forward by the cords and then dropping backwards, having the tube firmly implanted within me. To add to the sensations the end six inches of the tube had started to oscillate. I feared that the prongs would tear me, but they had been designed to rotate without damage. The rotating stopped and a prong appeared on the upper surface of the tube. Its blunt end came into contact with my clitoris, harder when I swung forward and more tantalisingly as I swung back.

So far there had been so many sensations to enjoy that I had almost been unable to distinguish one from the others, even the pumping liquid was masked by the rotation of the tube. The probing of my clitoris was a different matter, especially as it was accompanied by the emergence of another internal prong which hit my G spot and caused me to twist my body from the waist and gasp. I wanted to clutch my breasts as the pressure on both my G spot and my clit increased, but all I could do was sit precariously on the swing with my legs doubled back and my cunt invaded and manipulated as I leaned my head back and made a sound that seemed to me to be a wail of frustration. The entire process became more vigorous and faster. Despite being apparently fixed in my vagina, the tube had half an inch of movement so that its extension collided with my clit with more force and the probe at my G spot moved over its surface. It was a new experience for me to have a vaginal orgasm, but well before my clit answered the call of its stimulation, my vagina was pulsing with the pressure on my G spot. Liquid started to ooze from between the tube and the sealing petals of my cunt. I felt my belly begin to knot up, but the pressure within it was much greater than I had experienced hitherto. I began to breathe very quickly, gulping in as much air as I could manage. I was staring up at the ceiling, but my vision was quite out of focus and all I could feel was the mounting stress in my belly, my chest, my throat and then as if something had exploded, in my head. I must have tilted myself a long way back from my waist. I had closed my eyes and was howling when the full force of my orgasm hit me and I felt myself begin to crumple. I recall shaking my breasts and jerking my arms. I recall the thunderous noises in my ears. I thought my climax was finished, but the tube had more tricks to play and it continued its stimulation of my most sensitive areas. I screamed. I felt my breasts jerking up and down as I caught as much oxygen as I could. I felt as if I was running along a straight path which led up a steep hill. I felt as if I was falling apart. I knew that I was the plaything of this implacable machine. I knew that Mel and Kerr were watching, transfixed by my writhing, waiting to see if my response would be repeated. I couldn't muster the command to turn it off. In any case would they have done so? I lay back on the swing, my thighs pulled apart as I moved forward to encompass the tube. My head was thrown back my belly taut and my breasts pointing upwards. I wanted to give myself to the penetrating tube, I wanted to come and come again until I could feel no more, except that I had already had as much as I could stand and tears flowed from my eyes.

Mel and Kerr were less unyielding than I had feared. I felt Kerr's chest at my shoulder and I was aware that Mel had turned the machine off. At once I felt all the pressures begin to fade but I had not reduced my own grip on the now smooth tube and as I pulled myself into a slightly more upright position I thrust the tube out of me. Kerr encircled me just below my breasts with his arm. Mel released my now suddenly aching legs. Steadying the swing, Kerr lifted me off it, turned me round in his arms and clamped me against his chest. I realised that my legs had been under such tension that it would be several minutes before they would bear my weight. In the meantime I hung on to Kerr, who gently lowered me on to a large chest covered with a chenille throw.

Mel asked me if I was all right, and stroked my hair and sat on the chest next to me holding me close and telling me how well I had managed the encounter with the swing. I told her I couldn't have coped with any more, and she told me that the programme ran for three hours before it turned itself off. I began to wonder just what sort of person it was who had equipped his home with such devices and who he used them on. I had a curious feeling that Mel was well practised in their use. Perhaps it was her acceptance of them that made her echo my own, now open, desires. Then there was a further concern: our trip was nearly over, what would I do without the stimulation, satisfaction and the affection which I had enjoyed in the last ten days? I had a horrible feeling that I was becoming a sex junkie. I was almost ready to be concerned that I was an incipient nymphomaniac, except that most of my experiences had been thrust on me, willing as I was to enjoy each one however extreme and painful.

In the midst of these thoughts Mel said something to

me, but I missed what she said. I looked at her enquiringly. She repeated what she had said and looked at Kerr. I realised that she was asking Kerr if he would like to have the greatest orgasm of his life and her question to me was whether I would help. I had enjoyed my contact with the tube so I thought I owed him one. The arrangements struck me as a little bizarre. Kerr stood in front of a hoop of metal which was securely fixed in the floor. I was instructed to slide on my bottom so that my ankles were on either side of his feet. I sat up and my eyes were filled by Kerr's elegant torso but still flaccid cock. Kerr leaned forward over me. Mel secured his wrists and tied the cuffs with a cord which she attached to a column which supported the ceiling. I could see from Kerr's face that he was worried, but he relaxed when Mel instructed me to hold on to his balls with one hand and his cock with the other. Almost without thinking I cupped his balls in one hand and stroked his cock with the other. That seemed to start some interest, but despite my submerged position I didn't see how, even if I tried to swallow his cock, he would have the best orgasm of his life. Mel gave Kerr a hefty slap across his arse and told him that she was going to milk him of all he'd got. Perhaps I was supposed to attach some device to his cock, but there was no sign from Mel that I needed to do anything so I continued my gentle stroking and squeezing from which I noticed a slight change in his interest, but still nothing to fulfil Mel's promise.

Suddenly I heard Kerr gasp and attempt to straighten himself up. I squeezed his balls so that he gave up the idea of moving. Nothing much more happened for some seconds, though I could just make out Mel's presence behind Kerr. She called out, 'Action in ten seconds,' and started to count down, "Nine, eight, seven, six, five, four, three, two, one!"

I heard Kerr cry out and felt his cock become rigid in my

hand and then it started. Because I had my hands on his cock and balls I felt the tumult before his ejaculation started. I was about to get my mouth round the end of his cock when a spurt of jism splashed my face, followed by another and then a fountain such as I had never seen before rained down on me, covering my face, neck breasts, belly and thighs. Kerr was groaning and I was moving my head to keep the stream from my eyes. Such experience as I had and the reading that I had done told me that an ejaculation in a fit male was over in five seconds. I had started my own count when I felt his cock twitch and I reached fifteen before there was any apparent sign of a tailing off. Even then he was dribbling and giving the odd short spurt. His knees began to bend, but the bar, my ankles and the restraint at his wrists prevented much movement. Mel was quickly detaching the cuffs from his wrists as I struggled out from under him. She looked at me, laughed and asked me what I thought of Kerr's performance. Kerr stood up, glassy eyed and seemed to be amazed at the jism dripping off my body. I told Mel I'd never seen anything like it. She asked me if I knew anything about artificial insemination. I looked a bit blank. She grinned at me and sweetly enquired how they acquired a boar's semen. In my ignorance I suggested they had a bucket and then someone jerked the pig off. Mel laughed even louder and told me that pigs, unlike dogs, don't respond to hand jobs so the operator pushed a probe up its arse, firing it off to stimulate an erection and ejaculation. Kerr looked appalled. I began mopping myself with tissues which were quickly soaked. She asked Kerr what he thought of the performance. He looked embarrassed. She asked him if it wasn't the best ejaculation he had ever had. He looked at us both a little curiously.

'The ejaculation was OK,' he told us. 'But I missed the contact with your beautiful bodies.'

'You're not a pig,' Mel told him and pressed herself

against him. In other circumstances this would have been a signal for Kerr to become distinctly interested, but it was clear that he was played out, and I was covered in the evidence to prove it.

After an extensive shower I rejoined the other two and we settled again to the studies which had engrossed us before the interlude in the basement. After a while Kerr began to yawn and made his excuses about an early night. We grinned at each other as he made his way upstairs and Mel observed that the difference between men and women was that a woman could have any number of successive orgasms until she got bored with the whole thing, whereas if a man had four in a twelve hour period he was an acknowledged sexual athlete. Our conversation drifted into the nature of the female orgasm and how it as possible to prolong it and merge one with the next. Mel certainly knew her stuff. I hoped to experience all the satisfactions which she described.

We spent a restful night in each other's arms whilst Kerr rested from his exertions.

Friday May 11

This was a very quiet and studious day until after tea, when Mel suggested we should make another foray into the basement. Kerr and I looked at one another. He was quite frank about it and didn't think he could manage anything just yet. Mel told him that his role would merely be as an audience and that what she had in mind involved only herself and me. I, too, was doubtful of my renewed interest, but I didn't like to say anything because Mel had gone without when I hadn't. As hostess she had the right to at least as much pleasure as she had given us and I was determined that whatever pert I had to play I would do my best by her.

Mel led us into the all too familiar basement. She asked me to strip off and she did the same. She went to a drawer and pulled out a couple of contrivances with several straps attached. I realised that these were dildos and that I would be involved in some way with fucking Mel. She handed me one of them and I sorted through the straps and started to put it on. For some reason it really didn't feel right. I looked at Mel and was surprised to see that her dildo had disappeared. Stupidly, I asked. The answer was a single word, 'Inside.' I looked blank until I realised that she meant that I should arrange the straps so that the dildo could be accommodated within me. I got it right at last, but what was to happen next I had yet to discover. Mel had a whispered conversation with Kerr who looked up at her from his seat but said nothing.

We were standing with our backs to the wickerwork ball. Mel picked hold of a couple of tawses and opened a door in the side of the ball. She stepped in, gesturing me to follow her. As I stepped inside the ball it began to move, but Mel told me to stay still whilst she closed the door. She pointed at the hand holds which were liberally distributed over the inside surface of the ball. She handed me a tawse. 'The rules of the game are to score as many hits on your opponent as you can, and the dildos are remote controlled by Kerr. He has no idea how fierce they are, but you may well be stopped in your tracks. The end is called when one of us kneels down and gives up her tawse and is thrashed by the other one.' I wondered who this might be, but I knew that this was an unsteady environment in which chance would play a very great part.

I hung on to the hand hold above my shoulder to my left and hefted the tawse in my right hand. I thought it might be better to fend off Mel's first attempt to slash at me and get my bearings about how the ball moved. In this I was both right and wrong. Mel was holding on to a grip above her shoulder and was watching me whilst she swung the tawse from side to side. Abruptly she leaned forward and attempted to slice at me with the tawse. As she moved the ball started to roll towards me and I found myself becoming flat on my back at the lowest part of the ball whilst Mel rose in the air scrabbling with her feet to try to prevent herself dangling from one arm. It was very difficult for me to swing my tawse from a prone position, but I did my best, letting go of the hand hold and throwing myself to my left to avoid Mel's next strike. The ball was now wobbling towards my side, whilst rolling along.

Mel's feet came loose from the wickerwork when she was at the top of the ball and she let go of the handhold, landing in a heap beside me. I managed to get to my feet and caught her a resounding crack across the buttocks. She tried to jump to her feet, but the ball rolled on. She was running her feet backwards in an effort to slow the ball which was oscillating, making it very difficult for either of us to get in any accurate strikes. Mel gave up the idea of controlling the ball and swung the tawse horizontally as I brought mine down. I caught her across the shoulder and back, but her blow was more telling as she caught my breasts with the thick leather, momentarily knocking the wind out of my lungs.

The ball rolled and I tried to keep vertical, only that wasn't at all easy. The handholds were a snare. It was footwork which achieved most. As I twisted to get a better strike on Mel, she managed to get a double strike on my back and waist. I retaliated with a hefty blow across the top of her thighs which I suspected was instrumental in driving the dildo further into her. Without warning the ball hit the end wall and both of us fell in an untidy interlinking of limbs and bodies. I was head down and tried to bring my feet over my head to get into a position where I could stand up. Mel had quickly regained her feet and was striking my buttocks as hard as she could. My awkward position left me with no protection from the tawse and because my knees were apart I presented her with an easy target which she didn't refrain from attacking. I could hear the whistle of the tawse in the air which seemed to coincide with the crack against my skin and the scorching spread of the pain. Mel was quite merciless. I found a hand hold and put my other arm up to defend my face. As I managed to get to my feet she slashed me across my breasts, my waist, my thighs and my belly. It was as much as I could endure. I didn't want to give in and be thrashed as I knelt like a suppliant. On the other hand I was not able to get myself together to retaliate. I hung by one hand with my other still shielding my face as blow after blow struck me, shaking my body, bouncing my breasts and making me twist ineffectually to ride the blows.

Eventually, even Mel seemed to tire a little. Tears dripped down my cheeks. I had moved my free hand to another handhold and I presented the whole of my almost naked body to her cruel thrashing. In the midst of this I began to feel a strange sensation between my thighs. It corresponded with a couple of slashes which caught my cleft and made me howl and shake. This was different and made me cough and shake my head. I caught sight of Mel whose mouth was wide open. It dawned on me that the dildos had begun to work on us and had come alive with an increasing vibrating and pulsing action. Mel raised the tawse above her shoulder to strike down at me but a sudden spasm made her drop the leather and clap one hand over her cunt whilst the other grasped her breast. My own implant began to have a life of its own, but I hung as I had before. Mel's was apparently much more powerful than mine. It was good to have a relief from the whip, but I had no way of leaving my existing position whilst the dildo pumped and vibrated within me. I knew what it was that I wanted and if this kept on I should surely have it. Mel attempted to stand upright, but she was totally absorbed by the thing between her legs. Kerr was standing a few feet from the ball with both hands on what I at once thought was the control unit which had activated the dildos. He grinned at me and moved a dial. At once the pulsing inside me increased in violence and speed. Mel had managed to gain her feet and stood opposite me groping for something to hang on to. She took up the same pose as I had and I saw that her belly was reacting to the dildo. Some liquid had passed the lips of her sex and some dripped onto the floor whilst some gave the insides of her thighs a polish. I began to feel my own vagina pulsing under the stimulation of the vibrator. I now had enjoyed sufficient extravagant orgasms to know all the phases, including the convulsions in my belly, the rising tide of pressure through my body, the misting of my eyes, the roar in my ears and then the sudden release as if a sluice gate had been opened and everything gushed from me.

I began to go limp. The dildo continued its rhythm, but I

was incapable of any more response. This time Mel was wrong. The whipping and the stimulation had drained me. Mel was a different story and she writhed and shook, bucking her hips in response to the buzz between her legs, lifting first one knee and then the other and moving into what I took to be her third orgasm in a series which had started whilst she was kneeling, continued through her getting to a standing position and which would only end when there was no feeling left in her.

I watched her fourth orgasm and saw her eyes roll upwards. Her hands released their grip and she fell forward at my feet. Kerr looked at me through the wicker.

'Time for your revenge,' he told me but as I detached myself from the handholds all I wanted to do was hold Mel in my arms and kiss her and comfort her. Kerr stood back as I stepped down to Mel and stroked her hair. She made a little mewing noise and I pulled at the ties on the straps which held her dildo in place. It took little effort to detach them and I pulled out the dildo, accompanied by a rush of her juices. She gave a great sigh and I held her close to me.

My dildo had ceased to buzz, but I wasn't sure that I trusted Kerr not to increase the power and disable me. In any case I wanted to address all my efforts towards Mel. I held her shoulders with one arm whilst I used my free hand to undo the ties as best I could. Mel must have sensed what I was trying to do and she wearily lifted her right hand to my knee, slid it along my thigh and grasped the end of the dildo drawing it out of me in one long, relieving pull. I was glad to be rid of the intruder. It had managed to give me pleasure, but I now had a taste for the real thing.

Mel and I cuddled and kissed one another in the bottom of the big wicker ball. She looked up into my face and asked me if I forgave her.

'For what?' I asked her. A tear started in the corner of

her eye and she asked me to forgive her for thrashing me. 'I could have done the same to you, and I probably would have, only I wanted to see you flailing at me and hear the tawse cracking against my skin and feel the explosion of white hot pain shoot through my senses. I've never felt so alive!' I whispered in her ear. She turned her head and kissed me softly and firmly on my mouth, holding on to me as if I was a life-saving buoy.

In a little while we were both back to something like normal and by some mystery of mutual understanding we got to our feet and carefully left the confines of the ball. Kerr was still there, looking hard at us. He was fully dressed and we were naked, but that didn't matter. He stepped between us and put an arm round each of our shoulders, cupping a breast in his hand. He suggested that we go back to the house, have a drink, attend to any weals that required it and perhaps have an early night. And so it was.

Saturday 12th May

It has been my last full day here. I was sad at the thought that tomorrow I should leave this amazing place, that I should probably not see Kerr again and that my relationship with Mel would have to return to tutor and student. It all seemed very wrong to me. But then, I had been spoilt. More than that, I was not the person I was when I stepped into Mel's car. I really didn't know what sort of person I now was. I wondered if I loved Mel more than Kerr. Of course I did. But Kerr was growing on me. As we sat on the terrace with a big cafetiere between us, I looked at Mel and all that I saw filled me with pleasure and delight. I looked at Kerr, who from the very start of our meeting had treated me as an equal rather than the down trodden plain girl that… but wait a moment. I forgot that looking in the mirror this morning had shown me a woman with a toned figure and an attractive face with wonderful auburn hair. How was I going to pass that off back at college? In so short a time I had become used to my own attractiveness. I stood up straight and smiled. It was all very well, but I should have to go back to being the penniless student wearing dull clothes and ignored by the smart set at college. I got on with my work, quite surprised by how much I had managed to do in the few days since we arrived. Mel was correcting a chapter of her nearly completed thesis, Kerr had his eyes on a large academic tome, from which he was making notes.

We had lunch and I cleared up afterwards. When I reappeared on the terrace Mel closed her laptop and looked hard at me. She asked me if I had enjoyed my stay and if I was all right. I told her my concerns about being thrust out of paradise and the other changes which were inevitable. Mel came towards me and it was her turn to comfort me.

She suggested that we might spend half an hour in the wardrobe. At the end of it I had two suits which would be very suitable for work, a couple of silk dresses, several pairs of high waisted jeans, several tops, half a dozen pairs of shoes and some positively eye popping underwear. Kerr insisted on a fashion parade and in the pleasant sunshine I was happy to oblige. Kerr said I would knock them dead at the College. I wondered.

We discussed the last part of the semester. There were exams and some specialist lecturers to encounter. Then it was out of the college and into the world of employment. With a sinking feeling I realised that I hadn't got anything to go to. Still, there was always temporary work as a waitress or at worst dish washing. Come to that I could be a house cleaner. Kerr asked me if I was free to work anywhere. I had no ties and said so. He looked thoughtful. The sun got hotter, we unselfconsciously discarded clothes. Kerr looked at me again. He told me that he was trained as a painter and he'd like to paint me. I asked him when and he told me right now. I was down to a prettily decorated thong. I asked him if he wanted to paint me as I was. 'Fewer clothes,' was his reply.

He disappeared indoors. Mel told me that I would like this, but I couldn't see much fun in sitting still for a long time. Kerr reappeared with a wooden case in one hand and a bundle of brushes in the other.

'Come with me, please,' he asked, and I followed him. I was surprised that he hadn't brought his easel and canvas with him, but I thought that he wanted to pose me before he got down to painting. In that I was certainly right. There was a wide scaffolding made of rustic poles which looked as if it was intended for training roses. There were none on it, but Kerr came to a halt underneath it and beckoned to me. He took hold of my hands gently, told me to interlace my fingers and secured my wrists with a rope which hung from the top of the arch. He drew my arms up, not roughly but irresistibly, until I was standing on tiptoe. He turned away from me and opened the box. There were numerous bottles of paint in powerful poster colours. Mel arrived with a jug of lemonade and three glasses. She had brought a cushion with her and made herself comfortable sitting on it. I was about to point out that Kerr had forgotten his canvas when he turned to me with a long brush loaded with bright red paint and drew an arc on my chest from my throat to my lower ribs. My face must have given me away because Mel laughed and Kerr grinned. He did want to paint me, just as he said.

It is very seldom that we get a chance to investigate someone else's body in the most intimate detail. Even Mel, who I had watched in so many different circumstances, dressed, part dressed and wholly naked, I was used to seeing as a whole. I didn't have either the time or the opportunity to look at each part of her separately and concentrate my gaze on each area of her skin. I realised that this was exactly what Kerr was doing. His brush strokes were closely observed. I felt the tip of his brush travel along my collar bone as if he was pin striping my body. H filled in areas of skin with a wider brush, creating a pattern which meant nothing to me as I couldn't see it. He swept his brush over the upper part of my breasts and then went in for some elaborate work on my nipples. The touch of the brush and the close presence of this perfectly beautiful man began to make me stir in my loins.

The painting continued and Mel brought me a glass of lemonade with a straw in it. I sucked up the drink whilst Kerr washed out a couple of brushes. He had arrived at my belly and was painting the area enclosed by my hips. I wondered how far his painting would extend as he coloured the area between my thighs and stroked the brush slowly up and down my cleft making it exceptionally difficult for me to keep still. He did very little to my thighs, but he broke off and asked Mel to bring him something. He put what he described as a few finishing touches to the paint work and then stood back to admire his handiwork. Mel handed him a camera. He retreated a couple of yards and started to take pictures of me. I tilted my head back so that I would be unrecognisable. He seemed to like the pose and took pictures of me from both sides. Eventually he seemed satisfied and started reviewing the pictures he had taken.

Kerr seemed totally absorbed in the record of his work. I hung from the rope wondering what was to happen next and what his painting looked like. The paint had dried in the sun, but I was unsure if I could move. Mel said something to Kerr and he nodded. She came up to me and loosened the rope, letting my arms down slowly. I must have got used to being suspended as my arms very quickly came back to normal. They hadn't been painted so I rubbed them gently whilst I waited for Kerr to stop looking at the photos. He gave me the camera and instructed me to press the forward arrow when I wanted to move on. I sat next to Mel on the cushion and looked at the first frame. Kerr was a lot cleverer even than I had taken him for. He had painted my face on my skin. I was immediately recognisable despite the contours of my body.

I told him how talented he was. He had almost obliterated my body whilst making my face completely life like. I pressed the forward button and saw myself from various angles. Once I had got over the surprise of what he had achieved I became interested in how he had done it. At that point I pressed the button which showed me from the side. I was amazed at how slender I was, with the distance at my waist from my front to my back being only a very few inches. I was delighted with the line of my breasts as they stood out, high and firm from my chest. I could see the slight swell of my belly culminating at my navel and the round, high globes of my buttocks. I was intrigued by the visible promontory of my mons, something which I had never noticed before, but then, I'd never had my photo taken when I was naked. They were beautiful pictures. I looked good and felt good about myself. I had enjoyed Kerr's undivided attention to myself for an hour and a half. He had titillated me with his brushes. I felt beautifully decorated.

Kerr took his paints and brushes into the house, but not before he kissed me and told me I was beautiful. I lounged on the cushion with Mel. Idly I pressed the forward button. The sequence of photos started again at the beginning. Mine had been shots somewhere in the 50s. I found myself at number one. This was a scene in what I think the Australians call the outback. There was a view from an escarpment which included distant blue mountains, what looked like scrub and then something close to jungle. The view point was not at the top of the escarpment as the next shot showed the trunk of an ancient tree which had long ago fallen so that a great deal of it projected over the edge of the cliff. The third shot was straight down from the camera. The ground dropped away vertically. Small bushes grew from cracks in the rock. The trees at the bottom were half a mile down. The next shot was of an aborigine standing next to the fallen trunk just where it crossed the edge of the cliff. She was a tiny woman wearing a costume of what looked like painted feathers and coloured fur.

In the next picture she was standing on the tree trunk. It was difficult to make out her features. I wanted to see a close up. I was frightened by the next shot which showed her standing with her back to the end of the trunk with the stumps of two big branches either side of her. She was not holding on to anything and the dizzying drop beneath her feet was partly visible. I hardly dared press the button again.

Mel clutched my arm, afflicted as I was by the fear of the vertiginous drop. We gasped at the next frame which was something of a close up of the woman, sitting astride the end of the barkless trunk with her back to the drop. The white of the trunk contrasted with the deep black of her skin. I looked into her face and saw no sign of fear. She was undoubtedly a beautiful woman. She had her arms oddly crossed on her chest with her hands close to her neck. The next photo showed why she was holding her hands where they were as she had undone the front of her dress to reveal a body of exquisite proportions with breasts which protruded from her chest like dark cones, a narrow waist and spreading hips leading to muscular thighs. In the next picture we were to see just how important these were to her. She was lying back on the trunk with almost half her body hanging over the end of the timber with nothing but air below for the better part of 3,000 feet. I was reminded of the road to the top of Pike's Peak in Colorado where the rack railway ends at flimsy buffers within a few feet of a similar drop. I got the same strange feeling at the back of my thighs and in the pit of my bottom.

Her head was right back from her shoulders and her breasts pointed up into the sky. The feathers and fur were trapped under her whilst she gripped the trunk with her thighs and calves. Her hands were between her legs. Did I dare to look at the next frame? Mel took the camera and pushed the button. The woman was still in the same position but she had a hand at the top of each thigh holding back the black petals of her sex and revealing the bright pink contents of her cunt. The contrast between the outer and inner folds of her body was startling. Mel moved on to the next shot where her fingers were working against her very visible clit. Her eyes were closed and her mouth open, with her nipples now erect and pointing to the sky. She seemed to have moved her legs so that she was even more exposed than in the earlier photo. I wondered if she had made herself come. The next photo, obviously using a telephoto lens from the safety of the rocks showed her in a detailed close up with her fingers and thighs shiny with the spurting juices of her orgasm. The next shot showed only the empty white trunk until I saw, far below, the painted dress caught on a bush. I must have cried out and in a panic I clutched myself between my thighs, feeling my swollen clit and at once beginning to dribble juices in my uncontrolled dismay.

Kerr was just behind me.

'Funny how some people react to tension and fear. Men can have an ejaculation if they are sufficiently fearful, or just wet or soil themselves.'

I asked what had happened. 'Why not try the next frame and find out?' Mel shook as she pressed the forwards button.

The scene was a relief, at least in one way. There was naked Kerr sitting on a clump of grass whilst the black woman sat in his lap facing him with her arms round his neck and her arse just sufficiently raised to show her cunt engaged with Kerr's cock. Judging by the position of her legs she was bouncing herself up and down on him. All out of nowhere I was furious and jealous. I tried to prevent my emotions from becoming visible, but I was still dribbling and gasping from the shock and the stimulation of the earlier pictures as well as feeling my guts churning at Kerr's trick and its outcome with the black woman.

'We're not all virgins, you know,' he told me and I realised how little time ago that I had been a virgin and how I was delighted no longer to be one. My fury abated. He stood in the bright sunshine which caught a little curl in the hair at the back of his head. I put my face in my hands. I realised that I loved this man. I had no idea how he felt about me - just another bit of female flesh to be used and screwed and passed over in favour of the next opportunity, I thought. I must have let out an involuntary sob, and suddenly Mel and Kerr were all concern and tenderness.

I told them no more than that I was sad at having to leave this place. Mel assured me that I would always be welcome to return. It was more than that, as Mel realised. I had enjoyed my taste of Eden and t morrow it would be back to College. It seemed to me that I would suddenly lose everything that had made life wonderful.

Sunday 13th May

We packed our bags last night. My little rucksack was supplemented by a large leather suitcase which made up in opulence for its sheer weight. Mel and I drove back to College quietly thinking over the events of the last week and then, less happily for me, considering the future. Mel had given me a pair of designer jeans which would have cost as much as all my own clothes put together. With them she gave me a sleeveless top which clung to my figure like a second skin. She nearly persuaded me that I didn't need to wear a bra with it, but I feared my nipples would be all too apparent if I didn't.

We said goodbye to Kerr who gave me a powerful hug and kissed me for longer than I thought he might. I knew there were tears in my eyes and he wiped them away, telling me that we would meet again. I hoped so.

I struggled with my rucksack and the case, something of a new experience for me. In an hour or so it was time for dinner. This was an entirely informal affair on Sundays so I unpacked my rucksack and then sought out hangers for the dresses, skirts and tops which I had acquired from Mel. At the bottom of the case there was an envelope with my name on it. I opened it and found a note from Mel telling me how much she had enjoyed our week together and telling me that her uncle always insisted on giving her some money for looking after the house and she thought I should have half of it. To my amazement there were twenty five $20 bills. I had never seen so much money at one time and I almost considered taking it, but I slipped the envelope deep into the pocket of my jeans and thought I'd call on Mel after dinner.

I usually drifted into classes and meetings, to say nothing of meals, in an anonymous and forlorn sort of way. I looked in the mirror, combed out my short auburn hair, applied a little make up, made sure my top was neatly tucked into my jeans, put on a pair of sneakers with inch and a half heels and set off for the refectory. There were two of the rather snotty pony club girls ahead of me, dawdling along and gossiping. I caught them up and said 'Hallo.' I revelled in their expressions. I could see that they didn't recognise me, and then doubt came over them as they stumbled over a reply to my greeting and then Louie looked at me as if she had seen an apparition. 'It can't be,' but I was happy to tell her it was. They started asking me questions, but I told them virtually nothing.

For the first time in my life I made an entrance! I haven't any idea where I got the courage from but I held my head up high, smiled, ignored everyone and walked right through the diners to a table which I shared with two of my erstwhile tormentors. I heard an amazed pause in the conversation and then a substantially increased volume of sound. I had always courted the utmost privacy and kept away from the others, but now I was being talked about. I laughed inside to think what a bit of toning, a change of hair, some expensive clothes and most important, the confidence generated by all my experiences of the last weeks could do for me. I had seen and done thongs which my fellow students had not even thought about.

I went to see Mel who was working hard on her thesis, as I should have been on my books, and tried to return the envelope with the cash in it. For once Mel was forbiddingly fierce and told me that if I ever wanted to visit with her again I would accept her terms which were of equality and sharing. My thanks were sincere, but I cut them short and left her to her work, and went back to mine. However, things were not to be quite as straightforward as I had hoped. There was a knock at my door followed by the entry of Stella Gorangios, a very nose-in-the-air blonde who had never deigned to do more than make biting remarks in my direction before this. She came in, looked round and sat in my easy chair. She asked me how I'd spent the week and I told her I had visited some friends. She looked hard at me and asked how much they had given me. I could feel the envelope in my pocket, but I looked at her askance and told her that in my family we were brought up to think that discussing money was very vulgar. She got the message straight away and was up out of the chair in an instant. I knew that I had made an enemy by being smarter, in every sense, than she was. I just hoped I wouldn't have to endure her taunts again. I got on with my work, hoping to be able to revise everything before the exams started and hand in my dissertation, which was on deprived children and the effect of physical impoverishment on their education, at least two days early. I worked into the early hours, had a shower, bolted my door and slept.

Monday 14th May

I got through the lectures, worked in the library, missed Mel and Kerr and found my room so stuffy, even with the windows open, that I quietly went downstairs and out into the wilderness area of the college grounds. There is a bench facing the reedy lake. I sat on it and read over my notes, highlighting important passages. The light was fading and I put my file down beside me, closed my eyes and listened to the night noises. My drift into slumber was halted by the sound of voices. I recognised two of the speakers. One was definitely Stella. Something warned me to take notice. As I feared, they were talking about me and in very unfriendly terms. I very quietly left the bench and hid behind a very thick holly bush. Three of them approached. Stella saw the file which I had inadvertently left on the bench and snatched it up. She announced its ownership to her companions in words that included calling me a bitch. She then told them that if I didn't want the file then neither did she, and she threw it into the muddy water and reeds. I was overcome with a mix of horror and terror. Without any prompting tears ran down my cheeks. If they could do this to my precious revision file, what could they do to me? They walked on and in the gloom I left my hiding place, took off my trainers and stepped into the mud at the edge of the lake. My file hadn't submerged and I hoped I might be able to rescue it. At once my feet went from under me in the sticky ooze and I found myself sitting in the stagnant water with mud clinging to me up to my arm pits. I managed to regain my feet and reached my file. I held it high out of the water and struggled back to the bank, mud and stinking water running from my clothes. I made my way back to my block, hoping that I didn't meet anyone on the way. As I turned the corner of the building into the lamplight I was appalled to find Miss Readie in conversation with Stella and her friends. Worse, the Principal was facing me and looked horrified at my mud plastered clothes. All four of them turned to me. Stella looked as if she could murder me on the spot. Miss Readie asked me what had happened to me. I took a deep breath and told her that I had fallen in the lake whilst walking along the edge. A look of relief came into Stella's eyes, followed by an expression of triumph. Miss Readie issued instructions and took me to the side door of the gym, adjacent to the showers. In a moment I had stripped off my stinking clothes and had closed the cubicle door with the shower full on. One of the girls brought me a skirt and blouse and a large towel which she hung over the cubicle door. Stella arrived and mockingly asked if I'd like my file laundered. I wanted them all to go away. Eventually they did and I stepped out of the shower, dried myself and put on the clothes. I picked up my file and ran it, spine upwards, under the shower for a moment. It was time to return to my room and try to retrieve the pages as best I could. I went to bed eventually, deeply unhappy and very worried about my revision and the next thing that Stella could organise.

Tuesday 15 May

I worked on my dissertation all day today. In the evening I went to see Mel, having made sure I wasn't observed or followed. I told her something of what had happened the night before and asked her to look after my almost completed dissertation. Mel was very sympathetic and offered to confront Stella and her friends. I already had enough trouble and Stella's family had been benefactors of the college. My word would mean nothing compared with hers. I was very miserable and Mel suggested a quick work out to make me feel better. It was a good idea. She gave me a key to the gym and told me to help myself as she was at a crucial point in the editing of her thesis.

I went back to my room changed into shorts and a crop top and went to the gym. I realised that I hadn't been there since I was with Mel before we went away together. For some reason I felt a fluttering in my belly. I spent a good half hour using the apparatus which was out and doing press ups and stretching exercises. I managed to get up a fair sweat, especially when I was doing the aerobic exercises. I went into the shower cubicle I had used the night before and luxuriated in a sense of physical well-being and pleasant tiredness. As I stepped out of the shower, drying my face with my towel I felt hands on my arms gripping me fiercely. Standing in front of me was Stella. I tried to cover my nakedness with my towel, but as her friends secured my arms she snatched it away from me. 'You like your trips to the gym, don't you?' she asked me. I didn't reply. She reached forward and seized my left nipple between her thumb and forefinger pinching it painfully and pulling it towards her. I gasped, but was powerless to defend myself.

'Now tell us where you really went last week,' she

demanded, sinking her fingernails into my soft flesh.

'I told you,' I gasped out. 'Don't mess about with me. You were seen getting out of that PE woman's car on Sunday.'

'She gave me a lift,' I replied, wincing as her nails seemed almost to meet behind my nipple.

'You're a liar. Everyone knows Cotton's a dike, so you're her bit on the side.' Despite the pain she was inflicting I laughed and told her she was ridiculous.

'Ridiculous, am I?' She looked very threatening. 'Come on, you two, bring her over here and we'll swing her.' I tried to resist but they hoisted my arms up and Stella grasped me from behind round the waist hauling my feet off the floor. They tied each of my wrists to a rope and I hung there completely at their mercy.

'Well, look at this,' said Stella, poking at me between my legs. 'So that's how Cotton likes it, is it? All nicely shaved and ready for her.' I felt a wave of scarlet shame engulf my face. I wished Mel was here to deal with these bullies. There was nothing I could do to escape my fate.

Stella had disappeared into the store room. She came back with a sheaf of cords in her hand. She divided these between the three of them. She stood behind me and I felt a powerful shove in the small of my back. I began to swing forward, but despite the strength of the push I moved only a little way. Stella tied my ankles together with two cords. She told her friend to pull me forward as far as she could and then let go. Almost at once I began to swing back, only to find that Stella was dragging me backwards as far as she could. They set up a rhythm and I swung backwards and forwards. They dispensed with the tow ropes and kept me going with pushes at my front and back.

It was degrading, swinging like a naked puppet, but hardly unbearable. Stella gave me a very hard push and I swung forward nearly coming into contact with the girl who had been pulling my feet. As I swung back I suddenly felt the burning pain of a slash across my back inflicted by Stella using a bunch of the knotted cords. The shock of the unexpected attack made me gasp. As I swung forward my earlier tormentor whistled her handful of cords through the air and spread them over my belly and across the tops of my thighs. I cried out, drew up my knees and shook my body in response to the biting pain of this strike.

I heard Stella say, 'Now we're getting somewhere,' as I swung back to receive another set of stripes across my back. The stinging pain brought involuntary tears to my eyes, but as I swung forward the handful of cords were aimed across my breasts. They struck me like a swarm of wasps with sufficient force to buckle the soft tissue and for the knots to make indentations wherever they bit into my skin. I began to howl, but there was no let up in the ferocity of the assault on my body. The swinging was beginning to make me queasy. I feared the movement in each direction which ended in swift and violent pain. I lost count of the slashes which were delivered so harshly. I shook and twisted my whole body as each one bit home and I drew in my breath in gulps to try to pump oxygen round my system to dissipate the agony. Tears dripped down my cheeks, though I did not succumb to sobbing. I visualised what I must look like to the girls who were torturing me and at once, with my eyes closed I had the clearest possible vision of my naked body swinging between them. There must have been more to this powerful image than I had realised as endorphins began to kick in and I felt that tell-tale flutter between my legs and working its way up my belly.

I laid my head back between my arms, closed my eyes, opened my mouth and gave myself over to the ruthless punishment of the biting cords and the beginnings of my orgasm. It was not long coming and I felt the pressure build in my belly whilst the agony of the whipping decreased in its turn. I counted the swings. At three I was beginning to breathe more rapidly and more shallowly. At four I felt as if fingers were at my throat, at five the pressure mounted to my brain and I became unaware of anything except the desire for the release which would come with the fulfilment of my passion. I could hear the breath rasping in my throat. I could just make out the swish and crack of the cords against my flesh, I knew that I was shaking involuntarily at each blow; I tried opening my knees but failed. At the same time a handful of cords struck my cunt and I was filled with a choking all-enveloping gasping, weeping and then gushing orgasm.

They must have stopped whipping me when my belly went into a muscular spasm. I had no idea how long I gushed and spurted nor what happened next. I came to my senses when Stella was sneeringly telling me I was a lucky girl and that they would be thinking up new delights for me so that I could enjoy myself at their hands. They released me, but this time there was no pile of mats to collapse onto and no comforting hand to hold me. This time there were sneering faces staring down at my naked and abused body.

Stella and her friends left me to my shame and my pain. I struggled to my feet and went back to the shower room. I had a very cool shower and patted myself dry. I was in the process of dressing when the door behind me opened and I flinched.

'It's only me.' It was Mel's voice, and I turned to her. 'What on earth have you been up to?' she enquired. I told her what had happened. She looked furious, but thoughtful. 'First things first, I'll attend to those weals, and then...' She left the sentence incomplete, but I knew she was formulating a plan

Wednesday 16 May

I slept surprisingly well last night. I avoided Stella and her friends. I made sure I was never alone. I went to my room as soon as I could and sat to one side of the window working at my books, having salvaged all that was important of my revision file. I began the task of making an abbreviated copy of the pages of my crumpled file.

I had no contact with Mel during the whole day and missed her

Thursday 17 May

I didn't sleep very well last night. My mind was full of revision coupled with the events of the last three weeks and the fundamental changes in my life. I don't look like I once did, I have developed experience and the fulfilment of desires I didn't even know that I had, I have lovers who I love in return. I have been abused and hurt and to this I have reacted in a way which I could never have dreamed of less than a month ago. What's more, instead of being penniless, I have a secret stash which is enough to make me almost independent, at least for a while.

Tomorrow the exams begin so that there will be little time to record anything, not that much is likely to happen other than sitting in a desk for three hours at a time more often than is good for me.

Friday 18 May

I decided to get an early night yesterday, but just as I was comfortably settled in bed there was a tapping at my door and Mel called to me. I opened the door and she slipped in. She held her forefinger to her lips and I locked and bolted the door. We at once embraced and I felt the touch of her muscular body against me. She whispered that she had come to wish me all the very best of luck for the exams and also that she had sent off her thesis to her supervisor and now had her fingers crossed. We sat on the bed together. I was embarrassed to be wearing my old cotton nightie which was seriously worn in places and seemed to be too small across my breasts and unflatteringly baggy round my waist. Mel sat on my right and put her left arm round my shoulders drawing me towards her. Her right hand was on my right knee, but I was conscious that it was making its way up my thigh. I didn't resist, but Mel's close fitting top and tightly belted jeans made it very difficult to respond. I fumbled a bit but without success. Mel was concentrating all her attention on me. Her hand left my thigh for a moment and then returned.

'Open wide,' she breathed in my ear. I was not wrong that it was my knees she wanted to be parted. At once I felt her fingers at the top of my thighs and an unfamiliar touch which suddenly emitted a buzz as tiny flexible fingers were pressed against me and sought out my clit. I shuddered with the stimulation. Mel held the finger tip vibrator against me and increased the pressure. At once the sensations doubled in strength and I lay back on the bed drawing in breath in vigorous gulps as my clit responded. I thought it would not be long before I was forced to come. Just as I thought that a matter of seconds would do it for me, Mel removed her hand. I must have uttered a little cry of protest.

She bent over me and covered my mouth with hers in a deep kiss.

Almost at once her fingers were back again, but this time the angle was different and I felt her buzzing finger penetrate my vagina. It caught my G spot and I jerked my legs uncontrollably. To add to my pleasure she pressed her thumb, which was also equipped with a vibrator, against my clit. The effect was devastating. I began to twist and writhe, and I would have cried out in my ecstasy if Mel's lips hadn't sealed mine. As it was I felt that I was in the midst of a panic attack. I couldn't get enough air into my lungs through my nose, my heart was racing and my head seemed filled with explosive lights. The fear drove my orgasm forward and I felt myself falling into a chasm of iridescence. Then, as Mel had taught me, I let myself go and I felt the hot juices surging in my vagina and jetting out of my open cunt. Mel lifted her lips from mine and placed her forefinger across my mouth in a gesture of silence.

I hoped that she might spend the night with me, though my narrow bed would have made this difficult, but instead she stripped off my now more than damp nightie, mopped me between my thighs with it, swung me into bed, tucked me in with that most comforting of small services, kissed my eyes, turned off the bedside light and having unbolted the door she clicked back the Yale lock and was gone. Although I was still trembling and wanted nothing more than to lie in my bed and think about what had happened until I slipped into sleep, I hesitantly got out of bed and bolted the door.

That was an unlooked for prelude to the exams. I slept dreamlessly. I spent an early half hour on my hair and face. I checked my pens and went off to the exam hall without confidence except in my appearance. Surprisingly, the exams seemed to me to be much easier than I had expected.

The long two hour gap between the morning and afternoon sessions was trying. I decided to walk in the grounds, but only in the most visible parts. I came upon one of Stella's friends who was deep into a book and looking very worried. She looked up as I came near her and her worry turned to apprehension. I was delighted to think that she felt safe only in the company of the other two. I ignored her and went back to the library which seemed to be full of people who were doing last minute revision. The afternoon was much as the morning. I read the exam paper, picked out my four questions, three easy ones and the one I thought was the most difficult on the paper. I made sure that I had defined the terms used in the questions and finished writing with just over fifteen minutes to spare. A quick read through, two corrections and an addition and it was all over.

The exam ended at exactly five p.m. Our papers were collected and we were free to go until Monday afternoon when it would all start again. I went back to my room. On the carpet inside the door was an envelope. The message was from Mel. I was to book myself out and join her, complete with revision materials and my dissertation at the gym at six p.m. My heart leaped. A weekend with Mel! What could be better? Perhaps being with Kerr, but that was an idle dream.

I was shaking with excitement as we drove away from the College. I laid a hand on Mel's thigh, more as a gesture of friendship than an attempt to feel her body. She was, most unusually, wearing a thin cotton dress which ended four inches above her knees. I had put my hand on the cloth, but she moved it so that I was touching her skin. She smiled and I felt a constriction in my throat. We seemed to be going a different way from our previous journey together. I didn't like to ask, but Mel divined my question without a word being said.

'This time,' she told me, 'we're going to my place.' I

was even more delighted. We travelled the leafy roads of Cape Cod, turned off onto an unmade road and then onto a track. We followed the track into dense woodland. There were twists and turns and then rhododendrons in full flower, pink, white and red in huge clumps. Despite the opulence of the approach the house was small, with weatherboard walls and a south facing porch which ran almost the whole width of one side of the house. Mel opened the door and we went into a large room with a big cast iron stove set in the middle of it with the chimney going through the ceiling. There was a kitchen off to one side of this room but no signs of any electrical appliances. The stairs were steep and had no hand rail. We went upstairs to find another big room with mattresses on the floor and a big cupboard off to one side. In this room there were several candles. All the walls and the ceiling were of wood. The windows were on three sides of the room and looked out over more rhododendrons to the surrounding countryside. I saw a glint between two groups of shrubs. Mel explained that there was a stream which fed the lake. Downstairs again and Mel showed me the bathroom, only there was just a box seat with a hole in it. I must have looked dismayed. She pointed at the stream which supplied the house with water, and the lake which provided amusement, exercise and washing.

Mel unpacked the trunk of her car and brought in an assortment of food and drink. She told me to get on with my studies whilst she cooked up a little something. I went out on the porch and sat in the swing, letting the thick cushions envelop me. I was at the stage of the final edit of my dissertation. I went through it with my pen in my hand, but I must have been a very bad editor because I found very little to do. I was about half way through when Mel called me in. Her meal was delicious with salad and wholemeal bread and two unfamiliar cheeses. The dishes were compressed paper. I asked about the wastefulness, but Mel pointed to the stove which consumed all the domestic rubbish.

We sat in the dusk until there was no chance of reading any more.

'Bed with the setting sun. Up with it rising,' Mel said, and added, 'Bath time.' She fetched two towels and stripped off her clothes. I took mine off and she led me by the hand to the lake. We plunged in together and swam about for some minutes. I had just stood up on the bottom when I heard a loud splash behind me. I spun round and saw that there was another person swimming in the lake. I adopted the classic female modesty pose and turned to Mel, who was laughing.

'It's all right, he's seen you without your clothes before.' I hadn't time to recover when Kerr stood up with water streaming from his face and body. He took a couple of steps forward and kissed Mel and then turned to me and held me close whilst pressing his lips to mine. I hugged him for all I was worth.

Kerr often turned up at the cottage and looked after it at the weekends when Mel was at work. Serendipity had brought the three of us together. We left the lake and stood in the gloom towelling ourselves dry. Back at the cottage, Mel went upstairs and lit two of the candles. Kerr told me about his week which seemed to involve teaching and a great deal of administration. He asked me how I had got on with the exams and I truthfully told him that I thought I was on the low side of competent. We had a glass of rich red wine each and it was time for bed. Mel led the way up the stairs and we entered the beautiful room with its high gables and low walls all clad in golden cedar. Mel pulled a couple of the mattresses together, covered them with sheets, scattered pillows over one end and unfolded a vast quilt which she spread over the mattresses. I waited to see how the sleeping pattern was to be arranged and found myself in the middle.

Both Mel and Kerr turned towards me as I lay on my back. A small quick hand reached for my breasts, a big powerful hand was working its magic between my thighs. I was being kissed repeatedly. Kerr gently detached himself from me. In a voice not much above a whisper he asked me to kneel over him with my knees either side of his chest. In the candle light I looked at Mel for her approval, but she gave me a push to help me on my way. As soon as I had taken up my position I was aware that Mel was kneeling just behind me. Mel caught my arms at the elbow and pulled them behind me. She deftly cinched my elbows with a strap as I knelt up with my knees wide apart. Mel reached round my waist and her fingers delved between my thighs. Kerr reached up and took a breast in each of his big hands. For a moment I closed my eyes and gave myself over to the pleasure they were giving me. I felt something brush against my fingers and realised that Mel's belly was within my reach. I did not hesitate to hold her by the petals of her cunt and run my fingers between her inner lips. I heard her give a little cry and I increased the ferocity of my attack, whilst her fingers slipped against my clit and found their way deep into me. In the midst of this I found that her left hand was pressed against my buttocks and her finger was being thrust against my sphincter. I must already have provided enough lubricant to make penetration easy, but I feared the invasion of my arse by her accomplished fingers.

I looked down at Kerr's hands on my breasts, pushing them together and pulling my nipples between his thumbs and index fingers. I could see his teeth glinting in the candle light as he smiled up at me. The now familiar buzz was starting in my belly and I gasped at its rapid ascent towards my chest. I didn't know if I could stay kneeling up when I achieved orgasm. My head began to spin as Mel's fingers worked on me and Kerr massaged my breasts into fiery pleasure. I began to utter meaningless obscenities as my juices spilled from me on to Kerr's chest. Mel released my elbows and I sank back, lowering my bottom towards Kerr. I had not expected to sit on Kerr's rigid cock, but as my thighs began to sink I felt the thick head of his shaft at the cleft of my cunt and I willingly pressed myself down on it. I also did not expect a second arousal as I grasped his cock with my pelvic floor muscles, but in this also I was to be rewarded. It was not long before I came again, but this time I could do no more than collapse face down on Kerr who held me in a strong embrace and Mel released the strap on my arms. As I recovered I realised that neither Kerr nor Mel had matched my pleasure. I heard Mel tell me to change places. I lifted myself off Kerr and scrambled away from him as Mel took my place. I saw she was busy with her fingers between her thighs, but changing places meant changing places and I knelt behind her, doing to her as she had done to me. Right from the start Mel was impaled on Kerr's cock and I followed the bouncing movements of her arse whilst pleasuring her front and rear. It was amazing feeling Kerr's cock against my fingers as he penetrated Mel. She began to mew with pleasure and I felt her belly muscles contract as she started to come. Kerr bellowed a roar of triumph and added his juices to hers. As I had done, Mel fell forwards on to Kerr. I stroked her back and the heart shaped outline of her buttocks. Slowly she recovered and we found ourselves under the quilt with Kerr between us.

Saturday 19 May

As Mel had suggested, we were up with the sun. The day rolled on with close attention to my books until the middle of the morning, when Kerr and Mel approached me. They asked me about Stella and her two friends, but I told them of the apprehensive side kick and that I thought that Stella was the leader of the pack and the one who represented trouble on her own.

Mel looked thoughtful. 'Next Thursday, the exams are finished and Friday is the last day for handing in dissertations. Then those who have exams to mark have a week to do so and have them moderated. The following Friday is the Exam Board where the grades are sorted out and on Monday the results are published. Kerr and I have a plan. I am gong to invite Stella for a weekend at my uncle's place. Kerr will take you there on Friday morning. He has to be back at work on Monday morning, so he can return her to the College. You and I can stay on.' I must have looked dumbfounded.

'She ill treated you and sneered at you. We will not ill treat her, but we will get her to do it for herself. If I know anything about her character she won't be able to resist doing things she's told not to.' I had no idea exactly what they had in mind but I was sure that I trusted them, though revenge was not in my mind.

It was a quiet day. Mel went for a walk with Kerr and I wondered about their relationship. If it was as close as it seemed to be how could either of the put up with my presence, let alone allowing me into their closest intimacy. If it was not, what did that say for either of them and their regard for me? I really couldn't work it out, but then I cast my mind back over the last weeks and all that I had learned from them. I knew that I had blossomed and that I was now free in a way that I had never been in my life. On the other hand I was not free because I had fallen in love with both of them, though Kerr was my idol. I wondered if there was any chance of getting him for myself. If I did, how would that affect Mel? I didn't want to hurt her, nor did I want anything to impair the friendship and love between us.

These thoughts came between me and the work I was trying to do. Mel and Kerr returned as I was revising. Mel decided it was lunch time and in a few minutes the table was laid and we sat down together.

The afternoon followed the pattern of the morning, except that even someone as stolid as I am can become bored with sitting down all day. I gathered up my towel and wandered through the shrubs to the lake where I was delighted to find that Kerr and Mel had preceded me. I managed to get a quarter of the way across the lake, but began to feel tired and turned back to the shore. Once there I sat down on my towel on a grassy patch and watched the sparkling water glittering in the sunlight where the two of them cavorted and splashed each other like a couple of kids. Not for the first time I realised that both of them were beautiful physical specimens, strong and lithe and well toned, as well as exceptionally good looking.

I must have drifted into a doze in the warm sunshine and awoke to find the other two close to me towelling themselves dry. Mel asked me how the work was progressing and I told her I thought it was okay, but that I had needed a break. Kerr thought that was a very good idea, and told me to lay off the study until tomorrow and then finish everything I needed to do by four p.m. at the latest so that it would all have an opportunity to fall into place in my mind.

We spent the evening sipping wine and talking about our pasts and our hopes for the future. Mel wanted promotion at work, which she would deserve once her PhD was confirmed. Kerr had plans for making a change in the education and training of teachers. I suddenly realised that I had no idea what he did or where he did it. I thought it would be intrusive to ask and kept my mouth shut. They asked me what my hopes were and I told them that I hoped to get my degree and then get a job so that I could look after kids and get a bit of money together.

'No Mr Right?' Mel asked me. I felt myself blush and managed to tell her that I'd already met him. This was not clever because her reply was to ask if he was anyone they knew. I was filled with confusion and muttered something. As I looked up I saw Mel was winking at Kerr, but I couldn't fathom what this implied. We rolled into bed together, quite agreeably under the mild influence of the wine we had drunk and slept until the sun woke us in the morning.

Sunday 20 May

I woke up to find myself embraced by the still sleeping Kerr. Mel had already got up and I could hear her doing something in the kitchen. I needed the bathroom and gently detached myself from Kerr who made a little disconsolate noise but appeared to remain asleep. It was a cool morning, but I made use of the waters of the lake to wash myself and make me fully awake. I realised that all three of us had spent almost the whole day and certainly the whole night, quite naked. I hadn't thought of the reaction of anyone visiting. Would they follow suit or be shocked or offended? It hardly mattered. Tomorrow I would be back at the college and the grind of exams would follow. I was suddenly concerned that whatever Mel's plans were for Stella she might well not co-operate and then what? I should have to be very careful. I went into the kitchen. Mel had prepared breakfast and Kerr had appeared, complete with two days' stubble and a rather bleary look. He was wearing a pair of sandals and shorts which seemed slightly too tight in the leg for his muscular thighs. Mel was wearing a thong and an apron and I was using my towel as a sort of sarong.

I thought I would get it over with and ask just how Mel was going to deal with Stella. She told me the first thing she was going to do was to summon Stella to her room when Kerr was present. Mel knew something of Stella's proclivities when it came to men. I felt a pang of fear and jealousy.

She would invite Stella for the weekend with Kerr and me so that she could know just exactly what I had enjoyed, and she might enjoy it too. Mel thought that Stella would never credit any man with preferring someone other than herself; she also thought that Stella might see this as an opportunity to humiliate me. I was very doubtful about the whole affair.

Just as we finished breakfast we heard the crunch of tyres on the shingle outside. Mel looked out of the window and then ran to the door excitedly, telling us it was her uncle. I made shift to cover myself with the towel. Kerr followed Mel out of the door and all four of us stood in the sun. Mel, naked to the waist was embracing her uncle, who had her in a bear hug. Kerr shook his hand and stood back. I was introduced and was embraced in my turn. He must have been the most adept of pickpockets because as I stepped back I found that he was holding my towel and smiling at me in frank appreciation.

The three of them laughed until I realised that being self righteous would do me no good at all and I joined in. Uncle George was a neat figure of a man in his late sixties I thought, though I was to discover he was ten years older than that. He had a neatly trimmed beard, greying curly hair and a pale blue silk shirt and linen chinos in darker blue. His eyes twinkled and he gave out an impression of sincere charm. I could see that he would be devastatingly attractive to many women, especially as his dark green Bentley must have cost as much as I was likely to earn in the next ten years. He turned and pressed a remote and the boot opened. Among other things inside was a big wicker basket. He pointed to it and told us that he wasn't going to slum it and had brought lunch. I thought Uncle George was delightful, combining care with charm. There was only one thing I couldn't immediately fix and that was his accent, until I realised that it was British and it made his courtesy somehow slightly sinister.

This was a Sunday morning like no other I had experienced. Uncle George told us something of his latest adventure which had been among a remote Inuit tribe. I listened, fascinated, when he described the social position of women which was as things owned by their 'husbands.'

He had been invited to enjoy the sexual delights of his

host's wife. Uncle George admitted to liking a new encounter from time to time, but he pointed out that he had no idea how to go about fucking a woman who seemed to be sewn into a bear's pelt with the fur inside. I was shocked at the charmer's direct turn of phrase. By some means he had conveyed his difficulty to his host who pointed to laces at the shoulders and made a gesture of pulling, which is exactly what uncle George had done as his hostess stood unmoving before him. He wondered what was awaiting him as the fur slid down the woman's body, only to discover a strong but slender naked body with coffee colour skin and black body hair. She remained standing with her fur covering piled at her feet. She gave off a powerful odour peculiar to those who eat a great deal of fish and seldom change their clothes. George managed to convey that he liked her a lot, which was true, but the social customs of his society required that the woman should wash from head to foot before anything was attempted. His host had no trouble with that and grabbed his wife by the wrist, towing her out onto the ice. He took her to his fishing hole and swept his leg round behind her, taking her off balance so that she fell into the icy water. She struggled against the sides of the hole for a minute or so until her husband reached down and grasping one arm and her hair, hauled her out of the water. As she arrived on the ice he smacked her arse with his horny hand and directed her to the relative warmth of their home. It would have been very rude to have rejected this nubile shivering creature, even if Uncle George had been inclined to. He had grasped her wet body in his arms trying to warm her and put a stop to the shivering which possessed her. She made no effort to do anything, so as she warmed a little uncle George put his lips to hers, an expression of affection which she clearly didn't understand. He cupped her breasts in his hands and felt them full and solid. Still standing he twisted her slightly and reached a hand down between her thighs and penetrated her cunt. He found a well lubricated cleft and found her clitoris which he proceeded to manipulate with all the skill he could recruit for his second favourite task.

The woman looked at him with an expression of amazement. He found that she was holding on to his upper arms and gazing into his face with something akin to adoration. Her shivering had stopped and was replaced with trembling. Her breathing became more rapid and she closed her eyes. In a couple of minutes she showed every sign of beginning to ascend to a climax. Uncle George unzipped and took himself out of his pants. She at once began to move into a kneeling position. Uncle George had stopped that happening and had turned her round, still with his fingers in her, playing, as he put it, a familiar tune.

He felt her cunt tighten on his fingers. He was aware of juice trickling from it, so he pushed her shoulders forward and thrust himself into her wonderfully lubricated cleft. She let out a long cry. Uncle George began pumping into her as his fingers continued their work. Juices streamed onto the floor, she shook and cried out. He continued until she went limp in his arms and then mixed his fluids with hers. Quite how he managed such self control was a mystery to me. I would have to ask rather discreetly.

The morning was getting well on and it was a long time since breakfast. Mel suggested an early lunch and we carried Uncle George's basket, with another for plates and cups, to the edge of the lake. Mel asked if we wanted a swim first, but we were all hungry. Lunch was wonderful. There was delicious white wine from one of Uncle George's vineyards in California. Crisp baguettes, lobsters from Maine, Nicoise salad with French dressing, a potato salad in a mayonnaise of exquisite delicacy followed by strawberries and cream and coffee from stainless steel vacuum flasks. We collected up the debris and put it in the baskets, then lay back on the turf and looked at the cloudless sky. Uncle George was beside me. He asked me to tell him about myself. There was little to tell. Orphaned at an early age, brought up by a grandmother who didn't like my father. Plain, dowdy, uninteresting, hard up but hard working. Raised the money for college by working at any domestic job which would have me. Worked through college and then a few short weeks ago had dreams and had the dreams fulfilled in ways that I never could have imagined. Came to the attention of Mel who was kindness itself to me. Had experiences which were quite overwhelming. What more was there to say?

Uncle George asked me why I described myself as plain and dowdy, since I was beautiful. I was shocked, but told him that the transformation was achieved by Mel.

'Do you regret no longer being a virgin?' he asked me. I hardly knew what to say as my mind was on how he knew that I had been one until lately, and then how he knew that I no longer was. I whispered a quiet 'no' and then in a gush I told him that I was now free of the constrictions of my earlier life. As I looked up to see a single cloud in the sky, he leaned towards me and with his forefinger traced a line from my eyebrow, down my cheek and then across my lips. It was an amazingly sexy and stimulating gesture and made me tremble and buzz between my legs.

Uncle George smiled at me. 'You are beautiful and responsive and Mel tells me you are very bright and she backs up the idea that you are hard working. It is all a recipe for success and happiness.' No one had ever been so flattering to me. Instinctively I reached up my arms and took him round the neck, raising my lips to his and kissing him first with a gentle pressure and then more strongly as my body responded to my desire to take this man in my arms and press myself against him.

In the midst of this embrace I wondered what Kerr must

think of me. I loved Kerr, though he didn't know it, and here I was virtually offering myself to this elderly man.

I felt a pull on my arms and realised that Uncle George was trying to detach himself from me. I at once let go, fearing I had offended him.

'I should dearly like it if we all had a swim,' he said, and added that he didn't want to put off seeing me naked again for a moment longer.

Just for a moment I felt a sudden flush of embarrassment, but it passed as quickly as it arrived and I stood up and drew my T-shirt over my head and dropped my shorts on to the grass. I turned to Uncle George and for the very first time I was not embarrassed to be naked when there was someone else present fully clothed. I gave a twirl, laughed and ran into the water. I was splashing about when Mel and Kerr arrived, complete with an inflatable ball which was thrown from one to another. I was so taken up with the game we were playing that I quite lost track of Uncle George until he entered the game beside me. I was amazed at how toned and bronzed he was, with as smart a six pack as anyone a third his age. We played for a while until Kerr said he wanted a swim to the other side of the lake. Mel said she'd join him, which left Uncle George and me. We got out of the water and sat on the grass near our clothes. Uncle George told me I was beautiful, and I told him that he was extremely handsome, something I had never said to anyone before, but which was true in his case. He asked me if I had been to his house at Calumet. I told him I had.

'Then you will know that I have a remarkable collection of artefacts in the basement.' I blushed and admitted I had seen them. 'And not only seen them, but used them, I expect. Mel was brought up to be inured to pain, but you'll have seen that it is an essential part of her life and one from which she derives great satisfaction. I suspect it isn't so long since an idea like that would have been abhorrent to you, but now you understand, and perhaps you might even participate?'

I looked away, a blush ascending my cheeks. Uncle George had a singularly seductive voice and was graceful and gentle in his dealings with me. I nodded.

'I thought so. I'm also pretty much certain that you have found depths in your personality which you were unaware of before you got to know Mel.' I nodded again, my heart starting to thump in my chest.

'So you might even enjoy being stripped naked and you might like showing off your beautiful figure for the admiration of onlookers. And then,' he paused and my throat tightened, 'and then you might just like to feel the sharp kiss of the whip, the bite of the tawse, the fire of the cat, the cut of the riding crop, the heavy agony of the strap, whilst you hang, totally exposed and unable to resist the effects of the display and the mounting pain until the agony stokes your loins, boils in your vagina, spreads up your belly, seizes your heart in its consuming talons and tightens your throat before it blacks out your brain and your eyes grow dim whilst the great release is given to you and your cleft quivers and you gush beautiful lubricant.' As he was speaking I closed my eyes and began to have the sensations which he described. I realised that I would get nowhere without a whipping, at least, not on my own.

'So what you now desire is to be rendered helpless and to be thrashed by someone who has nothing in mind excerpt your ultimate pleasure.' It must have been very strong wine which so far affected my judgement that I turned to him and whispered 'Yes'. He reached an arm round my back and caught my breast in his hand, very gently, but effectively massaging it until it became solid and my nipple stood out in relief at the end.

'Come,' he said and stood up, holding out his hand to me. I clasped it and we walked hand in hand towards the house. In what passed for the back garden there was a couple of odd looking clothes line posts with a line running between them and clothes pins permanently attached to it. I stood under one of these as he began to check on my wish to be beaten.

'Yes', I breathed, 'I wish I with all my heart.'

We must have looked a strange pair as he took my hands gently in his and then used the trailing end of the laundry line to tie them together. He threw the loose line over the pulley which was fixed to the top of the post and pulled so that my hands were soon above my head and I was standing on tip toe.

'I never think it is fair not to prepare the victim for sacrifice.' He put his lips to mine and kissed me as his left hand grasped my breast and his right hand caught my buttock in his fingers. He kissed me several times and his fingers slid over my belly to my cunt, which they invaded. At once I felt the now familiar buzz as he stroked my clit and then used his thumb on my clit and his fingers to penetrate within me. I began to pant slightly and I felt a tightening in my belly as he had predicted. I licked my lips and looked hard at him as I saw his smiling face so close to mine. Before I was aware how far I had got I felt that insistent trickle which presaged my climax. Uncle George knew well what he was doing and very carefully slowed his caresses and gently withdrew his hands from my body.

'It is time,' he said, and turned away from me. I saw the muscles on his lean back twist as he reached under a small bush near the post. He extracted a long plaited leather whip, tapering from its thick handle to the last slender foot which terminated in a short length of knotted whip cord. I was very apprehensive. Uncle George assured me that he knew exactly what he was doing, and to demonstrate his expertise he cracked the whip several times with deafening reports.

He stood to my left side and behind me and suddenly I

felt a violent sting on my left buttock. I hadn't sensed that he had made any movement, and I hadn't heard the whip swish in its passage through the air. For a moment I thought that I had been stung by a hornet and I jerked my body to try to shake the insect off. Uncle George came and stood in front of me. I looked him full in the face.

He smiled at me and said, 'Now for target practice.' I had no idea what he meant, but I very soon found out. Uncle George was the full length of the whip away from me. I hardly saw the movement of his arm but I became frighteningly aware of the lightning approach of the end of the whip towards me. The sharp cord struck my right breast and stung it mercilessly. I cried out and shook my breasts to attempt to lessen the pain. Uncle George seemed to approve of the bouncing, jiggling orbs and waited until I was still again. Whatever else he was, and memories of his basement crowded into my mind, he was an expert with the whip. His next flick caught me in my navel. I didn't think that this was the most sensitive part of my body, but I could hear the screech that I let out as the burn from the cord cut across my belly and made me draw in and exhale breath in quick succession.

I became aware that Uncle George had changed his position. He was out of my sight so I assumed that he was behind me. I hung on to the rope like someone drowning, looking up into the sky and leaving myself open to any strike he might wish to give me. Almost at once I felt the cruel bite of the whip between my buttocks and the penetration of the loaded tip to my rosy crater. Involuntarily I sprang in the air kicking and screaming from the agony which was flowing up from my anus into my back and belly. On reflection I have no idea how he managed to penetrate to my fundament with such devastating power and accuracy, but Uncle George was not a man to be underestimated when it came to inflicting pain. Even the pauses between strikes were varied so that each vicious contact came as an anticipated terror. This was never truer than at this moment, when I was dancing with agony and I at once received another pain at my anus like a fire cracker exploding against my skin. I screamed and danced only to receive the coup de grace with a cut which came forward of the previous hits and burnt its way into my cleft, searing my inner and outer lips and flicking up to cauterise my clit. I had experienced pain before, but this was a new agony. I stood motionless with my breasts heaving from the rasping breaths I was taking and my waist and belly pulled in as if to consolidate the muscle and ward off another dreadful spike of pain. I had closed my eyes, but tears forced their way from under my lids and ran down my cheeks. I was lost in a world of jagged agony praying that the pain was at an end, but hoping that there might be a little more to drive me wild from the need to orgasm.

Coming back from the consuming anguish I heard voices. I realised that there were others present who had witnessed my immolation. I opened my eyes and looked down to find that Mel and Kerr were sprawled on a grassy bank watching Uncle George at work. Mel had obviously become quite excited by seeing me whipped and had one hand between her thighs whilst her other was holding her breast. Uncle George had come round to face me. In the midst of his words addressed to Mel and Kerr he flicked out the whip and caught my right nipple. The pain was such that I was convinced that he must have torn my skin, but as I looked down I could see nothing but my erect nipple exhibiting a bright red flush. Again I shook my breasts together to try to dissipate the pain, but this was not an effective move except that I saw that both the men were showing visible signs of excitement as they watched me shake and writhe.

Uncle George said something to Kerr and at once I felt

the bite of the tip of the whip on my right hip bone and almost immediately on my left. I knew I was done for and hung in my bonds waiting my fate. Uncle George caught me twice more a couple of inches below the first two strikes. He had moved his aim inwards so that he was cutting into the sides of my belly as they were held between my hips. I gave myself up to be a sacrifice and the word itself drew in my breath and I visualised myself hanging naked and displayed and being tortured until I lost my senses. The effect of the whipping and the drama of my thoughts about it made me feel a little buzz between my thighs. I knew that my endorphins had kicked in. My body was reacting on its own. My eyes were filled with the image of Mel frigging herself as she lay back on the bank with her legs apart watching Uncle George and myself as a tableau of torturer and victim. I saw that Kerr had a hand round his rigid cock and that Uncle George was almost all the way to a full erection with his long, slender cock bouncing with every move he made and wagging from his groin.

Ludicrously I was pleased with the effect I was having on the others, but Uncle George returned to his target practice and he struck again an inch below his previous contact and then another inch lower. The stings were converging as my belly narrowed towards my crotch. I could do nothing except breathe in raspingly, feel the bites of the whip and experience the mounting tension and palpitations in my belly. I knew it would not be long before his strikes landed on my mons, and what then? Horror at the impending torture of my cunt was paralleled by a perverse desire to see Mel bring herself to a climax, and my own wish for the release of the mounting pressure in my belly moving up my body. Uncle George knew exactly what he was doing and had described every step of my way to being an oblation. Mel was watching me through half closed eyes, her mouth was open and her finger nails were dug deep into her breast. I could not imagine why the ever-ready Kerr wasn't thrusting into her for all that he was worth.

The inevitable came and the stings came lower on my belly and then I knew what Uncle George's target was. The knowledge filled me with dripping terror, but my body wanted more and as the tip of the whip stung my mons once, twice, three times, I forced my knees apart and presented my just opening cleft to his mercy, hoping for none. I was not disappointed. My screams became an almost continuous howl as the knotted cord found its way between my thighs and into my cunt. The pain was so vivid that I could hardly feel each separate strike, but I guessed there were six of them before my harrowed cunt gave way to the release that I had sought when Uncle George had touched me earlier. Except that this was a release of a different magnitude. I could hear myself howling, I could see Mel on her few last strokes before she joined me, I could feel the juices gushing from my cunt onto the dust at my feet, I sensed that there was a dreadful pressure inside my skull and that I was losing contact with the world of senses. My last impression was the sight of Mel with her head thrown back and her rapid fingers bringing herself to a squirming, succulent climax baptised by a great squirt of ejaculated juices.

I suppose it wasn't long before I regained my senses, but I was totally confused by what now happened. I found Kerr standing in front of me. My legs were several inches further apart than when I had completed my orgasm. Kerr had thrust himself into me and had his hands on my hips. I was at once aware that this was not all that had happened to me and I realised that Uncle George was standing behind me holding my breasts cupped in his hands and with his long and now rigid cock thrust between my buttocks and buried in my rectum. Neither man moved for many seconds.

Then I felt Uncle George begin to pump his hips, so that my buttocks were struck by his hard belly and his cock forced its way into me. Kerr waited just a few moments to establish Uncle George's rhythm and then began to match it. I could feel the heads of their cocks bouncing almost together on the thin layer of tissue between the two of them. Mel was standing at my right side watching the two men as they penetrated me. I tried to think what I must look like, impaled on two hard cocks. The thought made me gasp. I hung on to the rope which bound my wrists as the two men forced themselves into the intimate openings of my body. I knew that I was a slave to my passion and to theirs. Even in the midst of the pistoning of my body I wondered if I was just a creature of my own lust and the object of theirs. I knew I didn't care and I gave up my body to their pumping cocks as willingly as I had presented my naked flesh to the excoriation of the whip.

My legs were already wobbly from the whipping and the orgasm, now they were becoming unable to support me and I sank on to their cocks as a support against falling and to enjoy the whole of their penetration. I compressed my vaginal muscles in a hard grip on Kerr and drew my buttocks together so that my sphincter clenched Uncle George's shaft. Kerr came first, and I watched his eyes roll up and his mouth open as jet after jet pumped into me. Even after he had come he continued to hold my hips and kissed me. Uncle George increased his speed and depth of penetration and I could feel my buttocks bouncing with each thrust. I was amazed that I was becoming excited at the thought of what he was doing to me. Kerr was still connected to me but had leaned back a little. I felt Mel's hand slip between our bellies and in an instant her fingers were on my clit and she was giving it her expert attention. I couldn't believe that I could again feel the flutter in my cunt and the pressure in my belly. I hoped that Uncle George could keep it up for just a little while longer whilst I enjoyed another orgasm. The thought itself was enough to drive me over the edge and I rushed into another thundering climax as Uncle George uttered a whistling cry behind me and I felt him pull out of me and spurt his jism over my buttocks and the back of my thighs.

Kerr reached up and slipped the knot of the rope that I was holding. He disengaged himself from me and both men took an arm and began to massage it until the pain of being suspended abated. Mel had disappeared briefly, but as we all sat on the grassy bank she returned with a bottle of champagne and poured four tumblers full. We sipped them slowly and I found myself leaning against Kerr, engulfed by one of his big arms lying between my breasts and I realised there was no need for words.

Monday 21 May

I'd spent what remained of Sunday being made a fuss of by all three of them and quietly getting on with my revision. I had finished my dissertation and printed it, enclosing it in a spring binder. I handed it in this morning and got a receipt for it, though it is on a CD which Mel has carefully locked in her filing cabinet. Outside the exam room I had a chat with Charlotte Clinton, in everyone's estimation one of the pleasantest, prettiest, brightest and most hard working girls in the College. We talked of next year and the jobs that we hoped to get. Then it was time to go in and face the exam paper and conjure up answers which we hoped would impress the examiner.

Most of the day was spent in the exam room and the rest of it was devoted to eating, a bit more revision and sleeping.

Tuesday 22 May

It rained today, otherwise it was very much the same as yesterday. I saw Stella for a few moments walking towards the gym. I had intended to have a short work out to liven up my sedentary body, but I decided not to in case I ran into her.

WEDNESDAY 23 MAY

It's nearly all over. The exam in the afternoon was very hard, but I managed to answer the five questions that I had picked out. When I got back to my room I found a slip of paper had been pushed under the door. There was a typed note: 'S is coming to Calumet with K on Friday. Come to my room after the exam tomorrow, ready to take off.' I hadn't spent any of my $500 on clothes, or, for that matter on anything else. I had the clothes I had been given from the Calumet wardrobe and some of my own, which were comfortable, if rather worn. I carefully put them in the only case I possessed. I realised that I must be ready to pack everything in a few days time as my college career would be over and I would have to get a temporary job and hope that I might secure a post for the next semester.

I became very depressed by the prospect of my future. I would probably have to go to Boston to work in a smart hotel and sleep at the Y. I would lose touch with Mel and Kerr and even Uncle George would be sadly missed. I took a firm grip on myself, went off to the bathroom and luxuriated in warm water for twenty minutes. I washed my hair in the shower and having dried it I went back to my room and attended to it with the colourings that I had been given at Calumet. It looked to me as if it could do with a trim, but I was delighted with its rich colour and the way it framed my face. In my room I stood naked in front of the wash basin and took shaving foam and a razor to my pussy. By the time I had finished it was a very bald pussy and the very sight of it and memories of what had been done to it made me shiver.

I thought an early night might be a good idea. I slept well.

Thursday 24 May

What a day! The exam in the morning was greeted by many gritty eyes and weary fingers. It was a very searching paper with what were seemingly quite simple questions which contained subtleties only apparent to me on a second reading. I did my usual routine and finished editing the paper at 1220. I re-read the questions which I had done and could find only one sentence which I thought it would be useful to add. I couldn't wait for 1230, but I knew I must be quiet for the sake of the others.

Then suddenly it was all over. Girls were chatting and giggling in the sun drenched yard. Several were on their way to the local village to make use of the bar. Being twenty one and to all intents and purposes no longer a student was great for them. They could have a week off at home; I just hoped that Mel would let me stay at Calumet until Sunday week. I was fully prepared to be housekeeper and gardener. I took my bag and went to Mel's room. There was a note on the door which I removed it simply said 'Staff Car Park.'

We were on our way to Uncle George's house. I shivered with excitement, only slightly clouded by my concern about Stella; and particularly Stella on her own with Kerr. I supposed I had little to complain about, having given myself to Uncle George as well as Kerr. My mind drifted to the previous weekend and I gave an involuntary tremble. Mel seemed beset by her own thoughts, and I hardly thought it my place to invade them.

I wondered how successful Mel's plan would be and whether there was any point in it now that the students were about to go their separate ways. A tiny doubt entered my mind; was this Mel and Kerr preparing another girl who they could amuse themselves with? For a moment my heart thumped and my throat became dry. Then I relaxed as Mel, having escaped from her reverie, put a friendly hand on my thigh and smiled at me. She told me she was just wondering if her plans for Stella would work.

'Either way,' I told her, 'she just might have the weekend of her life, or she might just be bored.'

Mel told me that there was little chance of that with Kerr on the premises, and I felt a touch of depression cloud my mind. It had been wonderful being transformed, it had been wonderful being introduced to an entirely new way of life, and it had been wonderful being whipped and fucked and loved. It had all been wonderful and had been a prelude to the tension of the exam week. Now I wanted my life to be governed by Kerr and Mel. I didn't mind being a plaything, a victim or a sacrifice, as long as I was caressed and kissed and at least the semblance of love was inherent in our relationship. My thoughts cast a black shadow over my mind and I could not repress a sob. Mel pulled the car off the road under some over hanging trees. She asked me what was wrong and I began to weep. Between my sobs I told her of my fears. She got out of the car, came round to my side, opened the door and none too gently drew me out onto the grass. I stood with my head down and my hands clasped in front of me. I expected to be told off. I wasn't disappointed except that the words were sympathetic. Mel told me not to worry about the future which always held more surprises than we expected. She had no intention of relinquishing her contact with me, and she knew Kerr hadn't either. Then there was Uncle George, who she said was besotted with me. I doubted it, but she then did what I really wanted, which was to clasp me in her arms and kiss me again and again. I wasn't slow to respond, but the appearance of another car led us to get under way again.

We arrived at Calumet at what the English used to call 'tea time'. I was surprised to see the green Bentley parked under the trees. As we drew up the front door opened and a forbidding looking woman appeared on the threshold. 'Uncle George's cousin and his companion,' Mel explained. I didn't know what to make of this so I got my bags out of the trunk and followed Mel up the steps.

The woman stepped back and then opened both arms to Mel enfolding her in a mass of drapery and wafting a most exotic perfume down to me. I was introduced and was treated to the same embrace.

I seemed to disappear into a sort of breathing duvet. I suppose that I had been standing a bit lower than the enveloping lady and somehow my face had come into contact, through the fabric, with a large and pillow-soft bust. For a moment it was like an old seaside postcard with my nose buried between two breasts which enveloped my head and covered my ears.

I soon realised why Uncle George had such a person for his companion. It was apparent that she was not only statuesque, but also highly intelligent and competent in everything she did. She knew a good deal about me and knew that we had a design to correct Stella's arrogance. Uncle George was out fixing some deal in New Bedford, so she told us that she had taken it upon herself to prepare a few interesting diversions for Stella and that she had rigged up a CCTV system so that we could monitor her if she decided to trespass. Mel pointed out to me that Aunt Dorothy had an engineering degree from MIT and that she had worked at White Sands as the leader of a technical innovations team. If Aunt Dorothy made something for a particular purpose, it worked every time.

Uncle George returned from his trip and greeted both of us with considerable enthusiasm. He suggested that we might like to go for a swim. I was rather embarrassed because I hadn't brought my costume with me, and in any case I was not happy at the prospect of stripping off in front of Aunt Dorothy. As usual, Mel was ahead of me.

Uncle George roared with laughter. 'Dorothy never wears clothes if she can help it. Those draperies were just to show that she possessed clothes. She will be very happy to swim with you, and so will I, but this time all my attention will be on Dorothy.' For a moment I was unexpectedly disappointed, but Mel took my hand and we all trooped out to the pool. Already in the water and giving an excellent imitation of a porpoise was Aunt Dorothy. I had no idea how powerful she was until I saw her lift herself out of the water in the middle of the length she was swimming. What a magnificent figure of a woman she presented. There were curves and muscles everywhere and those huge breasts were as solid and perky as if she was in her twenties rather than her fifties. I liked the look of her, but not half as much as Uncle George did as he plunged in and intercepted her passage down the pool. Mel and I dropped our clothes next to some loungers and dived in together. When we came up, Uncle George was embracing Aunt Dorothy, and Mel and I found each other's naked bodies and the pleasantly warm water to be powerful aphrodisiacs.

The day passed full of delight, only marred by my inability to ask if I could stay on after Monday, In the evening we sat on the porch and drank Aunt Dorothy's cocktails, which were as strong as she was and like her, needed to be treated with respect. Eventually Mel asked what exactly Aunt Dorothy had prepared for Stella. She warned us not to go into the basement in case we became the victim rather than Stella, but gave us no further information. Eventually it was bed time and I found Mel already in my bed as I came out of the bathroom. She looked at me enquiringly and asked if I could bear her company. My kiss was all the answer she needed and we spent the night in each other's arms.

Friday 25 May

The morning came in a haze which the sun just managed to penetrate. Very soon it was warm and then hot and then very hot. We sought shade and wore thin cotton to keep off the sun's burning rays. I was helping with the preparations for lunch when Kerr drove up and parked under the trees. He levered himself out of the car and opened the passenger door, letting out Stella who was wearing the most micro of micro dresses that I ever remember seeing. Its skirt reached just to the fork of her legs. As she walked towards us I thought that she was naked beneath it, but I realised that she was wearing a flesh coloured thong. The upper part of the dress was unbuttoned to the waist which afforded an excellent view of the entire curve of her breasts. I was racked with a jealous spasm when I thought of her with Kerr in the car. Still, as she hadn't a hair out of place not much could have happened.

Mel greeted her with a hug. Stella was obviously surprised. She looked at me with less than enthusiasm but was polite. Aunt Dorothy embraced her and Uncle George appeared on the scene and clasped her in a very friendly hug. Kerr had got their bags out of the trunk and was stalking across the gravel to the house steps. Aunt Dorothy took a bag and invited Stella to come with her so that she could get to know the house and would be able to locate her room. Mel and I greeted Kerr and then went back to our preparation of lunch. I had laid the table for four, but I quickly added a couple of places. Judging by the bowls of salad and the ham and chicken with French bread on a big wooden board there would be plenty for everyone. We had just finished carrying everything through into the dining room when both men appeared, obviously much enjoying each other's company. Aunt Dorothy appeared, trailing

Stella behind her. I heard a snatch of their conversation as the door opened.

'Yes, that's the door to the basement, but don't you go down there because it's dangerous,' followed by Stella's sharper tone. 'But Kerr said...' and then her voice trailed off.

We had lunch during which the conversation moved from life at college to future prospects for us all and Uncle George's next adventure. We sat on the patio after lunch and shared a huge jug of sangria. I noticed that Stella was steadily refilling her glass. At 3 o'clock uncle George and Aunt Dorothy excused themselves as they liked to have a siesta. Mel and Kerr walked off into the garden and I was left alone with Stella. She asked me what I was doing there and I said I was hoping to be their housekeeper during the summer. She asked me if that was all and I looked puzzled.

'Well there's that hunk Kerr and Uncle George looks if he might make good use of the hired help.'

I told her I was not that sort of girl and she snorted. 'I'd have believed that two months ago, but now you seem to be enchanted by Kerr and you've changed.'

I admitted to having my hair done. 'And that's not all. Remember I've seen you naked.' I pretended to be embarrassed, and told her that clothes were pretty much optional here. 'So I get to see Kerr au naturel, then?' I replied that it was likely, though they might change the rules for a visitor. Stella looked interested and asked me what else went on. I told her there was a good sized swimming pool and that there were some wonderful walks, but she didn't appear to be satisfied.

'What about this basement, then?' she asked. I looked down at my feet and simulated confusion. 'Come on, Kerr dropped several hints about it being the answer to everyone's darkest fantasies. What have they got down there, an orgy room?' I shook my head and looked embarrassed. Stella became insistent. 'Old mother Dorothy told me to keep away so it must be worth seeing.'

I told her I didn't know, which was so transparent a lie that she became quite aggressive. However, at that point Mel and Kerr reappeared. I thought that Mel was going to ask me if we were getting on all right, but I suspected that they had been waiting behind the half open door to choose a suitable moment to enter. Kerr asked Stella if she would like to see the grounds, patently leaving me out of the invitation. Mel asked if I would give her a hand with tidying up and we shifted the lunch things into the kitchen and filled the fridge and the dishwasher. Mel smiled at me and told me I'd done a brilliant job winding Stella up.

The day passed quietly enough until supper time. Uncle George told us that he and Dorothy were going to New Bedford the following day and were taking Mel with them. He asked if we could manage on our own. I looked a bit disappointed and said I'd like to come, too. This was promptly agreed. Uncle George asked Stella if she minded being on her own with Kerr and a rather feral glint came into her eyes. Had this not been part of the game I'd have been seriously worried about my relationship with Kerr. It was hot and sticky and even the air conditioning was struggling. Uncle George suggested we should all go for a swim. Stella looked coy and told him she'd have to borrow a costume. Uncle George laughed good naturedly and told her that he doubted if we owned a costume between us, but of course, if she was embarrassed he'd think of something else. Stella smiled sweetly and said that she thought it would be all right since there were so many of us.

We went out to the pool and shed such few clothes as we had on. Stella stood close to Kerr wearing only her thong and brushed his arm with her breasts. As he turned towards her she insolently removed her thong. Not the first time she'd done that, I reckoned. Certainly she had the whole of Kerr's attention and I suppose she deserved it as she had a remarkable figure with extravagant curves and a waist so tiny that it almost seemed that she might break in half. I hadn't realised how athletic she was and both Kerr and I were surprised when she did a back flip into the water. We all joined her and Uncle George produced a ball and suggested an impromptu game of volley ball. In a moment he had secured a net across the pool with himself Aunt Dorothy and Mel on one side and the three of us on the other. The game proceeded very much as I had expected with Stella between Kerr and myself. She did an inordinate amount of leaping up out of the water and came heavily into contact with Kerr on several occasions. I thought that tomorrow would be an interesting day for him.

Saturday 26 May

Last night I noticed that Stella left her bedroom door slightly ajar. Whether Kerr or even Uncle George availed themselves of the inherent invitation I didn't know. Mel and I had adjacent rooms, but until then I was unaware that the panelling concealed a connecting door. I had not expected that I would be lucky enough to have her company that night, but she slipped into my room very quietly and whispered an apology for not knocking and asking permission. I embraced her and kissed her and we took great pleasure in each other. Before we fell asleep Mel outlined the plan for the following day.

Things went exactly as Mel had described. We piled into the car and set off down the circuitous drive, but once out of sight of the house we turned off and entered what had been the stable yard. There were two open garage doors and we took the left hand one which closed as soon as the car was inside. Lights came on and we made our way up to a large, sparsely furnished room on the first floor. The room was dominated by a floor to ceiling plasma screen on which was an image of the door and steps of the basement. We settled ourselves on the settees and Aunt Dorothy produced cups of coffee and a plate of cookies. We awaited events. After about twenty minutes Uncle George took out his cell phone and pressed a couple of buttons. A count of three rings had an answer and a perfectly pointless conversation followed. Ten minutes later Kerr arrived downstairs and promptly joined us.

'She feigned disappointment that I had to go out for a couple of hours, but I reckon she couldn't get rid of me quickly enough. I wonder how long she'll give me to get out of the way before she goes exploring?'

I looked at my watch; it was almost exactly five minutes

before the picture in front of us began to change as the basement door opened. Stella stood on the top step looking at the assembly of equipment below her. She gathered her courage and carefully descended the stairs. As the bottom she stopped at the St Andrews cross and stepped up on the platform and spread her arms to the heavy wooden bars. In doing so she must have come into contact with the prong in the centre of the cross and she pressed herself against it. She got down and walked down the aisle picking up objects on the way. The light was as dim as when I was last there, but the cameras were able to pick up every detail. Stella approached the rack and got on to the table holding the ropes in her hands. She squirmed about and then got off. Up to this point I had been mesmerised by the screen and had failed to notice that Aunt Dorothy had an identical picture on her lap top. She seemed to be directing the cameras from the computer. Just as I became interested in what Aunt Dorothy was doing the sound of a scream filled the room.

I watched the big screen where the image was of Stella caught by her ankles and being inexorably towed upwards by cables which went above our line of sight. Stella was bending her body upwards so that she could free her ankles from the cuffs that held them. As she did so the cables moved apart, until she was virtually doing the splits. She pulled on her legs to get a purchase at her ankle, but apparently unexpected help was at hand. A hook descended behind her and moved forward until it seemed to engage with the neck of her T-shirt. Stella then became aware of it and twisted to see if she could make use of it to free herself. She was not quick enough and already the hook was sliding up towards her legs. At first I didn't realise that it was cutting its way through the cloth. It moved on relentlessly ripping everything in its path including the micro shorts she so favoured. Having run out of material to tear on its upward journey it descended and this time tore another path through her shorts. The next tear left her naked with the T-shirt in a pile on the floor beneath her and her shorts a few tattered shreds. She was twisting and writhing trying to find some means of escaping but without success. Aunt Dorothy switched to another camera and we had our view of the naked Stella from the front.

I began to be sorry for her and was about to say something to Aunt Dorothy when a forbidding figure appeared at the top of the basement steps. Hooded and dressed entirely in black I could only think that Kerr had stolen away and returned to the house – a quick glance round confirmed that he had gone. I doubted if Stella would recognise him. She was twisting as far as she could, but without any effect to free herself. She was moaning, gasping and crying out, very different from the Stella who despised me so bitterly. Kerr approached her from behind. Without warning he put a big gloved hand across her cunt and another in the small of her back and started to push her so that she swung backwards and forwards with her hair trailing and her arms trying to grasp Kerr or anything to steady herself. Kerr moved round to face her. She lashed out at him with crooked fingers, her sharp talons just scraping down the front of his sweat shirt. Kerr grabbed her wrist and she tried to strike at him with the hand that was free. This was a mistake because he was able to get hold of her other wrist. She was powerless to resist the clutch of his big hand. He took a strap from the table next to him and tightened it around her wrists. He pulled down another cable and attached it to the strap. The cable started to ascend and Stella's body was brought up with it. For a little while she was folded in half with her big round breasts jutting over her widespread thighs. Then her feet, still held wide apart, started to descend so that she became almost vertical.

Kerr took a long whip from its stand and cracked it before

her. Stella shook her head and cried out not to be whipped. Kerr looked at her through the slits in his hood as she shook and tried to writhe in her bonds. He put the whip down and drew out a box from a pile which was at the head of the rack. He undid the clips which secured the lid and opened it in front of Stella's fear-filled eyes. He drew out a neatly tied bundle of thistles which looked to be in the prime of their growth and which were covered in scintillating prickles. He waved it in her face. I heard her say 'You wouldn't dare,' but she was to be proved wrong. Kerr stood behind her and gave her a double slash across the buttocks. Stella shrieked and shook. Aunt Dorothy zoomed in and it was possible to see Stella's skin glittering with the hundreds of embedded spikes. He followed up with a couple of lashes to her back and then moved round to face her. Tears were running down her face and she was whimpering. Kerr pushed the bunch of thistles against her belly and then, moving slightly back, he whistled the bunch through the air and it caught her left breast.

It was obvious that the shock of this blow had left her speechless. She was trying to drag air into her lungs to counteract the pain and the shock. She had just managed to fill her lungs when Kerr caught her the return blow across her right breast. Her scream was out of this world in its strength and duration. Kerr ignored her and swept the thistles up between her open thighs so that she was pierced by hundreds of prickles in her most delicate tissues. Stella was almost beyond writhing and screaming. Kerr put down the thistles and Aunt Dorothy lowered Stella's legs until they were almost vertical. Stella was moaning and gasping from the effects of the imbedded thistles. I turned to Mel and asked if she had suffered enough. Mel replied that Stella had a long history of bullying students who were not able to protect themselves and this had to be a lesson for her that abusing her host's trust and using her strength and the status which her money conferred to make the lives of other students unbearable was not something that could just be overlooked.

I was unaware that she had driven girls who she did not like out of the college and at least one to the brink of suicide. Unfortunately her father was a major donor to the college and her uncle was a governor. I wondered what would happen when she reported what had happened to her. I thought that Mel was playing a very dangerous game and my concern that they were overdoing Stella's punishment was matched by my concern that there might be a price to pay.

Kerr had taken something else out of the box. Uncle George muttered 'Nettles,' and I saw that Kerr was showing Stella the thick bunch of nettles he held up before her. There was no arrogant reply this time. Stella's eyes opened wide with terror. Kerr drew the bunch over her left breast. Stella did nothing for an appreciable time and then as the poison entered her system and excited her nerves she began to make a guttural sound deep in her throat. Kerr waited until she had got used to the pain and the shock and repeated his brushing, but this time over her right breast. There was the same pause and much the same constricted grunting gurgling noise. I saw that her breasts were becoming bright pink and that they appeared fuller and heavier than when she had first been stripped. Her nipples stood out like tiny rigid phalluses and her waist was even narrower than it had been before the punishment started. Kerr had stood back and was watching the effect of thousands of poisonous piercings. Stella's head was back between her arms. Her eyes were closed and her mouth open to emit a tearful howl of pain and despair. Her pose was unbelievably erotic, as if she was willingly giving up her body to the torture, her breasts pushed out from her chest and her mons thrust forward.

It was then that I noticed that Aunt Dorothy had drawn Stella's legs apart. She had split the image on the big screen, the left side showing Stella's naked body and the right filled with an image of her face. I knew it would be inevitable that Kerr would apply the ultimate torture. Aunt Dorothy zoomed in on Kerr's right hand. He was holding the nettles inches below Stella's throat. Very gently he touched the leaves between Stella's breasts, and with infinite slowness he drew them down her body, leaving her rib cage and crossing her diaphragm and starting on her belly. He was almost stationary at her navel when Stella gave a jerk, which must have brought her even more pain. The bunch descended to her mons and Kerr gave a little flick to ensure total penetration of the neatly trimmed fleece. All the while Stella had kept up a strange, deep, gasping sound, but apart from the single jerk she had made no movement. The moment of final agony had come and the four of us watched in complete silence as Kerr pushed the bunch between her thighs and thrust it upwards against her slightly opened petals. He removed it and Stella uttered a growl of unutterable agony, gasping and groaning as the poison sank into her tissues making them swell and feel as if they were being burnt. Her face told it all with an expression of total abandonment to the pain which had been inflicted on her.

Aunt Dorothy lowered Stella's feet to the floor and Kerr detached the cuffs and cables. He reached up and detached her wrists, catching her body in the crook of his left arm. Stella was in no position to stand on her own and Kerr deftly picked her up in his arms and carried her across to a table on which he laid her face down. She made no attempt to move, but sobbed quietly. Kerr took a pad of cloth in one hand and a bottle in the other and spread a viscous liquid over her back. He put the pad and cloth down and turned Stella over on her back. Aunt Dorothy explained that the liquid would dissolve the spines from the thistles and it contained the essence of the chemical ingredient in dock leaves which relieved the pain of stinging nettles. Stella lay supine as Kerr attended to her. Not even when he pressed the pad between her thighs did she respond. I looked at Mel who assured me that Stella would be all right. When I looked back at the now single image on the screen I saw that Kerr had attached her wrists and ankles to the rollers of the rack.

Stella was beginning to show signs of recovering. Her eyes flicked open and she licked her lips. She turned her head to look at Kerr who was standing beside her. Her body gleamed with the mucilaginous paste which Kerr had applied to her skin. She tried to move, but was constrained by the ropes which held her in place. There was no tension on her body, but also little room for movement. Kerr leaned across and stroked her face. I thought I heard him say 'There's my brave girl,' but I might have misinterpreted his whisper. We all watched very closely to see what was to happen next.

Kerr stood at the end of the rack. He turned the wheel until there was a click on the ratchet. With his free hand he stroked Stella's face. After some seconds he moved the wheel until the ratchet clicked again. He continued his stroking, this time moving down Stella's body to the upper part of her breasts. I tried to count the pause, which seemed to be about ten seconds. There was a third click and the drum was just beginning to take up the slack in the ropes. Kerr was stroking Stella's breasts. She was looking up at him as he brushed his gloved fingers over her erect nipples.

There was another click and the ropes became a little tighter. Kerr continued to fondle Stella's breasts and it seemed that her breathing had become slightly quicker and deeper. A further click began to put tension on the ropes. Kerr's hand strayed down to Stella's belly and she attempted to lift her buttocks as if offering her cunt to his hand. Another click began to pull at Stella's arms, and she again tried lifting her buttocks, but Kerr returned his hand to her breasts. We waited for another click and when it came we saw that Stella's belly had gone quite flat, her mons was protruding higher than the ends of her pelvis and her ribs were standing out under her skin. The only part of her she could move was her head which she was turning from side to side. I couldn't work out if she was suffering much pain, but she certainly seemed to want Kerr to take her between her thighs with his hand.

There was a longer pause than usual and then I saw that Kerr had removed his right glove and that he had attached something to his second finger. He very slowly bore down on the wheel and Stella began to utter a hollow moan. Most of her body was now above the level of the table and her ribs looked as if they were about to burst through her skin. Her belly was sunken and looked drum tight. Her mons protruded even more as her hips tilted and the muscles of her legs were thrown up into sharp relief. Stella had her mouth open and there was a tiny trickle of drool at the corner of her lips. She was obviously having to make an effort to breathe. Kerr stood with his left hand on her breasts and his right on her left thigh. He slid his hand along her thigh until his fingers touched the cleft at the base of her belly. He pressed his fingers into her and a powerful buzzing noise filled our ears. Stella's face was crimson. Kerr moved his fingers and she began to open and close her mouth. She made a curious growling sound as he penetrated her cunt and then a high pitched whine as the vibrator contacted her clitoris. Kerr applied his free hand to the petals of her sex and drew them apart, revealing the pink interior with the unsheathed nub of flesh poking up in response to Kerr's stimulation.

She seemed to me, given her athletic prowess and general air of being on the go, to be the sort of woman who likes to move about a great deal when sexually stimulated. However, this was impossible in her present situation and she seemed to be transferring all her usual writhing and jerking to the expressions on her face. She looked as if she was dying for an orgasm, and the way that Kerr was fingering her ensured that she wouldn't have to wait long. Her face went from crimson to a momentary purple which spread down her neck. She seemed to stop breathing as Kerr lifted his hand away from her cunt and we saw gouts of lubricant ejected from it on to the table. I had to admit to myself that in her passion she appeared quite beautiful stretched out under Kerr's total control. Her ejaculations continued for many seconds and then her head lolled back on to the board.

I thought that Kerr would release her, but this was not the end of the performance. From another box he extracted a can and a razor. He squirted the foam over her mons and the sides of her cunt and then slowly and carefully began to shave it until it was quite free from any trace of the fleece which had covered it. He gave a final squirt with the foam can and rubbed it into her skin, wiping off the surplus with the pad of cloth which he had used as an emollient. He stood back and loosened the roller a couple of clicks. To my surprise he wound a handle at the side of the rack and it seemed to fold in on itself from under Stella's buttocks, leaving her body flat on the table but her legs drawn down and outwards. This had the effect of presenting Stella's open cunt to the viewers and making it accessible to Kerr. The buzzing began again and Stella turned her head and rolled her eyes, She was evidently becoming ready to orgasm again, but as we watched Kerr pulled a flap from his tights, exposing a monstrous erection which he introduced to the gates of Stella's sex. He thrust himself into her causing her to howl. I was almost convinced that I could see the head of his cock pressing up into her tense belly. Kerr leaned forward with a big hand on each of her breasts and began to pump into her slowly and deliberately. He decreased the speed of his penetrations, but increased their depth. Stella cried out as his big legs forced her tense thighs even further apart and then uttered a long drawn out screech as Kerr pumped jism into her and she achieved another climax. I just wished it could have been me.

Kerr stepped back from the ravished Stella and then released her from the torment of the rack. She couldn't stand so he picked her up and sat her on the table and massaged her legs with his bare hands. She put her hands round his neck ostensibly to steady herself, but I was sufficiently like her to know that she needed contact with him and some sign of his affection. The victim all too often falls in love with her persecutor. I wondered vaguely if that was what had happened to me.

The four of us were talking about what we had just seen. Aunt Dorothy had recorded the entire affair on her laptop and was busy picking out the most startling parts of the performance. She was not short of choices. She switched back to the scene in the basement and we saw that Kerr and Stella had left it. Within a few minutes there was a knock on the door and the still naked Stella was thrust in, followed by Kerr. He was holding her wrist and he pulled her round to face us. Mel looked hard at Stella whose head was cast down and whose shoulders were bowed. Mel began to speak:

'Now, Stella, this is my uncle's house and you were expressly forbidden to enter the basement. It is an abuse of the hospitality which has been extended to you that you sneaked off to pry into the secrets which were not yours to share. For this you have had some punishment, but there is more. When you came to the college you were spoilt and immature. We thought that contact with many other people of your own age would prove to you that there were many who were a lot brighter than you and many who accepted discipline and worked hard. No one had any objection to you enjoying yourself, but your enjoyment seemed to be based on acquiring a coterie of sycophants who joined you in tormenting those who were weaker and much more vulnerable than yourself. We asked your father to discipline you as we had no means of doing so other than by expelling you. However, it became clear that he was unable to penetrate your carapace of smug sadism. This is why you were invited here this weekend. You have to learn some humility, experience physical pain and be changed forever. If what we have in mind makes no difference then you will be ruined for the rest of your life. You have always considered yourself to be one of those superior people to whom no rules other than their own apply. In your estimation of life rules are for the little people and you need have no part in them. For the remainder of your time here you will do just as we say. If, when you return home, or to the college you feel it is worth complaining please remember that without a fundamental change it is the opinion of everyone who has been in contact with you, that you are not only unsuited to be a teacher, but also that your misdemeanours over the past years should now be made public.'

The last sentence struck home with Stella and she seemed about to protest, but thought better of it.

There was silence for a few moments and then Aunt Dorothy drew Stella's attention to the screen where she was seen furtively entering the basement. The rest was a repeat of the highlights.

Stella gasped as she saw herself displayed and tortured. Aunt Dorothy told her that what she had experienced was nothing compared to what might have been done to her if we had been as vicious as she was.

Stella stood in a penitent pose before us and whispered

an apology for her past misdeeds. She added that she was willing to be punished to any extent that we felt was appropriate. This amazed me, but a sudden insight into my own condition pointed to her as deriving an arcane pleasure from the pain and humiliation which she had endured. There was more than a bit of the exhibitionist in her, too, as her clothes had indicated when she arrived.

Uncle George looked at her almost benignly. 'You know, my dear Stella, there is no pleasure without pain and no pain without pleasure. Pain is what tells us that we are alive. You have everything to live for. We could have ignored you, but instead we have taken the trouble to help you to have new experiences. I suspect that your cruelty to others was the result of no one ever having been cruel to you. I wonder if your father merely gives you what you ask for so that you will go away. I know nothing of your mother but I think she may well be busy leading her own life and be unconcerned about yours.' At this Stella let out a great sob and pressed her hands against her face. I felt very sorry for her despite her past wickedness and wanted to put my arms round her and reassure her. Mel caught my eye and frowned. 'We will give all our attention to you from now until you leave.'

'Thank you,' Stella whispered but didn't look up.

Mel looked at Stella's diminished figure standing before her. I wondered if Stella was going along with what she might think of as a charade until she could break free and return to the college with Kerr. He had slipped away and returned dressed in shorts and a polo shirt. He looked positively edible. I hoped that he would not be employed in further correctional activities. Aunt Dorothy suggested it was time for Stella to have some new experiences. The men stayed behind, but the four of us women returned to the basement. Aunt Dorothy lifted a metal cover from the floor. Beneath there was a dark hole. She ordered Stella to get into it. Stella hesitated. Aunt Dorothy told her that she wasn't going to be killed, just made a little uncomfortable. Stella sat on the edge of the hole and lowered her legs into it. Aunt Dorothy quickly clipped her hands behind her back. A slight pressure from her made her slip into the hole. She must have landed on something solid as she stood looking up. Aunt Dorothy turned on a powerful overhead light which cast shadows from her breasts down her belly. Stella turned round to look at us with her head only just above the level of the floor. Aunt Dorothy told her she was about to have the wash of her life time.

Stella looked apprehensive and Mel picked up a remote control and pressed the green button. At once I saw dozens of thin tubes extend from the sides of the hole and make contact with Stella's skin. Two or three clustered at her cunt and a couple at her anus. She shivered at their touch, but there were so many of them that she was virtually unable to move. Four were pressing on each breast. Mel was doing some extensive programming and then she pressed the green button. Water poured from the jets from Stella's shoulders downwards. There seemed to be very little in the way of pressure and such splashes which fell on my legs were pleasantly warm.

We stared at Stella, and she looked back at us. It looked to me as if the pressure had increased, and I found that a small splash was quite hot, whilst the next one was very cold. Mel turned to Dorothy and told her that she had set the jets on alternate pulse. I guessed this meant that Stella was receiving a hot spray at one moment and an icy shower at the next. She was unable to escape the powerful jets some of which must be penetrating the secret passages between her legs. Stella was moving as if she was jogging. Her mouth was open and above the noise of the spray I could hear her grunting. Mel altered the programmer so that Stella was receiving hot water all over and inside her body. I was fearful that the water would scald her but Mel told me it was failsafe at 47 degrees-quite hot enough, but not dangerous. Stella was showing signs of exhaustion in the hot water and steam so that Mel turned the gauge so that she was receiving cooler water and then cold water again. This made her shake but it also revived her so that she was fully able to experience the shock of the cold water particularly in her anus and cleft.

Aunt Dorothy decided that Stella had suffered enough so the water was turned off and the tubes withdrawn. She stood in the hole, miserably shivering. Aunt Dorothy knelt at the edge of the hole and reached down to unstrap Stella's wrists. She was too cold to make the effort to heave herself out of the pit, so Mel and I caught an arm each and drew her upwards. Aunt Dorothy secured a powerful grip on her waist and Stella was swung on to the floor. Mel produced some towels and she and I began to towel Stella dry. She said nothing but stood unresisting as we returned warm blood to her skin. I was attending to her legs and worked up from her feet. I passed her knees and was vigorously drying her thighs when the back of my hand touched her cleft which, sadly, felt as if she was dead.

Our towelling and her release from the icy water did much to restore Stella's circulation and prevented her from suffering any of the effects of hypothermia. Mel found a thick cloak on the coat stand at the bottom of the stairs and wrapped Stella in it. Colour came back to her cheeks and she was able to get up the stairs under her own steam. Back in the warm room upstairs Stella returned to being fully functioning. Uncle George brought her a hot toddy, now that her surface temperature was back to normal and she sipped it with evident pleasure.

I asked Mel if I could stay on after tomorrow and she looked at Uncle George and Aunt Dorothy for their permission. Both of them seemed to be very pleased to have us both there. Stella whispered something to Mel who smiled and asked if it was all right if Stella stayed, too. If they were surprised it didn't show. Kerr told us he would have to leave early in the morning and Uncle George told us that the two of them would be going to Ottawa in the early afternoon, so that we would be on our own, only really on our own this time.

I spent the night with Mel, but we were both quite drained so that sleep came swiftly, but all the more sweetly in each other's company.

Monday 27 May

I am utterly unused to not having to study and be subject to a strict timetable. I picked up one of Mel's books and began to read it finding the subject matter fascinating, but the style arid and boring. But since the subject was to do with sexual deviations I supposed that it would have to be dealt with in a non-emotional way. I usually avoid the prefaces of academic books, but on this occasion I read it with interest, particularly the first sentences:

'It is as well to define our terms. Deviancy is whatever I don't do or want to do.'

This made me feel a whole lot better, given its implications in connection with my own desires. Stella had been very polite during the morning and was dressed in pedal pushers and a halter top when Aunt Dorothy and Uncle George left. As the car swept down the drive Stella turned to Mel and asked her if she was to be punished any more. Mel replied that according to the original arrangements she would have gone back to the college with Kerr, so that her official punishment was now over. Stella looked thoughtful. 'I know I shouldn't suggest this as I was warned not to enter the basement, but there were so many things there that I'd never seen or even imagined. I just wondered if we could have a look and possibly try one or two?'

Mel and I looked at each other in amazement. Could it be, I wondered, that Stella had got more out of her punishment than we suspected? Had it opened some barriers in her desire for experience and life, as it had for me? Mel pointed out that not all the implements in the basement were safe to use as it was a museum as well as a workshop. However…

For a while we lolled in the sunshine companionably

enough, wearing only the least of garments. We were surprised by the sound of a car horn from the front of the house. Mel pulled on a T-shirt and went round the corner of the wall to see who had arrived. Stella and I put on enough clothes to be decent. Mel came back with a familiar couple in tow. They were the two we had first met at the party which seemed so long ago. Pietro was as handsome and striking as ever and Alys was just amazing in a green and scarlet dress cut to reveal. I wondered if all her wardrobe was like that. They were introduced to Stella and both of them seemed to regard her with a slightly wolfish expression. They really were so sophisticated and stylish that even the super-confident Stella seemed to pale before them, or perhaps Stella wasn't quite as confident as she had been until so recently.

I went into the house to fetch a pitcher of iced lemonade and glasses. On my return I heard Pietro tell Mel and Stella that he was disappointed because he had hoped that on a hot afternoon we should all be sunbathing and if it was too hot we might be sampling the basement. I hadn't realised that Pietro was quite as well informed about Mel and Uncle George as he appeared to be. Mel laughed and told him that had we known they were coming we would have laid on a special show for them. Alys was sitting in the shade of a large umbrella. I supposed that the lack of pigmentation in her skin made it quite dangerous for her to expose herself to the sun. As she sat up to receive her glass of lemonade I saw that the dress that she was wearing was a wrap over secured by a single decorative button at her left shoulder. Judging by the way it followed every curve of her body it was a very expensive printed satin.

Pietro was wearing a skin tight T-shirt and black jeans which must have been specially made as they fitted him with such perfection that it was possible to trace every line of his body through them. The bulge at his crotch was as reassuringly large as I remembered. He asked us if we minded and removed his T-shirt. His skin was a good deal darker than I remembered, but the curly body hair and the muscles were as I recalled them. My wish was to see more, even if Alys was our chaperone. I glanced at Stella who was openly staring at him. She asked if... and before she had time to finish the sentence, Mel was removing her T-shirt, I took mine off and Alys undid the button on her dress and let it fall from her shoulders. There could hardly have been four more beautiful but different figures. Mel was as toned as ever and pale coffee coloured all over, Stella was strong but not visibly muscular, though her breasts, placed high on her rib cage were sizeable and round with no hint of droop. I considered myself and thought that I was about average but it was Alys who was sensational. Her skin was a glittering white with sheen on it as if it had been coated in tiny crystals. Her wide shoulders led to breasts each of which were far too large to be held in a single hand, either Kerr's or Pietro's. They thrust out from her chest in a quite glorious plethora of curves, surmounted by large pink areolas from which protruded nipples which were both long and thick. As she moved her breasts bounced slightly and I wondered what might happen if she was to run. Her waist was remarkably small for so tall and powerful a woman. Her belly had the slightest of convexities to it and led to a very prominent mons with a naked cleft below it. Her legs were long and elegant and for once I saw that here was a woman with knees which were not ugly, humorous or silly. Her ankles were fine and her unblemished feet were long and slender.

Alys remained in the shade whilst the rest of us relieved ourselves of our remaining garments and then sat in the sun. Pietro had his knees together, which was something of a disappointment to Stella, and me. Stella, on the other hand, sat up facing Pietro with her ankles drawn up towards her and her knees splayed out. Pietro turned to Mel and said that she had not told him that Stella had joined the club. Mel looked slightly confused. Stella had shifted her position so that the petals at the base of her belly were slightly parted, a very slight evidence of the beginnings of her arousal was evident in the erection of her nipples and the glistening of her cleft. Pietro looked hard at Stella who was shocked by his next sentence. 'What's she like under the whip, that one?'

Mel said she didn't know.

'What do you mean, you don't know?' he asked almost angrily.

Mel pointed out that it was only a day since Stella had achieved her transformation. Pietro stood up, his body outlined against the horizon and his substantial cock dangling in front of his scrotum.

'This is no way to do things; she must be initiated at once. It is our duty and our pleasure. You'd like that, wouldn't you, Stella?' Stella's face was pale. She lowered her eyes and nodded. Another exhibition and the delights of a good thrashing. I wished I had to suffer the same fate. I felt the need to be admired and whipped into a frenzy. No such luck, apparently. It was just as I feared, novelty taking its place over the desires of the deserving.

Mel seemed concerned about Stella and told Pietro it was chance that she was there.

'By her own desire, I am sure,' Pietro replied, revealing a great deal about his ability to size up a situation. He asked Stella if she preferred the open air or indoors. Here it would make little difference because we were as isolated and private as it was possible to be. We could activate the electric gate on the drive to make sure there were no unwelcome interruptions. Stella stood before Pietro with her eyes cast down and her head bent forward. In that moment of submission she looked like a little girl who is being told off for raiding the cookie jar.

Pietro decided for her and he chose the outdoors. He went to his car and took a sports bag from the trunk. Alys had slipped her dress on but had not fastened it. Pietro told Mel and me to take one of Stella's arms each and follow him. He obviously knew the grounds well and led us to an ancient oak tree. Once there he opened the zip on the bag and drew out a coil of rope. At one end there was a pair of padded cuffs. He threw them towards us. We did not need to be told to attach them to Stella's wrists. Meanwhile Pietro had thrown the line over a branch of the oak. We walked Stella to stand under the branch and Pietro started to haul on the rope. Stella's body began to elongate. Her feet had been flat on the ground, but very soon she was standing on tip toe. That seemed to satisfy Pietro and he tied his end of the rope off on the stub of a lower branch.

We all looked at Stella. Her face was filled with apprehension about what was to happen to her, but she looked back at us bravely enough. Her arms were stretched to their limit and framed her head between them. Her shoulders were pulled up so that her collar bones resembled a wishbone. They pulled her breasts up and together so that the substantial globes were pressed against one another with her nipples pointing upwards. I counted Stella's ribs below her breasts as they shone beneath her skin. Her belly was drawn in and her buttocks seemed to have tightened into two hard balls. The tension on her belly threw her mons into relief and her cleft was pushed a little forward at the top of her thighs. These were endowed with substantial muscles as were her calves, though the effect was of slender shapely legs and feet to match with her toes bent forward and looking for an easy place to stand. Pietro was obviously pleased with what he saw and approached Stella from behind, running his hands over her tense, naked body and grasping her breasts in his fingers. He seemed to like her buttocks and fingered them for some time, squeezing and stroking as Stella attempted to move, but couldn't find a footing. Eventually he stood back.

He looked at me and said, 'Choose your weapon.' I failed to realise what he meant and looked at him with a mix of enquiry and surprise. He told me it was my turn to use the whip. I stuttered that I couldn't whip Stella, but he insisted and we heard Stella say 'Please.'

There was plenty to choose from, but I was shaking and my mouth was dry with the prospect of hurting Stella, whatever the purpose was. I felt slightly sick as I handled the well oiled leather implements. There was a long braided whip, but I knew I didn't have the skill to use it properly. There was a riding crop, stiff and unyielding, which might break the skin if used with any vigour. I tried a tawse and was nearly convinced that the thick leather strap was my choice, but I found a cat with numerous strands, each of which was knotted. I feared that this would mark Stella so badly that she would have to be attended to frequently for the next couple of days. I didn't mind the idea of handling Stella's naked body, but I hardly thought it was fair that she should suffer in this way, given what she had already endured. Eventually I picked up a lightweight whip with a wooden handle and two plain strands attached to its end. These were a couple of feet in length and looked as if they would sting, but not cut or leave marks other than temporary weals. I hoped I was right. Alys nodded and told me I had made a good choice.

Pietro, Alys and Mel sat on the grass in a semi circle round Stella's naked hanging body. Stella was shifting her feet as far as she could but it hardly seemed to affect her pose. I raised the whip and caught her across the back with the long strands. She shook, but it had been a gentle slash. I counted to ten and repeated the strike but from her right side. I whistled the thongs round her waist and despite the fact that it was a fairly gentle blow, Stella bucked her hips and thrust out her buttocks. I liked the look of these pink orbs and stood well to one side of her so that I could give her a slice across both of them. In this I was wholly successful and two long white weals appeared on her skin. Stella reacted well to this slash. So far she had remained silent. I realised that it was time to increase the power of my strokes. In any case I was getting a taste for inflicting pain, particularly as there was an appreciative audience admiring both our naked bodies.

The following three slashes were a good deal harder and were laid across Stella's back, round the small of her back and across her buttocks. Stella began to dance and utter small noises. I liked the effect so much that I caught her again across her buttocks with a left and then a right handed strike which produced a howl and within the limits of her toes touching the ground, a great deal more tramping and movement. I walked round to her side and was surprised at the extent of the projection of her breasts from her ribcage and the projection of her mons from between her hips. So far my targets had been conventional, but I now became determined to give the audience something to watch. I flicked the strands of the whip across Stella's flat belly. This must have hurt more than I expected as she drew in her breath and gasped and howled. I thought that this was an excellent target so I struck it again and immediately again and then again. Stella was crying out on an almost continuous high note and she was lifting her feet alternately, bending her leg at the knee and stamping her toes down into the grass as hard as she could. Each jolt of her foot sent her breasts leaping and bouncing.

Consequently I made them my next target. I had become used to handling the whip so I judged that I would be able to stand back a couple of feet and whistle the whip at her so that her nipple on her right breast was struck by the fine tips of the strands. I was pleased with the accuracy of my strike, but Stella's ear piercing yelp of pain was louder than I had expected. I had already aimed at striking her left breast and there seemed no way in which I could avoid doing so. Stella had drawn her head back between her arms and was gasping and yelping. I struck her belly twice more and her high pitched shrieks became lower pitched groans. Even though there was nothing to be gained by doing so she rubbed her knees together and stamped and shook. She began to turn on the end of the rope and I rewarded her movement with a slash to her ribs below her arms and then across her back and buttocks. These were full on strikes which left a criss-cross of weals and made her shake from her knees up to her shoulders so that her body seemed to be undulating.

As she turned towards me again I saw that her feet had parted and that there was a narrow gap between her legs all the way to her cleft. I caught sight of Alys who made a swinging upward gesture with her hand. I had seen it before, and felt it. I swung the whip back beside me and brought it forward with as much speed as I could muster. I hoped that my strike would be accurate and that it would go all the way. Stella's head was right back as far as it would go and I could see only her throat with its knotted muscles. My aim had been perfect and the two whistling ends of the whip caught Stella's cleft where one seemed to penetrate beyond the outer petals. I hadn't expected Stella to leap in the air, nor had I reckoned on her screaming and opening her legs wide. As she did so I let her have another, but much harder, strike in the same place. She came down to earth with a thud and I watched as her belly contracted and she drew in a great gasp of breath. She tilted her pelvis so that her cleft was presented to me rather than being secured between her thighs. I struck her again and was rewarded, as she was, by a stream of juice issuing from between her legs. Her screams and cries had changed to a series of powerful grunts as each breath of air was expelled. Alys had stood up and had taken Stella's head in her hands and had bent her own head forward to kiss her as she swooned in her ecstasy.

Pietro was on his feet, undoing his end of the rope and gently lowering Stella's arms whilst Alys held her from falling. Mel undid the cuffs. Pietro hauled the rope out of the way and neatly folded it and put it in his bag. Alys led Stella to where she had been sitting and lowered her to a sitting position on the ground. She gestured at us and as she kneeled behind Stella, holding her body against her thighs and with Stella's head on her soft belly, we knelt either side of Stella and stroked and kissed her. Pietro brought across a bottle of some preparation from his bag and indicated that we should spread it all over Stella's skin. She had set up a soft, almost continuous sound which we interpreted as an indication of her pleasure. Pietro knelt between her open legs. 'She will need to be fucked,' he said and I knew just how right he was. Stella's eyes opened and her lips smiled. I kissed her and Pietro lifted Stella's unresisting hips and thrust his sports bag under her buttocks. Alys gently lowered Stella's head until it was on the grass and held between her thighs. Pietro took his rigid phallus in his hand, and moved so that he could cover Stella's naked body, the highest point of which was her cleft. He rubbed the end of his cock against her cleft which opened like as flower to admit him. Slowly he pushed himself into her foreshortened vagina as she mewed and gasped at his penetration. Eventually he must have felt the neck of her womb contacting the head of his cock and for a brief moment he continued to push forward and she opened her mouth to cry out, but before she was able to do this he was pulling slowly back until only the tip of his cock was holding open the gates of her sex. Then he began penetrating her again. He sank all his weight into pushing his cock as far as it would go into her. I knew what it was like to be penetrated like this and felt her mix of delight and terror as he stabbed her again and again deep into her guts. There was nothing like giving one's self to a man whose very sexual act feels like a passionate murder. I watched as Stella's breathing became more rapid and then her eyes rolled up in their sockets and the ecstasy of passion was on her again.

Mel and I released her arms and she put them round Pietro's neck, pulling his head towards her. They kissed long and deep and Stella seemed to go limp with the satisfaction of her most extreme desires. Pietro lifted his head and then kissed her again, gently. He carefully extricated himself from between her legs, removing the bag that had elevated her hips. He lowered her buttocks to the grass and Alys cast her floating dress over Stella's body. She gestured to me to get up and she took my place next to Stella, cradling her head on her arm and gently kissing her cheek and then her closed eyes. I knelt for a moment until I felt an unexpected touch on my shoulder. I glanced back to see Pietro's muscular thighs and his glistening rigid cock. He reached down and hauled m up to stand in front of him.

'I have something for you,' he told me. He took my hand and rested it on his cock whilst he looked deep into my eyes.

As I stood there I felt myself utterly filled with lust. I desired this man and wanted to give myself to him without question. He could do anything to me provided that in the end he satisfied my overwhelming wish to be fucked until I was as senseless as Stella.

He led me back to the tree. For a moment I wondered if I was going to be whipped, but all he did was back me against the trunk and tie my wrists behind me. He went to his sports bag and took out a box. He came close to me and bent his head and kissed me. I tried to press myself against him but I was unable to move sufficiently. I felt a sudden pain at my left nipple and saw that he had applied a spring clip to it. Another dangled from a fine chain attached to the first one. I prepared myself for the second bite and it was not long coming. He was pushing my thighs apart and I willingly opened them so that he could enter me more easily. This was not what he had in mind, at

least not just yet. He had hold of the left hand petal of my cunt. He stretched it out and applied another clip. It was a ferocious bite and I cried out in protest, but before I had finished my howl, another clip had been added to the right petal. The pain was making me draw in my breath in quick gasps. I could bear the pain but I wanted him smothering me with his body and penetrating me mercilessly. An image of him thrusting himself into me filled my mind.

He drew what felt like another chain round my buttocks. One end was attached to the left hand clip. I felt him pull on the chain until my petal was unfurled and drawn back towards my thigh. He attached the other end of the chain to the other clip, did some adjustments and I stood with my outer lips drawn back and the pink membranes of my inner lips parted and on show. His finger was between my inner lips and working on my clitoris. This was more like what I wanted. I began to get a buzz at the base of my belly and my breasts grew heavier. I was hoping for Pietro to work up a bit of lubricant and then stab me with his cock. I wanted his next move to be painful, but I was unprepared for it to be utterly agonising. He attached another spring clip to my clitoris. The jaws of the clip were serrated and were piercing my soft flesh in the very place where there was the greatest number of nerve endings. I screamed long and shrill and saw that I had woken Stella who was looking at me as if I was a ritual sacrifice.

Pietro gave a jerk on the chain connecting my nipples and then tugged the lower clips. I thought that I was going to faint, but eventually the blackness cleared from my sight. Pietro produced a buzzing tube and pushed into my cunt. I felt it vibrate against the walls of my vagina and then he pushed it further until it came into contact with my cervix. I was gasping and tears were running down my cheeks. Pietro's response was to turn up the power and push even harder. I felt that I ought to be able to stand this affliction, but it made me shake and cough. I could feel the rough bark of the tree scraping my buttocks as I tried to reduce the pressure within me. He started to move the tube about and explored my vagina with its tip. Either by luck or his mastery of female anatomy he hit my G spot and I jerked helplessly as my vagina clenched on to the tube. He pulled the chains that held my instruments of torment, but at the same time pressed home his probe so that I could hardly breathe. I began to shake uncontrollably at the continuing pressure deep within me. My knees began to buckle and I started to utter a continuous stream of low pitched wails.

This was all too cruel. I still wanted Pietro to hold me in his arms and thrust himself into me. Caught against the tree which so recently had supported Stella's naked, dangling body I was displayed in the most obscene and vivid way and had far too many painful stimuli to cope with. All I wanted now was to be released and comforted or to sink into a welcome oblivion.

I felt Pietro withdraw his probe and I at once thought that the torture was coming to an end when he unclipped my clitoris which ached as the constricted blood flow returned to normal. He stood back and looked at me as I stood against the tree. The other three were equally attentive to my torture. I was almost right about my release. Pietro took another tube from his box. This was no bigger than a fat fountain pen. He took Alys's hand and pressed a button at one end of the tube whilst holding the other against her knuckle. Alys let out a little cry and tried to snatch her hand away. Pietro smiled at her.

'This is nothing,' he said. 'It is designed to reduce pain by projecting a little electric spark into the body. It summons the endorphins by providing a sudden and very localised pain. The endorphins work on a larger scale so once it has achieved its aim it ensures that a large area is free from pain. Let me show you.'

He held the tip of the tube against my left nipple and repeatedly pressed the button. The pain was sharp and added to the agony of the clip, but after a few seconds the pain from the little implement and from the clip subsided.

'It is no use keeping her nipple clipped as she can feel no pain.'

He squeezed the ends of the clip so that it opened and released my nipple. He did the same for my right breast, but the pain was intense and my nipple ached from the pressure of the clip.

'Now we will try a more delicate area.' He touched my pitifully aching clitoris with the tip of the tube. I was prepared for a little bite, but I was utterly unprepared for the pain he inflicted. The skin must be very thin and my clit was damp. The two led to the sparks being much more powerful and the shock swept up my belly and made me cough and gasp. Pietro removed the clip and continued to fire the shocks into me. The pain was excruciating at first, but as he proceeded I felt it diminish and I even started to find a now familiar stimulation between my thighs. I tried to count the sparks he was generating, but I concentrated instead on the stimulation which the little tool was producing. For a moment it stopped and I felt the tube penetrate my vagina. He had already located my G spot and now he fired sparks into it. I didn't think I could stand this agony, but it too began to diminish and then I felt the beginnings of a climax induced in my vagina rather than my clit. I didn't care what he did so long as he went on firing electric current into me and the beating of the eagle's wings in my belly transformed themselves into the rush of pressure up my body to my chest and then my throat and finally my brain was enveloped with the totality of my climax and the pressure released itself into a spurting orgasm.

I realised that I was repeating over and over, 'Please, please, please.' I saw the grim smile on Pietro's face as he pressed the button in time to my pleading words. I opened my legs as far as I could and waited for those few long seconds before I could neither see nor hear and then my engulfing climax burst upon me. I poured my juices over Pietro's hand and stood gasping and inarticulately mouthing meaningless words. I didn't know that Pietro had released me from my tormenting clips and the tree trunk until I fell forward into his arms. He held me firmly in front of him with my feet just off the ground. I could feel his hard cock pressed against my belly and I hung on to his neck and kissed him. He took two or three steps and lowered me to the grass. He lay beside me and cushioned my head on his arm. He kissed me and stroked my face. He touched my sore breast and bent to kiss and suck the nipple. I found myself repeating the word which had presaged my climax and at last he knelt between my thighs and I felt his victorious cock slide into my well lubricated cunt. He kissed me and took his weight on his forearms whilst he pumped into me. Pietro must have been possessed of the most amazing self control because long after I had climaxed again he was continuing his thrusting until suddenly he jerked his body upwards and thrust completely into me with a triumphant yell.

Tuesday 28 May

There's no doubt that sharing Pietro between us has made Stella a great deal pleasanter to live with. Yesterday evening was quiet and comfortable after the visitors had departed. Mel said that she would have done a lot to get her hands on Alys. Stella amused us by saying that if Alys had not wanted the attention Mel would have been no match for her. I was inclined to agree.

Today was unusually cloudy with a little drizzle. It was still warm and after lunch we stripped off and rolled in the wet grass. This was very invigorating, but soon palled. Mel suggested that a visit to the basement might be amusing so we descended the stairs and stood among the myriad artefacts. Stella pointed at a fine wooden armchair apparently of Shaker design and manufacture. The space between the legs was boxed in. Stella asked what it was for other than just sitting on. Mel said she would show us and sat on the seat. She picked up a remote control on a lead beside the chair and pressed a button. There was a sound but nothing seemed to happen. She pressed another button and there was a mechanical whirring sound. She adjusted herself on the seat and we became aware that something was moving her from the waist down. She pressed another button and there was an oscillating sound. At this point we realised that dildos had risen from below the seat and had penetrated Mel. She increased the speed of the oscillation and looked very pleased with the result.

'Mustn't expend all our energies on the first toy,' Mel said, gasping a little. She pressed what must have been the cancel button and the chair returned to its original innocent appearance.

There was a thick piece of timber like a horizontal telegraph post with a trestle at each end keeping it about three feet off the ground. In the middle was a metal contraption which was a mystery to Stella and to me. Mel laughed.

'This wouldn't be any use to you,' she told us, 'or perhaps it would if you fancied a bit of femdom.' Stella and I looked confused.

'Quite easy. You wanted to keep some guy in one place. Strip him naked. Mount him on the post with a leg either side. Close the trap over his scrotum with his balls on one side of the clamp. Close the padlock and you can do pretty much anything with him, and even more if you tie his arms behind his back.'

Stella said this sounded very cruel, but Mel told her it was nothing compared with the ingenious devices which men had invented for torturing women. She showed us one which filled us with horror. It was two semicircular plates on a tube about eighteen inches long with a handle on one end. The tube itself was about two inches in diameter. Mel told us that this was thrust into a woman's cunt and the handle was turned until the two plates were forced apart against the walls of her vagina. We looked at each other in horror but I couldn't help seeing, in my mind's eye, Pietro's steady gaze fixed on me as he carefully turned the handle and opened my cunt impossibly wide. I felt a treacherous tingle of excitement.

Mel went on to show us terrifying breast clamps and frames; seats that allowed weights to be hung from the woman's genitals. Then finally she came to a narrow drum mounted horizontally on an axle with a pulley on one side and a waxed cord running from the pulley to another, larger pulley with a handle like an old fashioned mangle. Stella and I hoped this wasn't anything too dreadful. There was an elaborate framework behind the drum.

'This,' said Mel, 'is a most remarkable piece of work. I've always wanted to try it. Perhaps this is my big opportunity.' She gave us instructions as she climbed over the horizontal bars behind the drum. There was a flat piece of metal about two inches wide connecting the bars. Mel sat on it, her graceful, toned body looking vulnerable amongst all the ironwork of this contraption. She told us to, move the vertical column behind her so that it touched her spine. We attached her wrists to a cross piece above her head and wound up the column so that she was well stretched upwards. We had seen a very odd piece of ironwork hinged to the column which looked like oversized spectacles. Mel instructed us on adjusting this and we closed it over her breasts so that the rims neatly encircled each breast and the separate smaller rings with three bolts in the circumference fitted over her nipples. She told us to screw in the bolts until they held her nipples, but my experience yesterday made me unwilling at first. She insisted and we did as we were told. Last of all we strapped her knees to the two side bars and stood back to admire our work.

Mel was completely at our mercy. She looked beautiful imprisoned in the iron framework with her back straight and her pretty breasts lifted by the pull on her arms and secured in the circles. Her belly was drawn in and her cleft thrust slightly forward by her perch on the flat iron bar, and opened just perceptibly by the separation of her thighs. Having achieved all this we were now instructed to move the drum forward until it was less than an inch from her cunt. This wasn't difficult and we easily tightened up the adjusting screws. Mel told Stella to turn the handle on the pulley and the drum revolved. I had an insight that this was similar to the wheels that had been applied to my breasts and cunt. Mel asked for an increase in speed. As the drum started to revolve, faster flexible prongs appeared on its circumference and began to touch Mel's mons, stroking downwards towards her thighs. This was not what

Mel had in mind and she told Stella to stop the wheel and then wind it the reverse way. This time the prongs came up between Mel's thighs and stroked her cleft. As Stella increased the speed of the wheel the prongs extended and were clearly contacting Mel's clitoris. Her eyes closed and she began breathing deeply through her mouth. Stella kept the speed steady for a couple of minutes and then increased it. At this Mel began to make a series of staccato wordless noises and sweat began to run down her face and on to her body. A further increase in the speed made Mel push her head back against the column behind her, close her eyes and opened her mouth so that she could draw in great gulps of air. It was obvious that the constant brushing and poking provided by the prongs was having just the effect that the machine was intended for, there was no way she could escape its attentions. Her breath was rasping in her throat and as she began to come to her climax she opened her eyes and gazed straight at Stella who was about to stop turning the handle as Mel roared into her orgasm, every muscle of her body tensed. I told Stella to go on turning so that Mel's orgasm could be prolonged and we might perhaps manage to reduce her to the condition in which Pietro had left us.

Mel screamed as the hyper stimulation took over her senses. She could move only her head, though she tried twisting in her seat it was no use because she was held by the framework at her breasts and by her knees and wrists. She started to try to bounce her buttocks on the iron seat rail, but the frames and screws which held her breasts in place fixed her implacably. She seemed to keep her orgasm going, but after another twenty or thirty turns of the wheel she started to cry out as she had done before and this time we could see the gathering of juices at her open cleft. Stella increased the speed of the drum and edged it forward so that the prongs began to bury themselves between Mel's open petals. She was gasping and moaning alternately. I stood behind her and reached round and tightened the bolts which secured her nipples. She screamed with the pain that I had inflicted and I wished that I had Pietro's little sparking device. I found an unexpected and hitherto unknown streak of cruelty in my nature and thought of wetting Mel's nipples and enjoying the pain that I was inflicting. Somehow I liked feeling that Mel was in my power and that I could order her to be brought to an orgasm or to be tortured to the limits of her endurance.

It took longer this time, but after Mel's head had slumped forward and then returned to the vertical I reached round the column and Mel's body and took the tips of her nipples in my finger nails, scratching and tweaking them unmercifully. Mel had begun to babble and I watched over her shoulder as the prongs swept between the folds of her cleft and caught her clitoris. Whatever Mel was saying was incomprehensible. A thin trace of drool escaped her lips and trickled down her chin, disappearing under the metal which imprisoned her breasts. Stella went on turning the handle and the prongs swept against her inexorably. Mel began to show signs of distress, but I thought that this was no more than the passage up to her third orgasm. Just for once I seemed to be right. This time Mel howled, she moved so that her tortured breasts were elongated in the framework, she screamed with the pain and then, suddenly, Stella and I saw her spurting her juices on to the floor. Stella went on turning the wheel as Mel cried out and then her head fell forward and she became silent.

We withdrew the drum and reversed the order of her imprisonment and freed her knees, her nipples, her breasts and last of all her wrists. We caught her and managed to lift her over the bars and placed her feet on the floor. At once her knees gave up any pretence of being able to hold her up, so between us we carried her up the stairs and then another flight to my bedroom. Stella held her up as I flung back the bed clothes and we laid her in the middle of the bed. Stella looked abashed as I slid into the bed beside Mel, so I gestured to her to join us. Within a very little time Mel recovered enough to say 'Thank you,' and then she moved her arms so that she could clasp one of us in each of them. I could not resist stroking her and kissing her and I found that Stella was doing the same. Mel told us that she loved us and we redoubled our attentions. Mel asked for a drink and I slid out of the bed and fetched a jug of apple juice laced with vodka and three glasses.

When I got back I found that Mel had moved across to what was her usual side of the bed. Stella seemed to have moved with her. I poured out the drinks and got into the bed beside Stella. She whispered to ask if I wanted to be next to Mel, but I was happy to be next to Stella. I knew that in a very few minutes Mel would be sound asleep, whereas both Stella and I would have done no more than lose our inhibitions. In this I was quite right. We finished our drinks and I turned towards Stella. I kissed her mouth and she put her arms round me. I pulled back the sheet and exposed her breasts. I took one in my hand and laid my lips over the other one and tongued here nipple. Once more I felt the pleasure of being, unexpectedly, in control. I moved and knelt between her knees. I leaned forward and kissed her mouth. She gasped as I gently squeezed her breast. I kissed both of her breasts and held her nipples, tantalisingly, in my teeth. I moved down her body, touching her skin continuously with my lips. I did a little shuffle down the bed and kissed her navel. It was a short distance to her cleft. I pulled back the petals with my thumbs and put out my tongue to penetrate her inner lips. I almost at once found her clitoris and started to lick it. Stella lay back in the bed quite unmoving when I began, but she soon had her fingers on her breasts and was pulling at her nipples with her finger nails. I nodded my head to make my licking faster and deeper and I felt her hips move. I transferred my hands to her buttocks and gripped them fiercely. I heard her begin to whimper but was caught out by the unexpected spurt of her juices. I received them in my mouth and lingered over tasting them. Stella's juices were scented like jasmine and tasted like a mix of something slightly savoury blended with honey. I licked all round her cunt not wanting to waste an iota.

Stella pulled me to her and we lay in each other's arms until hunger drove us to the kitchen and Mel began to wake up.

Wednesday 30 May

I now realise that had circumstances been different I could have made a good friend out of Stella. As it is she is now rather more than a friend. Mel was having a shower prior to bed and, having had mine, I was lying in bed reading. There was a tap on the door and Stella came in wearing her short night dress. She blushed and stood at the end of the bed and asked if she could come to bed with me as she felt lonely. Before I had a chance to reply, Mel came in with a towel round her hair, and as usual, nothing else. Stella pressed the back of her hand against her mouth and started to back out of the bedroom. Mel asked her where she was going and Stella came over very confused. Mel laughed and told her she would be most welcome, provided she got rid of the silly night dress. Stella hauled the offending garment over her head and looked quizzically at us. We decided she should be in the middle. It is surprising how much pleasure three naked women can enjoy with each other's bodies.

The sun was well up when we showered and had breakfast. Stella and I tidied everything away and joined Mel who was lying on a lounger in the sun. We lay and read and dozed until lunchtime and repeated the process in the afternoon. In the evening Stella hesitantly asked if she could try the machine we had used on Mel yesterday. The effect was as devastating for her as it had been for Mel which allowed me to do to Mel what I had done to Stella the day before. The difference was that Mel's juices were slightly salty and a little thicker than Stella's. I wondered how this worked. It's amazing how little we seem to know about the workings of our own bodies.

Mel says she has organised a treat for us all for tomorrow.

Thursday 31 May

How right she was. At 1030 a car drew up outside the house. Out of it got a woman who I thought I recognised, two other women and an oriental man. As they approached the steps I realised that this was the woman who had cut and coloured my hair. The others turned out to be a manicurist, a make-up artist and a masseur. We all trooped out on to the terrace and the visitors donned white coats. Bags and cases contained a mass of equipment and the masseur brought in a folding treatment table. It was decided that we should be treated all at once. Whilst I was having my hair trimmed and styled and then the colour renewed, Stella was enjoying the attentions of the masseur and Mel was having her hands and feet beautified. The make-up artist fetched and carried at this stage. We stopped for lunch at 1230. I was about to go into the kitchen to sort out something for the seven of us, but I was prevented from doing so by the oriental. From the trunk of their car they brought in a big wicker hamper and unpacked a sumptuous meal. It had already been a treat. This was gilding the lily.

In the afternoon, as soon as each of us had her hair suitably tended, the make-up artist started to work. She described exactly what she was doing and gave each of us a sheet of paper with instructions and all the make-up we needed to copy her effect. The masseur shaved us, gliding his razor over every area of our skin so deftly that we felt nothing except a pleasant buzz when he attended to us between our legs. At last they said they were satisfied, if we were. I felt wonderful and said so. We trooped in to look at ourselves in the big mirror in the hall. Three wonderfully attractive women blooming with health and, dare I add, happiness. The team departed. Mel took us upstairs and I was reacquainted with the huge wardrobe of exotic clothes. She told us we were going to a fantasy dance that evening and we could pick our clothes to suit our fantasy character. Mel disappeared into a corner and came out with a dress and shoes which she carried into her bedroom. Stella was absolutely overcome with the range of wonderful dresses. I picked out a black Lycra body suit cut low at the front and with a neat Velcro fastening down the back from neck to buttocks. I went into my bedroom and was pulling it on very carefully when Stella arrived wearing a dress which would not have gone amiss in a painting by Boucher. She was in a bust revealing, tight waisted, wide skirted, flowery dress which made her look like an exceptionally glamorous lady of the court. The dress had to be done up at the back. No wonder they had dressers in the eighteenth century! She looked perfect, especially as she had found a pretty mask on a stick. Mel joined us dressed in a dark green velvet floor length gown cut so low at the front and back that adhesive attachments had to be applied to her skin. I had exactly her reverse problem. Every bit of me from ankle to wrist was covered in a second skin.

Friday 1 June

The ball was held at a wayside inn on a side road to Boston. There were perhaps a hundred people present and a very good band played covers from just about anyone who was requested. The costumes were amazing, varying from a savage in his loincloth to a large man in an admiral's uniform, dripping with gold braid and medals. The women were no less varied. At one extreme we had Stella's big floating dress, at the other there were several women in what appeared to be versions of fetish wear. At least one of them revealed both her breasts and was wearing a leather thong with a vibrator fixed into it. Her high-heeled, knee length boots and a black leather mask completed the ensemble. Despite the fact that my own costume felt and looked as if it had been sprayed on, I really felt rather overdressed.

There were several 'spare' men circulating, each of whom claimed a dance from us, but they were discouraged by the fact that we kept together. Once they found that none of us was keen on a look at the grounds in the moonlight we were approached by three of the prettiest women present. I didn't click for a moment, but I then realised that they, too, would like to take us somewhere quiet and explore the scenery. All three of us were quite happy with the other two and hadn't considered random relationships. We enjoyed their company briefly, retired to the buffet and at midnight decided we had much in common with Cinderella.

Today has passed quietly enough with some discussion of the people from last night. We sunbathed, swam, and lolled in the sun reading books and magazines. We also talked about Monday and what would follow. I was overtaken by sadness. I suppose I had been spoilt by the experiences of the last few weeks. I didn't want to let go.

On the other hand, I couldn't live on fresh air, so as soon as I had my results I could get on the phone to the place which had offered me a conditional temporary job and see if they still wanted me. I knew that I had only a limited chance as my results were likely to be average, though I thought I'd done quite well on the course work.

Stella had been offered a post by a friend of her mother's back home. I suddenly realised that I should be sorry to see her go. Sharing a bed and torments had brought us together.

Saturday 2 June

Tomorrow we pack up and return to college. Today we have spent the morning cleaning, polishing and putting everything to rights. The washing machine has been going great guns and a breeze and hot sun has meant that Stella, who seemed to be unexpectedly expert at it, had been ironing and folding everything that we have used. By the time lunchtime arrived there was a strong odour of furniture polish and every room had been cleaned. We had a slightly dismal lunch but then Mel suggested that we should play in the sun. We didn't know what the game was that she had in mind, but we very soon found out.

We played a game that she said the Greeks invented. It was intended to strengthen young people to endure pain and keep their resolve to be steadfast. Each of us was equipped with a five foot long leather strap. We drew lots for who was to go first and it fell to me. I was to stand with my hands clasped behind my head and each of the others was to give me two strikes with their strap. I was quite prepared to prove that I was the most enduring of the three of them, but I wasn't prepared for how much the strap hurt. Stella stood behind me and Mel in front. Stella caught me across the back and left a trail of fire on my skin. Mel stood to my right and the strap caught me across my waist, making me gasp. Stella's second strike was upwards on to my buttocks. I felt the bounce of my orbs and then the pain burst across my arse, causing me to draw in my breath. Mel followed this up with a slash across my belly, making my skin and muscle pucker and then release. This was painful, but I would have time to recover whilst Stella received her treatment.

This time Mel stood behind Stella and I took up the front position. Stella looked lovely, her naked body gleaming in the sun light and her curves as inviting and seductive as any I had seen. As usual her expression was apprehensive, but this swiftly changed to a grimace of pain as Mel brought her strap down hard on her skin. I at once followed this up with a strike across the top of Stella's thighs. Stella's belly was being pulled in and let out in rapid succession. Before she had time to recover from the initial two strikes Mel had caught her across the back and I slashed her across her waist. Stella let out a cry of pain but stood her ground for the requisite ten seconds.

It was Mel's turn and we both had a chance to admire her wonderfully toned body. Stella stood behind Mel and I stood in front. Stella hit her hard across the upper part of her back and I left a weal across her belly. Stella followed this up with a sharp cut to her buttocks and I missed my aim, which was the upper part of Mel's thighs and caught her across her belly. Mel puffed a few times but gave no other sign of having been affected.

For the next round the number of strokes was doubled and they would be delivered by each person as a four. I stood and waited for the pain to begin. Stella struck me across the buttocks, across the small of my back and then across my shoulder blades twice. The blows were in quick succession and there was no time for recovery between each of them. I gasped and I could feel a tear at the corner of my eye. I had no time to do more than endure as Mel began her assault with a slash to my thighs, one to my belly and another just below my breasts and finally one which wrapped itself round my waist. I just managed to hold my pose until the ten seconds was up, but I burned fiercely where the straps had caught me and I wanted to crouch down and hope I would have no more pain.

Stella's mouth was a firm line and she closed her eyes. I was to deal with her back and did so at speed, watching the criss-cross weals show up on her skin. She shook and whimpered, but endured. Mel stood further away from Stella and brought the end of her strap into play on her navel, mons, thighs and ribs. Stella began to unlace her fingers, but Mel warned her and she just about managed to keep standing. How would she manage with the next round?

I knew that Mel was a different case. Mel was hard. Mel was tough. Mel enjoyed being looked at, naked, and showing that she could resist any amount of pain. Stella and I did our best, but she again showed a stoic indifference to our efforts.

It was my turn again. This time it was to be eight on either side. Stella had become more expert with the strap and fiery slash after burning cut blazed across my skin. I knew that I was crying out and that I was frightened of not being able to take the sixteen blows. I didn't want to be the first one down and I dug my fingernails into my wrists to divert my attention from the whipping I was receiving. Mel gave me an explosive cut to the navel, followed by two to my mons, two to my thighs and then two more to my waist and then one to my right breast which bounced and burnt under her onslaught and left me unable even to cry out. How I managed to keep standing I have no idea, but my determination drove me on.

Stella was looking distinctly frightened, but she stood with her hands behind her head, her heels off the ground, tensing the muscles in her calves and thighs and with her head up and her belly drawn in and her chest expanded. It was my turn to stand behind her and I at once started out to make my attack as quick as I could. I slashed her from left to right across the back and then right to left. I followed this up with a double slash to the buttocks and then the small of her back, completing the sequence, to the accompaniment of her howls, with two hard cuts brought up from the ground to under her buttocks which bounced invitingly. Stella showed every sign of being about to totter, but no sooner had I completed my eight than Mel started out on hers. I had expected Mel to go a little easy, but her attack was as ferocious as mine had been. Double cuts to Stella's thighs were followed by two to her waist, two to her belly and two across her breasts. I moved so that I could catch Stella if she fell, but to my amazement she held her position.

We waited a while until Stella had recovered enough to be able to ply her whip on Mel's back. I stood in front and watched her face as Stella swept the whip against her. Stella was taking her time and allowed a substantial pause between each strike. This was probably worse than the rapid and continuous assault that we had both just managed to endure. Stella put a lot of strength into each biting slash and Mel gasped and breathed heavily through her mouth. She rocked on her feet as each blow landed, but in the end she only began to howl at the seventh strike. It was my turn. I waited until Mel had stabilised her position and then caught her across the belly so hard that it drove all the air out of her lungs. Mel coughed and choked but kept her place. I had intended a second cut in the same place but for some reason I missed my target and the end of the heavy strap caught Mel at the top of her thighs and buried itself in her cunt. She was utterly silent for several seconds and then, to my horror, I saw her knees begin to bend as she crumpled towards the ground. I thought she had fainted and was quick to cradle her in my arms. Very soon she revived and rubbed herself between her thighs. 'I'm yours to do what you want now,' she whispered to us. I looked at Stella who was quietly tearful. We instinctively knew that this was no real victory, and in any case we both wanted to kiss and caress her.

Sunday 3 June

We all shared a bed last night and made much of each other until the sun rose and we knew that our lives were about to change for ever. The journey back to the college was quiet and sad. A note on Mel's door requested that she should drive again and go and see her external examiner. Stella and I were surprisingly miserable without Mel. We adjourned to my room, which was stale and overheated and talked about tomorrow. Eventually we took cool showers and lay on the bed. For some reason I kissed Stella, who burst into tears and told me how sorry she was for being so vile in the past. She said she had learned a great deal in the past week and was only sorry that she had no one now to share her experiences with and repeat them. Darkness fell and our conversation became desultory. We fell asleep happy with each other's company.

Monday 4 June

Stella went back to her own room this morning so that I was on my own. The results would be posted on the board at 1 p.m. I didn't know whether to get there early or wait until the others had departed. I went to the cafeteria for a coffee and found myself sitting opposite Charlotte. I had no doubt that her name would be at the top of the list. She seemed to have everything going for her and was also one of the most agreeable students in the college. She complimented me on my tan and on my new appearance. We talked about the last years and what the next would bring. We discussed our favourite books and then our favourite teachers.

Suddenly it was five past one! We looked ruefully at one another and walked across to the admin building. The list had obviously been put up exactly on time and nearly everybody had gone, though I was surprised to see Stella some yards away. In bold type at the top of the list was Charlotte's name followed by the news that she had been offered the Dixon Research scholarship. I looked at the middle of the list but failed to find my name. I turned to Charlotte and hugged her, congratulating her on her success, but saying I'd have to look on the other board to see what I'd failed. I couldn't believe that Charlotte was laughing at me.

She took my right hand and used my forefinger to point at the list. As she did so I saw that my own name was directly under Charlotte's and that I, too, had been awarded a research scholarship. I staggered back as if I had been struck and tears poured from my eyes as I bent forward with my hands over my face. I needed time to recover. Suddenly I felt familiar arms holding me and realised it was Stella who was kissing my cheek.

Charlotte congratulated me and said how much she was looking forward to working with me. Seeing that I was being looked after by Stella who had taken me across to the long bench in the reception area, she departed to tell her family. Stella was kindness itself. Eventually I had the sense to ask her how she had got on.

'Failed two. Got to repeat next session.' I was about to commiserate with her when I realised that she was smiling and appeared delighted.

'Just think,' she said, 'you and me and possibly visits to some exotic locations. I might even prolong it to two years.' She kissed me and then pointed to the staff notice board. 'You know who has had her thesis approved; I wonder if she'd be a member of our group?'

Curiosity may have killed the cat but for Sarah it leads to a life changing experience. When she decides to try on a piece of fetish clothing her boyfriend brings home for a photo shoot, her punishment launches them both onto a bizarre career path.

Performing for ever more demanding audiences, Sarah sinks deeper and deeper into the role of submissive.
But once she is taken away to train for a mysterious club and from then on there is no turning back…

In 'Pain Ordained' Richard Garwood creates visions of powerfully erotic submission and domination. Some are unusual and surprising, some are dark and thrilling, but all are highly charged reading for those who relish excursions into the farther reaches of sexuality.

THE VICAR'S DAUGHTER.
A girl wakes in a strange bedroom with no recollection of how she got there. And the strangeness increases as she comes to realise that the girl she sees in the mirror, is a very different one to the girl she remembers being!

What ensues is a deeply erotic journey of self-discovery that leads her down the paths of submission…

DEAR JOHN.
A sea cruise like no other is revealed bit by bit in a series of letters home! Richard Garwood's original and vivid imagination creates erotic scenes and performances that transform the heroine in page after page of intensely erotic action.

Two erotica-packed novellas in one volume!

When Karin's mother marries Nikolai, Karin immediately feels uneasy. The man is sinister and she soon finds out how he dominates the women around him. Then she herself becomes the target of his domination and she is blackmailed into accepting a husband from the remote Eastern European country he comes from.

Her journey there and her arrival are traumatic enough but en route she discovers the journals of Zatina, a princess from long ago.

Zatina was 'The Girl in the Golden Mask' but through her journal she reaches out to the present and Karin finds her life is irrevocably changed and she must also learn complete submission.

Suspected of the murder of her master, Syra was forced to go the run in the USA.

What followed was a sexual odyssey of extraordinary power and honesty. From adventure to adventure, Syra moves aimlessly across the States, always seeking fulfilment.

She meets a succession of dominant men and submissive women all of whom help her towards an understanding of her own nature.

Seductive hitch-hikers, a biker gang and a football team are among the people she meets, and they all help her explore her need for submission and suffering.

'True Confessions' is a stark and powerful work of erotica. Not to be missed!

Syra is back in the iron grip of a harsh master and has to escape. A stranger helps her and once again she takes off across America on a voyage of discovery. This time her encounters drive her ever deeper into her own nature and into her desperate need for submission and humiliation.

In vividly recalled surroundings with beautiful and dangerous strangers, Syra recounts her descent into a final understanding of her true nature. Graphic and fast moving as only Syra Bond can write; the second volume of True Confessions expands the boundaries of erotic literature!

Princess Melanie Stroskova flees her own country and arrives in England. She enrols in a secretarial course and falls in love with her first employer, Craig Weston.

He introduces her to the delights of submission and sm and she joyfully submits to him.

However, she is recognised and her previous life threatens her present happiness. Her only escape is to submerse herself ever deeper into slavery...

When Claire comes to in hospital after a minor traffic accident, she finds that her behaviour seems to have altered dramatically. She also finds that she is the focus of attention of a mysterious stranger who commands her sexually in a way she has never experienced before.

As she recovers he leads her into more and more extreme encounters that she finds herself taking more and more pleasure in. But then she goes on holiday with her husband and he disappears just as the mysterious 'X' makes ever more stern calls on her body.

Stephanie Kenny makes an impressive debut with this tale of lost innocence and pleasure gained through submission.

There are over 100 stunningly erotic novels of domination and submission in the Silver Moon catalogue. You can see the full range, including Club and Illustrated editions by writing to:

Silver Moon Reader Services
Shadowline Publishing Ltd,
Box 101
City Business Centre
Station Rise
York
YO1 6HT

You will receive a copy of the latest issue of the Readers' Club magazine, with articles, features, reviews, adverts and news plus a full list of our publications and an order form.